I0679194

Other Titles by Joe Cacciotti

Hurricane Cores the Big Apple

Hurricane Rocks Wisconsin

Poems for the Heart II

Poems for the Heart

Blue Collar Real Estate Mogul

Coming Soon

Hurricane Strikes Rhode Island

Hurricane Mashes Idaho

Hurricane Gold Rushes California

Hurricane Volunteers in Tennessee

Poems for the Heart III

HURRICANE
Strips Las Vegas

joseph j. cacciotti

Marbry Books

Hurricane Strips Las Vegas

By Joseph J. Cacciotti

Copyright © 2012 Joseph J. Cacciotti

All rights reserved. No part of this publication may be reproduced, stored in or introduced into a retrieval system, or transmitted, in any form, or by any means (electronic, mechanical, photocopying, recording or otherwise) without the prior written permission of the publisher. Any person who commits any unauthorized act in relation to this publication may be liable to criminal prosecution and civil claims for damages.

All characters and events in this book are completely fictional and a product of the author's own imagination.

Paperback Book: ISBN: 978-1-938526-14-5
E-Book: ISBN: 978-1-938526-15-2

This book is sold subject to the condition that it shall not, by way of trade or otherwise, be lent, re-sold, hired out, or otherwise circulated without the publisher's prior consent in any form of binding or cover other than that in which it is published and without a similar condition including this condition being imposed on the subsequent purchaser.

Cover by Jennifer Tipton Cappoen
Edited by Camille Miller and Nancy E. Williams

Published by:

 Marbry Books
P.O. Box 894
Locust Grove, Georgia 30248 USA
www.MarbryBooks.com

This book may be purchased from TheLaurusCompany.com, Amazon.com, and other retailers around the world.

Dedication

To my mother and father,
Irene Rusniak Cacciotti and Joseph Cacciotti,
for giving me the courage to always go after
what I believed in.

To a very special friend, Harold A. Schink,
who asked me for a special favor, and inspired me
to keep on writing.

To my wife, Diane,
my three daughters, Wendy, Stacy, and Jennifer,
and my son, Joel Curran,
for believing in me.

Chapter One

Janice Jenkins had not stopped looking out the window of the plane since it had taken off from Mitchell International Airport in Milwaukee, Wisconsin, headed for Las Vegas. Now, as the airplane soared high above the clouds, Sam Rufus knew he needed to pry her nails loose from his arm. He couldn't believe how strong she was for such a little woman.

"Janice, why don't we switch seats so you can relax? I don't think my arm will be of any use if you keep looking out that window."

Janice turned toward Sam for the first time since the plane left the ground. She noticed a tiny spot of blood on his arm and realized what she had done. Releasing her grip, she grabbed a tissue and began to apologize, "I'm sorry, Sam. This is my first flight, and I was a bit scared when we left the ground."

"I figured that out, but that was almost an hour ago," Sam teased.

"We've been up here an hour already?" Janice exclaimed in disbelief. "It seems like we just left the airport."

She was like a kid in a candy store enjoying the view. When they flew over the Grand Canyon, she let out a gasp. "I had no idea it was this big. It spreads out forever." She was mesmerized until they were over the big mountain, "Look at how big the desert is, Sam!"

"Yeah, it seems to go on forever." Sam was really thinking, *Look at all that land where you could bury someone. I'll bet if I had a big earthmover, I could find plenty of bodies down there.*

Sam was always on the job and always thinking like a detective. Janice had told him as much after the call came in from Wayne Newman asking him to come to Las Vegas. He didn't know the extent of the problem yet, but he knew it had to be serious. He wasn't usually called unless circumstances were dire.

Since his training in the Green Berets, Sam knew he had to stay focused at all times to survive, especially since Janice was now in his life. He had not had a serious girlfriend before, so he would have to be extra careful. This woman had a power over him that he had never experienced before, and it could be very disconcerting.

Janice was beside herself as they approached Las Vegas. The sight of all the hotels and casinos was breathtaking.

As the plane started to land, Janice grabbed Sam's arm again. *Good thing it's my left arm, just in case I have to use my gun*, Sam thought to himself. Janice was like a little kid seeing Disneyland for the first time. She finally released Sam's arm from her grip to snap her seatbelt. She was so intrigued with the sights on the ground that she didn't even feel Sam reach around her for the belt.

When the airplane finally stopped moving, Janice looked at Sam and said, "Thank you, Sam, for bringing me. This is the most beautiful sight I've ever seen."

Sam smiled. "I feel blessed. This is the second most beautiful thing I've seen in the past few weeks."

Janice turned and gave him a smile that almost melted his heart. Like Charles Reade once said "Beauty is power; a smile is its sword." Sam had to pinch himself as it dawned on him that standing right next to him was a five-foot-eight, one-hundred-and-twenty-five-pound angel with an hourglass figure. The wind was blowing her shoulder-length fluffy brunette hair all around as they exited the plane. Sam thought of another quote once said by Martin Luther that went, "The hair is the richest ornament of women." Sam knew he was a lucky man. *Is this what it feels like to be in love*, he wondered. He knew he had never felt this way before. He was even becoming poetic.

After they retrieved their luggage, Sam was just about to flag down a taxi when he saw a young fellow standing by a limousine holding a sign that read, "Hurricane." They walked over to the young man and introduced themselves. He held the door open, and Janice entered first. The young man patted Sam on the shoulder and said, "You're a very lucky man, sir," nodding his head toward Janice. Sam looked at him and smiled as he nodded in agreement.

"Sam, I never realized Nevada was so big. I wonder how many people live here?" Janice asked after their luggage has been placed in the luggage compartment.

"Well, it just happens that I did some research on this lovely state before we left Wisconsin. Nevada is nicknamed "The Silver State," with a land mass of over 100,000 square miles. It is the seventh largest state, with a population of 2.2 million and growing, ranking it thirty-fifth in the charts. Las Vegas is the largest city, with a population of 508,000 people."

"Wow, Sam, I'm impressed. You sound like a walking encyclopedia. How did you have time to find this out when you were with me?"

"Hold on, I'm not finished yet." Sam pulled a sheet of paper from his pocket and started reading. He knew Janice would love the information.

"The Mormon Missionaries settled in Las Vegas in 1855. They built a fort that covered one hundred and fifty square feet, built of clay, soil, and sand, now known as 'adobe.' Between 1830 and 1884, the name 'Vegas' was changed to 'Las Vegas,' which means 'The Meadows' in Spanish. In 1890 railroad developers decided that with all the water here, it would be a prime location for a depot and even a town. In 1864, Nevada had been admitted into the Union. October 1, 1910, an anti-gambling law was enforced, and it was strict. It was against the law to even flip a coin for a drink. In the 1940s, a mobster named 'Bugsy' Siegel built the Flamingo Hotel with a member of the Meyer Lansky crime organization. In 1946, New Year's Eve, six months after 'Bugsy' Siegel was murdered, a giant pink neon sign, with replicas of pink flamingos, stood in front as the first gambling casino that was opened."

"Now, look at how big it is." Sam finished.

"I wonder if Siegel ever envisioned this being as big as it is now, and think about the guts it took to take desert land and turn it into beauty."

Janice was speechless as the taxi drove down Las Vegas Boulevard. She kept reading the casino and hotel signs—New York New York, Sands Hotel, Riviera, Moulin Rouge, Stardust, and Tropicana. The limousine stopped in front of Harrah's Hotel and Casino.

The driver jumped out, opened their door, and insisted on carrying their luggage inside the building where the concierge met them. "Mr. Hurricane, welcome to our establishment. You have the VIP room on the fifteenth floor." He led them to the front desk clerk to sign the register. The desk clerk turned to the uniformed young man standing next to him and handed him the room key. "Howie, escort our guests to their room, please."

Sam looked at the three men, "Excuse me, but I've never seen you before. How do you know who I am?" Sam asked, puzzled.

"Are you kidding me, Mr. Hurricane?" the young bellhop answered. "I've read all about you in the newspapers. You're a big hero in these parts. Are you here on business or pleasure?" the young man naively asked.

After a slight pause, Sam said, "Just call me 'Sam.' All of my friends do," as he held out his hand toward the fellow behind the counter.

"Henry, sir. My name is Henry, and it is a real pleasure to meet you, Sam." Henry had a firm grip, and Sam liked that. He could tell if a person had respect by their handshake. That trait has come from his Italian father. His Shoshone mother was much more wary of people.

"Is Mr. Wayne Newman here yet, Henry?"

"No, Sam, he isn't, but as soon as he comes in, I'll tell him you're here."

"Good enough, my friend. We might be in the casino for a while in case we don't answer the phone."

Henry gave a slight smile and shook his head as Janice and Sam went around the corner. Sam decided Henry was a good man; he understood without a word. *Discretion*, Sam thought, and a smile tickled the corner of his mouth.

They entered the elevator expecting a long ride to the fifteen floor and maybe a few stops along the way. But as soon as the doors closed, Sam was almost scraping himself off the floor. They were on the fifteenth floor within mere seconds.

"That's the fastest elevator I've ever been on," Sam stated. Janice shook her head in agreement. He couldn't help noticing that she looked a little wobbly as they started walking.

When Howie opened the door to enter the room, they couldn't believe their eyes. The bed inside the room was big enough to sleep three or four people. There was plush carpeting throughout the room, a big refrigerator, a microwave, a hair dryer, and a cabinet stocked with all kinds of candy bars, nuts, and refreshments. On further investigation, they even had a safe inside their closet to hide their important stuff. The most impressive part of the room was the view out their window. They could practically see down the whole strip, and it was a breathtaking sight.

Howie unloaded their luggage and instructed them to call if they needed anything. Sam handed him a nice tip as he started to leave, but Howie raised both hands and stated politely, "On the house, Mr. Hurricane." He bowed slightly and left the room.

Sam stared after him for a moment before turning back to Janice. "Well, kiddo, what do you say about going downstairs? Let's see if lady luck is on our side tonight," Sam said as he placed his gun in the safe.

"That sounds good. Maybe if you play your cards right, Mr. Hurricane, Lady Luck will strike twice tonight." A wicked little grin crossed her face as she looked at him.

Sam felt his body react and grinned ear to ear, his mind too preoccupied to answer. Janice noticed his sudden silence and smiled at Sam's facial expression. She reached out and took Sam's hand into hers. He tickled the inside of her palm, and she playfully hit him on the shoulder as she whispered, "Maybe later, baby. Right now, I want to see the bright lights."

They were still smiling at each other when they entered the elevator, and then they were clutching the handrails. The elevator descended even faster than it had gone up. Sam felt like he would go through the roof. When the elevator finally stopped, Janice exited first and asked, "Are you getting off with me?"

"I thought I'd go back up and get my stomach," Sam said. They laughed as they walked out the door. "What will it be, my princess? Roulette, Black Jack, Poker, or the slot machines?"

"With so much to choose from, I'm not sure where to start. Why don't we start out slow and try the slot machines first?"

Walking over to the machines Janice observed, "They have every kind of machine imaginable, from a penny to well over a dollar. Which one shall we play?"

"Well, we may never get back here again, so let's go big and try the dollar machines," Sam said.

They each picked a machine and inserted their twenty dollar bills. "Oh, that's great," Sam said, "another decision. Do I bet one dollar or three dollars?" Then he shrugged his shoulders and played one dollar. He pulled the handle and won on the first spin. He slapped his leg as he won fifty dollars. If he had played three dollars, he would have more than five hundred.

Sam heard Janice scream and ran over to see if she was all right. "Sam! Sam! I won five hundred dollars on my third pull. I love this game."

Sam knew he would never live this down, but he was grateful that she was on his side. Sam went back to his own machine and lost. Just as he was about to insert another twenty, a voice called out to him.

"Mr. Hurricane, I presume."

Sam turned around to see who had called him. He saw a man standing about five feet ten and weighing around a hundred eighty-five pounds. His complexion was smooth and clear. He figured he must have been part Cherokee Indian. Sam knew this man had a voice so unique that when he sang, you could almost envision being there. He was a sellout every time he came to Vegas. Sam didn't know for sure if he was the owner of Harrah's, or if he just entertained there. He had been there so long that most people figured he owned the casino. Sam knew one thing, if Wayne Newman wanted to, he could probably own it and more.

Sam walked over with his hand extended and said, "Mr. Wayne Newman. I've been a fan of yours ever since I saw you and your brother Jerry sing on a local TV show back in the 60s. Then I heard you sing 'Danke Schoen' and 'Red Roses for a Blue Lady.' You made those songs hits at age twenty-one, and now you are a legend at the age of … thirty, is it?"

"I'm very impressed, Hurricane. I had heard you were a stickler for details. I guess what I heard was correct." Wayne's face grew serious. "I need some help, and I wasn't sure which way to turn. Henry, our hotel manager, told me to give you a call. After what he told me before and what I've observed so far, I think he was right. I'm hoping you will be able to help."

"First of all, Mr. Newman, call me 'Sam'."

"On one condition only, if you call me 'Wayne' from now on."

"Fair enough, Wayne. Now you can tell me what you need, and I'll let you know if I can help."

Wayne glanced around to see if they were alone. "Sam, I'm having problems keeping my dancing girls."

This is out of my league, Sam thought to himself, wondering why they would call him about employment problems. He nodded and kept listening.

"I mean they have disappeared. Nobody has seen hide nor hair of them. I replace them, but sooner or later, they disappear as well. I'm afraid of putting any more girls in harm's way. It's almost like someone is trying to ruin my reputation and my business. Now I'm afraid to hire any more dancers for fear of losing them, too, and not knowing where they are or what has happened to them."

"Have you spoken to the police?"

"Yes, but they are short staffed. They've tried to investigate it, but with nothing to go on, they figured the girls went back home or found other employment."

"That's a possibility, isn't it?"

"I've always paid my dancers well, and if they needed more, all they had to do was ask. I treated them like they were my own kids. I just couldn't see them leaving without at least telling me first. I can't help thinking they were kidnapped, but why? I haven't been contacted for ransom money."

"When was the last time they were seen?"

"So, you'll take the job then?"

"I'll let you know for sure tomorrow. How can I get hold of you if I find out something?"

"I'll give you my private phone number. Just don't let it get out. I love my fans, but I also need my sleep. Who would want to kidnap these girls, Sam?"

"I'm just going on a hunch. I hope I'm wrong. Either way, I'll let you know. By the way, Wayne, my girlfriend is with me, and she's also a big fan of yours. May I bring her over and introduce you?"

"Anyone who's your friend is also mine. I'd love to meet her."

Sam stepped closer to Janice and tapped her shoulder. "Janice, could you come over here, please? There is someone I'd like you to meet."

Janice turned toward him, and they walked over to the gentleman standing with his back to them.

"You have to promise me you will not scream," Sam told her.

"Why would I scream, unless you're talking about meeting *him*?"

"Him? To whom are you referring?" Sam teased.

"You know full well, Sam Rufus. Is Wayne Newman here yet?"

Just as she asked that, Wayne turned around, and Janice fainted dead away. "Do all the ladies have this reaction when they meet you?" Sam asked.

"Let's get her up to your room, Sam."

"Do I have you to thank for the VIP room, Wayne?"

"That's the least I could do for you, since you may be helping me out."

When they were finally up in the room and Janice was back with the program, she was feeling terribly embarrassed at her reaction. She hoped she had not caused a scene. She was not usually such an emotional person. Wayne finally broke her out of her spell and put her at ease, "Janice, I hear you are a big fan of mine." She shook her head yes. "Here are two front row tickets for my show tonight. Do you think you could make it?"

Janice glanced at Sam and replied, "Absolutely! Thank you." She was still having trouble believing it was really Wayne Newman.

Wayne just laughed as he said, "Now, Sam, I'd like you to make sure you and this beautiful woman make it to my show tonight."

"Are you kidding me? Getting her there, that's no problem. Getting her to leave will be like taking a scared cat out of a tree."

They both laughed as Wayne left to get ready for his show. Janice decided to take a short nap to recuperate from her shock. It was still early, and Sam wanted to look around a bit. He decided to fish around in some other casinos to see if they had been having trouble, too. He found out that several others were also losing performers. How could all these people disappear from sight? Sam decided to check with the local police to see if they might have something they could add to the question at hand.

When Sam finally found the police station and walked in the front door, five officers were sitting behind their desks. "Officers, could you please tell the captain that Sam Rufus would like to chat with him?" One of the men stood up and walked around the corner. He returned with another gentleman close behind.

"Mr. Rufus, I'm Sheriff John Adams. How can I help you?" he said, extending his hand.

"I'd like to ask if you have found anything that could help with all of the girls who have gone missing lately."

"I see, and may I ask what business it is of yours?"

"I've been asked to check on this case by a close friend of mine. I told him I wanted to ask you and see if you've found out anything first. I was told you were understaffed and might need a hand in solving this case."

"I'm not quite sure I'm following you, Mr. Rufus. Are you a police officer?"

"I was once, but now I'm a private detective. I was wondering if you would like to work together in solving this case. If not, I'm more than willing to tackle it alone."

"What do you want, Mr. Rufus? We barely have enough manpower to cover the strip the way it is now. I really can't afford to give up any help."

"I don't need any more men, Captain. All I need is your permission to use your computer, along with your expertise, if I need a few questions answered."

"I guess we can work together then, Mr. Rufus."

"Great, maybe we can crack this case together. If I come up with anything, I'll keep in touch with you. I hope you'll return the favor to me, out of respect for the uniform. From now on, please, either call me 'Sam' or 'Hurricane'."

Captain Adams and all his men looked startled. They had heard stories about a man named Hurricane. They all thought he was a fictitious character someone made up to sell newspapers. Captain Adams finally broke the silence. "So, the Hurricane really does exist? We thought it was a made-up story. Well, as long as we'll be working together, let me introduce my men. Over in the corner to your right is Detective Charlie Watts. Next to him is Billy Connors, and in the middle row Sam Huston and John Silvers. Over there behind that corner desk is Sandy Logan, our dispatcher. We have eight others on second and third shifts. I'll introduce them to you later. Let me recant on what I said before. I'll see if I can clear some possible overtime from the mayor and have a couple men lend you a hand."

"I appreciate that, Captain. Wow, is it really seven o'clock already? I have a date tonight, and if I'm late, I might just be missing in action. I'll talk to you tomorrow, Captain."

They all laughed as Sam raced out of the building and headed back to Harrah's.

Janice was waiting by the door ready to go when Sam walked in. Her expression said it all. With only fifteen minutes before show time, they raced toward the elevator, grateful that the show was in the same building. He yelled as the elevator door started to close. A young lady heard him and stopped the doors from closing.

Inside the theater, the lights went out just as the usher seated them on the front row, center stage. The show was ready to begin. The curtain rose, and the band started playing. There was a full arrangement of instruments.

Three violin players had a sound of angels skipping on clouds, along with the trumpets, saxophones, trombones, clarinets, a percussionist, a regular drummer, and a lead guitarist. There were three microphones on stage but only two backup singers. Then Wayne's voice echoed as he entered from the back of the room.

All the ladies' eyes were glued on Wayne as he strolled around singing "Hello Dolly." *What a lucky man*, Sam thought. Wayne went around the room shaking hands with the men and kissing the women, and before the song was over, he was standing on the stage looking at Sam and Janice. He waved and smiled at them as he addressed the audience.

"Ladies and gentlemen, thank you for coming tonight. Unfortunately, one of my backup singers became ill before the show." Wayne looked toward Sam in a way that let him know there was more to it, and then he continued, "I promise to give you a great show tonight, so please, sit back and let us entertain you."

The audience was mesmerized as Wayne sang his most popular songs. His backup singers also sang some solos, and he took time to introduce all of his stage people. He even threw in some comedy. It was easy to tell he was well liked by his band as they joked around with each other on stage. It was a great show, and Wayne thanked all of his fans for coming when the show ended. Sam glanced at his watch and couldn't believe Wayne had sung for a solid two hours.

Sam and Janice remained seated as most of the fans exited the room. Several minutes later, the stage door opened, and a security guard invited those who had been waiting to meet Wayne to follow him inside. Sam's mind was spinning with thoughts of a disloyal guard, but not that guy. He looked like a seasoned gentleman. Twenty minutes later, Sam's name was called. He and Janice were escorted backstage to Wayne's dressing room. After shaking Sam's hand, Wayne looked intently into Janice's eyes and kissed her on the lips.

"Hold it, Wayne. She's mine."

"Not until I see a ring on her finger, my friend."

"All in good time," Sam answered, slipping his arm around her waist and drawing her close.

Janice was on cloud nine and probably would remain there for a while.

"I'd really love to see you two make this permanent. You have a beautiful lady here, and if you aren't interested ..." Wayne's voice trailed off as he gave Janice another admiring look. "Well, we'll talk about that later. Have you found out anything yet about my problem?"

"It looks like it's not just your problem. Several other casinos are also missing girls from their acts. It's like they disappeared into thin air. I talked to Captain John Adams at the police department about what's happening to these girls. There is no solid evidence to indicate foul play.

"I'm going to check around and make a few notes. Maybe I can come up with something. I will report anything I find to the Captain, and he's going to return the favor if he uncovers anything. I think if we work together, we will find out something. He's going to authorize some overtime to help us out. I just need a place to start. I'll canvas the area tonight and ask a few questions. Maybe someone heard or saw something."

"Stay on the strip," Wayne advised. "If you wander past the perimeter, you may not like what you find, especially if you're walking alone."

"I'm not alone, my friend. I have Janice with me."

"You're kidding me, right? How can this angel possibly protect you?"

"She looks like an angel, but she fights like a tornado."

Janice lowered her chin and blushed a bright red as she elbowed Sam in the ribs.

"Great! We go from a peaceful community to a possible tropical storm," Wayne said with a sinister grin on his face. "All right, my friend, but don't hold anything back from me. You know how to get in touch with me. I just hope you have good news when you call."

"Don't worry, Mr. Newman. I mean, Wayne. I'll make sure he keeps in touch with you," Janice promised.

"Thank you, darling. Do me a favor and watch your backs."

They both nodded as they exited the door. Sam knew it was going to be a long night. If they only had some place to start looking.

It was a beautiful night, in the high eighties, and the air was still. Sam looked puzzled as to where to start. Janice suggested they start at the beginning. Flagging down a taxi, they headed for the Riviera. Sam felt lost without his little friend strapped to his side, but he didn't think he'd need it until they had something more solid to indicate a crime had actually taken place.

The cabby dropped them off at the back of the casino. After a short elevator ride, it was a sight to behold. This casino had to be at least two football fields long and had everything imaginable. They even had televisions in the far west corner for people to bet on the sports being played. Sam and Janice decided to split up to cover more ground. They would meet by the bar in the center of the casino.

It wasn't long before three guys approached Sam. "Hey, mister," one of the men yelled, "what are you doing here?"

Not knowing they were security guards, Sam stood his ground. "Minding my own business, and I suggest you boys do the same."

"If you're not gambling you need to leave."

"I'll leave when I find what I'm looking for."

The biggest guy made the mistake of grabbing Sam by the arm. Sam spun around and twisted the big guy's arm behind his back. "I don't want to hurt you guys. Just let me finish what I'm doing, and then I'll go peaceably."

Just as the other two were circling Sam for the kill, Janice came running in. She dropped down, sweeping the legs out from under guard number two. Sam brought a straight right into number three's jaw, and he went crashing down. "Tornado, did you find out the owner's name yet?"

"Nobody knows who it is, Hurricane."

"Wait," one of the guards said. "Why didn't you tell us you wanted to see the owner? It would have saved a lot of pain and suffering."

"You know who we're looking for, son?"

"Know him, we work for him. We are his best security guards. At least, I thought we were up until now."

"Relax, kid, we're professionals. Next time, instead of acting like a jerk, try a little conversation first. It's not as painful. This is my partner, Tornado, and I'm the Hurricane."

"I'm Jason. This is Rick and John." After shaking hands, John asked, "You're not really the Hurricane we read about, are you? I thought that was just a bunch of stories."

"No, John, it's really me. But now I'm twice as dangerous with my new partner, Tornado."

"The boss will see you now," Rick said.

"How does he know we are here?"

"You can't hide in a casino, sir. Eyes are everywhere," John answered.

Sam and Janice followed the trio toward the back of the casino. They entered a small room and walked toward the desk in the back. Jason pulled a book from the bookshelf, and a panel slid sideways giving entrance to a huge room. One of the walls was the size of three outdoor theater screens. It was loaded with all kinds of computer screens. You could see the whole casino floor from just inside these walls. Sam wondered if they had taped any trouble lately that may have happened in their establishment. Just as he was about to roll out the question, a voice changed his mind.

"I'm Stacy Sanders, part owner of the casino. Who do I have the honor of meeting?"

"Well, Mister Sanders, I'm Sam Rufus, and this is Janice Jenkins. We'd like to ask you a few questions if we could."

"I'll try to answer the best I can. What are your questions? Nothing personal I hope," he chuckled.

"Just a few standard questions, Mr. Sanders," Sam started, "like, have you lost any showgirls within the past few months?"

"Now that you mentioned it, yes. I just figured they went elsewhere. Don't tell me it's more serious."

"Janice and I were called in to check out the situation. So far, almost every casino has lost a few showgirls. We were hoping maybe you had caught some funny stuff in the casino on the videotapes."

"You're welcome to look at anything you'd like. Just make sure you keep them in order, please. We have to account for every activity every day, just in case something like this happens. I'll set you up in the corner over by the far wall. Please, let me know if you find anything. Is there any place special you'd want to look? As you can see we have tapes in all the surrounding areas. We should try to narrow it down to a certain place, or you could be here for six months viewing tapes."

"Well, the last abduction we know of happened after the last show at Harrah's. She was last seen headed for the casino."

"When the show is on, the bright lights affect the cameras. So we turn them off until the people exit the showroom. It will be like finding a needle in a haystack."

"How many shows are there in one day?" Sam asked.

"Five shows, maybe six on the weekends, not to mention all the free shows from others on the casino floors."

"When was the last time a girl was a no show here?"

"Two weeks ago, I believe," Stacy answered. "She was one of the best dancers we had."

"That's where we start looking then. Please let us see the tapes from when she was last seen."

After showing Sam and Janice how to work the equipment, they were left alone to view the tapes. Sam looked at his watch. It was nearly ten o'clock at night. They were there for almost twelve straight hours. Just as they were getting ready to give it up, Janice jumped up saying, "What was that, Sam?" They backed up the tape and slowly ran it forward. "There, did you see the arm come out from nowhere and grab the girl?"

After going back and forth a few times, they found the time on the tape was after the last show. One of the computer guys helped bring the screen in for a closer look. It was a dark corner and hard to get a clear shot, but one thing that stood out was a Rolex watch on the wrist. However, whoever the mystery person was, he was smart. He had on long sleeves and white gloves. It was impossible to tell his race.

"Sorry about that, Sam," Stacy said. "I wish there was more on the tape."

"No need to be sorry, Mr. Sanders. We have proof that someone is collecting these girls. All we have to do now is figure out who and hope these girls are still alive."

After a copy of the picture was made, Janice asked, "Where to now, partner?"

"We have to see if the other casinos have a tape of this person. Maybe we will see his face or some skin. It's going to be a long night, Janice."

"How many casinos are on this strip, Mr. Sanders?" Janice asked.

"Not counting the ones on the rise and not yet completed, I believe twelve to fifteen."

"We're going to need help, partner."

Sam pulled out his cell phone and called the police department. After a few seconds of silence, Sam's voice echoed. "Captain John Adams, please."

"Yes, Captain, we may have found our needle in the haystack. Could you spare a few of your good men and give us a hand surveying a few videotapes? I'll fill you in tomorrow. Right now, maybe four guys, if you can. Thank you again, sir. Could you please send them over to the Riviera, and I'll explain what we are doing."

"Sam, if you need men, I'll ask if anyone on my staff would like to help out," Sanders said.

"I appreciate that, sir. Normally, I would say no, but after what it's taken so far just to find a watch, we would love to have extra help."

Four men pulled up in a police car and walked up to Sam. "Mr. Hurricane?"

"'Sam,' please. All of you call me 'Sam.' Here's what we have going." Sam explained the situation and what he was looking for. When he was finished, he asked, "Gentlemen, let me see if I have the names right." He called out as he pointed, "Charlie Watts, Billy Connors, Sam Huston, John Silvers, and the gorgeous Sandy Logan."

"That was good, sir. How did you remember our names so fast?"

"Almost fifteen years of practice, my friends. You'll get there in a few more years," Sam replied, smiling. Then he added, "Good luck, ladies and gentlemen. If you find anything, get hold of me on my cell phone." He passed out the number. "No matter how small it looks, it may be bigger than you think."

While Sam was addressing the officers, Mr. Sanders was busy calling the other casinos. They were all willing to pitch in and help. Sam was just hoping this wasn't a big waste of time. His head was saying, "Maybe," but his gut kept saying, "Try it." Lately, his instincts were right on the money. If only they had more to go on than just a blasted watch. Granted, it was more than they had before, but this was Las Vegas, and Rolex watches were as common here as slot machines. Sam decided to ask around the jewelry stores and find out what makes these watches so intriguing.

After entering several stores and looking at the watches, he noticed each watch had its own unique style. Some had little diamonds in them. Others had different faces, such as a compass or a calendar etched into them. Other than the price, they all looked pretty much the same. Sam noticed someone coming toward him in the reflection in the glass case. Then a voice spoke, "May I help you, sir?"

Glancing at the name tag on his pocket, Sam answered, "Yes, Jesse. Why are these watches so much more expensive than the others?"

"If you have to ask that question, these are not for you," he said in a snobbish tone.

"That's not a very polite response, Jesse. Are you like this with all your customers, or just the ones who look like me?"

"This is the United States, and it's still a free country. I can talk to whomever I want how I want."

"I think somebody in this store needs an attitude adjustment," Sam said.

"I think you better leave this establishment before I call the police."

Sam flipped out his badge. "I am the police, Jesse, and I don't appreciate the abuse I have just gone through. This will be on my report unless you answer a few questions."

"I'm sorry, officer. I had no idea. I'll answer anything you want."

"Now that we understand one another, let's try this again, shall we? What's so different about these watches?"

"Each watch has its own personality. You can tell by the graphics on it. They are all hand crafted and made in the USA, and they are all guaranteed to keep perfect time."

"They all look the same to me, how can you tell the difference?"

Jesse took out four watches that all looked the same and spread them out on the counter. "Yes, if you look at them like this, they all look the same, but look them over a bit closer. Do you see how each diamond is a little different, some larger than others or a little off center? Then look at the hands on the watch, one has a diamond on the tip, the other has a silver line, and this one has a little hole at the top. The second hands are also different, and they have either a compass or a calendar on the face."

"So, each watch has its own identity, so to speak?"

"Yes, and not only that, each watch is registered in case it gets lost or stolen."

"If I brought you a picture of a watch, could you trace it back to its owner?"

"Yes, it's possible, depending on how clear the picture is and if I can read the face of the watch. It may take a while to find due to the fact that there are possibly close to a million, if not more, of these watches out there."

"Now, Jesse, this is how you should talk to all of your customers all of the time. I may be back in a few days to ask you for a favor. Maybe we can become good friends and help each other. Until then, I have a lot of work to do. I thank you for the information. You've been a big help to a complicated mission." It was a long shot, but at least they had something to shoot for.

Sam walked out fast, flagged down a taxi, and headed for Harrah's. He had a few questions for Wayne. He couldn't believe how people drove in Las

Vegas, as the cab driver darted from one lane to the other all the way down the strip to the casino. He never missed a beat as he zigged and zagged down the street, very seldom slowing for traffic and only stopping for the lights if he just happened to miss them. He did it so smoothly, as if he had been doing this for years, but Sam found out he had been driving for only three years. He shook his head in disbelief and asked, "Was it difficult to drive here when you first started?"

"For the first couple hours. Then you learn not to think about it and just do it."

By the time he finished his sentence they were at Harrah's. "What time is your shift over, Ivan, is it?"

"Yes, sir, my name is Ivan. I just started my shift, and I'll be working until four in the morning."

"How would you like to work for me tonight, Ivan? I like how you drive in a no nonsense style."

"I would like to, sir."

"Just call me 'Sam'."

"All right, Sam. Let me contact my supervisor and let him know where I'll be." Ivan reached for his car radio and asked for his supervisor. When he responded to the call, Ivan explained what was asked of him.

"I have no problem with that, just make sure he pays you when it's over," the supervisor said.

Sam grabbed the radio mike from Ivan's hand and spoke up. "This is the guy who would like to retain Ivan for a few hours tonight. I'll pay him well when I've completed my business. My name is Sam Rufus. If you would like to check up on me, please call Captain John Adams at the Las Vegas Police Department, and he'll verify who I am."

"Very good, Mr. Rufus, you may have Ivan as long as it takes tonight. We've been a bit slow tonight anyway."

Sam instructed Ivan to keep a running account of what he owed him. Ivan was already doing just that as he marked it down in his logbook. Sam snickered and headed back into the casino.

Janice saw Sam as he entered the room. He seemed to have something on his mind, as he had walked right passed her.

"Well, excuse me, Mr. Hurricane!" she yelled out.

Sam stopped in his tracks and looked back at Janice. He apologized for walking by her, as he grabbed her arm and started walking fast down the aisle. She had never seen Sam like this and knew it had to be important. They finally stopped by the elevator and Janice had a chance to catch her breath. Sam reached for the buttons and pushed the twentieth floor.

"Who's on that floor?" she asked.

"Wayne told me he'd be staying there for a few hours before his show. I just hope he's still there."

When they reached Wayne's room, Sam knocked hard in case he had the radio or television on. They heard footsteps, and the door opened slowly.

"Sam and Janice, this is a nice surprise. Please, come on in. I hope this is a social call." Then he saw the look in Sam's eyes. "I guess this is a business call. Have you found out something already?"

"Wayne, what kind of watch do you own?"

"It's a Rolex. Why do you ask?"

"Whoever grabbed the girls has a Rolex watch. That's the only bit of evidence we have so far. I have to see if any other surveillance cameras caught a piece of this guy."

"Sam, almost everyone in this town owns a Rolex watch, either a real one or a knock-off. If that's what you have so far, it's very slim."

"Yes, but that's all we have so far. If we can get a clear picture of it, they may be able to chase down who owns it."

"If it's fake, you'll have done a lot of work for nothing."

"But if it's real, I'll have some place to start."

"Can't argue that logic, my friends. I wish you well. I'd like to stay and chat some more, but I have a show to do. Please stay, and we'll talk later. Better yet, why not come and watch the show?"

"I have to check on the other guys. Janice can go, and I'll join you as soon as I'm done."

Janice gladly accepted Wayne's extended arm, and they headed down toward the stage. Sam headed back down to the casino. Ivan looked happy to see him enter his cab.

"Ivan, could you please take me to police headquarters?" He paid Ivan and took down his phone number. "I might be a bit longer with the Captain, so I'll call you when I need you."

"Very good, Sam. I'll just be a phone call away," Ivan said.

Sam was in front of the building within a few minutes. Captain Adams hurried toward him and said, "Sam, I was just going to call you. I think we might have something here. When John and Billy were checking on the casino tapes at Circus Circus, they stumbled on someone pulling one of the missing girls out a door. But they only have his arm to go by."

"Did he have a Rolex watch on?" Sam interrupted.

"Why, yes, he did! How do you know that?"

"I saw the same arm on the Riviera tape, but it wasn't a very clear picture."

"We didn't think ours was good either until Sandy put it on her computer, and presto! Take a look for yourself."

Sam couldn't believe how clear the picture was. "Sandy, could you make a close up photo as clear as this? I have someone who may be able to help us out."

Sandy shook her head yes and proceeded to make the copy. Captain Adams asked Sam, "Did you find out something without letting me know?"

"I just found out a couple hours ago myself. I was checking out other tapes as well, hoping to get a clean copy. One of the owners in a downtown jewelry store said he could possibly find the owner if we had a clear enough photo."

After the copy was complete, Sam and Captain Adams were on the move. Sam thought the guy at the jewelry store was going to pass out when he saw Sam enter his store again.

"Hey, Jesse, remember me? I have that picture you said you needed."

"What picture?" he asked dumbly.

"The picture of the watch you said you could trace back to the owner."

"Oh, yes, now I remember. You were looking at the Rolex watches. I didn't recognize you at first."

Sam and Captain Adams both heard a bit of nervousness in the tone of his voice. Slowly, Captain Adams started circling the store, acting like he was looking for something in particular. Sam was checking out his big picture mirror hanging on the wall in back of the counter. Something didn't feel right to Sam. Observing Jesse's behavior, he wondered if they had possibly interrupted a robbery in progress.

"You don't have any surprises for us, now do you, Jesse?" He nodded in a slow yes motion. "I bet it's all behind you now, isn't it?" Jesse just grinned wide. "Well, when you have something, please call either Captain John

Adams or myself."

"If I call you, for whom should I ask ?"

"Just ask for the Hurricane, kid." As he said that, he spun around knocking Jesse to the floor. He drew his gun and pointed it toward the mirror. "If you want to live, I'd suggest you come out now. If not, you're dead where you stand."

There was some shuffling, and then Sam heard a familiar voice, "You're surrounded. Come out with your hands up." It was Captain Adams who had slipped out the back door and had them boxed in from the rear entrance.

One by one, they exited toward the front of the store. "I told you he was only one man. Let's take him down," the tougher-looking guy said.

Sam released the bolt action of his gun and put it away in his shoulder holster. Then he motioned for the guy with the big mouth to come on down. "I have a deal for you since you're the tough guy here."

"Let's hear it, Mr. Policeman!"

"First of all, I'm not a policeman. I'm the Hurricane. Second of all, if you win, I will set all of you free. But when you lose, you all come along peacefully, and we book you for theft."

"You're not the Hurricane. He's a myth, not a real person. I was told he's a cartoon character."

"You were told wrong, my young friend. Would you like to find out the hard way?"

"First of all, I'm not your friend. And second of all, I'm going to enjoy kicking your butt." He took a big swing at Sam. Sam ducked and came up with a roundhouse right, sending the young man flying backward against the wall. "Not hard enough, pop. I can still get up, and now you've made me mad." He began running toward Sam, who let the thief hit him in the jaw. Sam didn't budge. He just stood there and smiled.

"If that's all you have, kid, this will not take long at all." Sam hit the young man so hard that he flew back and hit the wall again. He wasn't as fast getting up this time. "Just stay down, kid, unless you want to feel some real pain."

The punk didn't listen. He picked up a broken mirror piece and started swinging it toward Sam. He saw Sam laughing and charged at him. Sam brought up his leg and kicked the glass back into the kid's stomach. Sam figured it was over and made the mistake of turning his back. Two shots rang out. One bullet hit Sam in the left arm, and the other one killed the kid. "Stupid kid," Sam remarked. "I hate it when it ends this way."

The other thieves surrendered and waited for the paddy wagon to arrive. Captain Adams and Sam tied them back-to-back and displayed them out on the curb. People were walking past and laughing at them as they struggled to get comfortable. When they were finally loaded and headed to jail, Sam and Captain Adams returned to see how shaken up Jesse was. When they entered, they heard Jesse say, "Man, that was cool. Not to sound ungrateful, but how did you know those guys were back there? Was it something I said?"

"Not *what* you said, but how you said it, my friend." Sam answered. "I'm just glad I decided to go back up to the room and get my gun. Now, do you happen to have a first aid kit around here so I can patch up this arm?"

Jesse retrieved the first aid box from the back and started dressing Sam's wound. "It's a superficial flesh wound, I'm pretty sure," he said as he cleaned the blood from Sam's arm and pulled out the gauze bandages. "By the way, I think this is a fake watch. The watchband looks too original. I'll send it in anyway, just in case I'm wrong. I should hear something back from them in two or three days."

"We don't have two or three days, Jesse. This may be the guy who's been kidnapping the showgirls from the casinos. The faster we find him the better chance they have of finding the girls alive," Captain Adams said.

"I'll fax it to them and let them know it's urgent. Maybe I'll know in a couple hours."

"Thank you, Jesse," Sam stated. "We'll be back in a few hours and check on it."

"No, Mr. Hurricane, it is I who should thank you for saving my store from being robbed and possibly for saving my life. Let me have your numbers, and when I hear something, I'll call you."

They all shook hands and parted ways. Captain Adams and Sam still had a lot of chasing to do. Sam was quiet as his thoughts turned to why the girls were being kidnapped. Who would benefit from all of this? Was there a serial killer lurking around, and if so, why hadn't any bodies turned up yet?

"I can tell by that look on your face what you are thinking, Sam," Captain Adams said. "I've beaten my head against the wall asking the same questions. What really boggles my mind the most is why we haven't found one shred of evidence of what is really going on?"

"Not only have we found no evidence, Captain, but we have not found anyone who has seen anything strange going on. I'm wondering if we haven't stumbled upon a slave market for beautiful women. The next question is how many people are in on it."

"Good point, Sam. I'm just hoping that all of those arms in the pictures are of the same person."

When Sam and the Captain arrived back at Headquarters, Sam asked. "Captain, how many photo images did we get so far?"

"We have twelve or more. Why do you ask?"

"About what time did these kidnappings take place?"

"Oh, yes, now I see what you're driving at. If these are all around the same day and time, there is more than one guy. And if not, we could set a trap and wait for the next abduction to take place. Very clever, my friend, but where do we start?"

"Captain, could I make a long distance phone call?"

Captain Adams gave his approval, and Sam started dialing. When he finally asked for his connection, everyone in the police station froze, trying to listen in on what was going on.

"Hello, could you please connect me with Colonel John Jones?" After a moment's silence, "Hello, Colonel, this is Sam Rufus, and I need your help."

"Who did you say you were?

"It's the Hurricane, Colonel. I need a favor."

"Hurricane! Why didn't you say so in the first place? It's good to hear from you. How can I help you?"

"I need a few of those transmitting devices the service has these days. I was wondering if I could influence you to send me a half dozen, or whatever you can spare. I'd sure appreciate it, and I'll owe you a favor."

"Are you kidding me, Hurricane? I still owe you big time for what you did for us in Rhode Island. Where shall I send the devices you want?" Sam gave the colonel the address, and the colonel added, "It just so happens that my wife and I will be in Las Vegas tomorrow. I'll bring them with me. I'll call you when we land. Then you can tell me the story behind this, and maybe I can help you this time."

"Those transmitters will be a big enough help, but I could always use a good military mind for moral support. I'll see you tomorrow, Colonel. Have a safe flight."

After Sam hung up the phone, he noticed all eyes were on him. "Do I look that bad?"

"We can't believe you actually called a full-fledged colonel. What are those transmitter things you were talking about?"

"Everyone will hold one, and when you see something suspicious, like a stranger looking all around or a car running, you will find a way to attach it to that person or vehicle. Then we can follow them and find out where they go. Maybe we'll find the missing piece we are looking for."

Just as Sam was getting ready to leave, his phone started ringing. "Hello, Sam here."

"You found out something already?"

"Stay there. Captain Adams and I will be right there."

"Jesse has something for us."

Captain Adams grabbed his hat as they ran out to the car. "Maybe we won't need those transmitters," the Captain said.

"I'm hoping you're right, Captain. I'll just wait until it's a sure thing."

Within a few minutes they entered Jesse's store. Jesse was standing behind the counter waiting.

"Well, guys, I have good news and bad news. Which do you want first?"

"Well, let's get the bad news out of the way," Sam said.

"It's authentic all right. However, it was stolen from a guy named Harold Schink. He lives in Wisconsin somewhere. He reported it stolen almost a year ago when he was here last."

"Now, what's the good news?"

"We contacted him, and he will send you a hundred dollar finder's fee. Where do you want it sent?"

"You take it, kid. You've earned it."

Turning to the Captain, Sam said, "Well, John, it's back to square one."

They walked out with their heads hung. All hopes were crushed, and the waiting game continued.

"Looks like we'll need those transmitters after all," Captain Adams said.

"Hopefully, things will improve tomorrow when we get the transmitters."

Sam said his goodbyes, stating that he had a couple friends he had to see. Maybe in the morning things would look better.

Sam and the Captain left the store, and Jesse stood there looked stunned. It had dawned on him that all he was holding was a picture and not the watch.

Chapter Two

When Sam woke up, the sun was peeking through the draperies. He couldn't remember going to bed last night. When he looked over and Janice was still sleeping, he knew something was wrong. He couldn't remember Janice being with him. *What kind of drink was I given last night?* he wondered.

Sam decided to try to get some answers in the bar in the casino. When he entered the room, the bartender asked, "How are you feeling today, Mr. Hurricane?"

"What happened to me last night, son?" Sam asked.

"You passed out after Manny served you your drink. Mr. Newman and your wife helped carry you up to your room."

"I don't recall ordering a drink last night, especially since I don't drink alcohol. Would you happen to know what I ordered?"

"I'm sorry, but our cash register tapes only tell us the dollar amount, not what was served. I wish I was able to help you more.

"When does Manny work again?"

"He should be here tonight. He works the middle hours, two in the afternoon to twelve midnight."

"Has he been working here long?"

"Almost a year I think, maybe longer. He likes the hours because he's finished working when all the shows are over."

"What difference would it make what time the shows are over?"

"Manny likes dating show girls. He's gone out with so many girls I can't even keep count."

"How would you know?"

"Because I relieve Manny every day he works. My name is Danny. I work from twelve midnight until nine or ten in the morning. I always see Manny walking out with another hot babe. Not to be rude, Mr. Hurricane, but your lady is also hot."

"Thank you, Danny. If I showed you some pictures, would you be able to remember if Manny has dated them?" Sam reached into his shirt pocket and took out pictures of the missing girls and handed them to Danny. Danny carefully looked at each one of the pictures and pulled a few out of the pile. "He's dated these five girls for sure. They used to work here."

"They don't work here anymore?"

"No. I found it kind of strange myself that, after their date with Manny, they never came back. When I asked him, he told me they found work somewhere else."

"Have you seen any of the people he hangs out with?"

"Once, when I came in about an hour early to stock the coolers. Manny didn't know I was here at first. I overheard him having a conversation with another scary-looking guy."

"Do you remember what was said?"

"I'll never forget it. He told Manny if he wanted his family to stay unharmed, he'd do what he was told. He also said if anyone found out about what they were doing from him, that they'd make sure his family would disappear without a trace."

"Did you ever question him about it?"

"No, but every now and then before he leaves, he'll get a phone call, and he gets all nervous. Once he just said, 'When will this end? I can't do this anymore.' I'll ask him if he needs help, and he just says the kind of help he needs I can't give him. Manny's a good man, Mr. Hurricane. I wish I could help him."

"What does he do after he receives the phone call? Where does he go?"

"I don't know. A couple of days ago he mentioned that he had a date with a hot girl from Harrah's. I asked him what she did here, and he told me she was a backup singer for Mr. Newman. She had just started a couple weeks ago, and she was really pretty."

"Does Manny have a Rolex watch?"

"Yes, he does. How did you know that?"

"Just a hunch, Danny. Thanks for the information. Here's twenty dollars for your trouble."

"Not that I want to sound ungrateful, Mr. Hurricane, but what did I do for this?"

"You helped Manny and gave me the next step in my investigation. Remember that help Manny was asking for?" Danny nodded his head yes. "I'm going to see that he gets all the help he needs. Where can I find him at this hour?"

Even though it was against the policy of the casino, Danny felt that helping a friend was more important than their policy and gave Hurricane Manny's address. Sam called Captain Adams and told him he needed to see him. He didn't want to tell him what he had found out over the phone.

Twenty minutes later, Sam walked into the Captain's office. He told him everything Danny had told him about Manny, the bartender. After a little bit of name calling and a few choice words that could be heard outside the closed door, Sam finally said, "Captain, please, let me talk to Manny first and find out what his story is. Maybe I can talk him into turning himself in. From what I've heard, his whole family has been threatened. Let's not get them killed before we find out what is going on. I'll let you know everything when I'm finished with him. He needs help, and since I'm an unknown in this area, I'll have a better chance of helping him. He just might be the piece of the puzzle we've been looking for. Let's bust the whole gang, not just a little fish in the big pond. What do you say, Captain?"

Even though Captain Adams wanted to arrest Manny, he knew what Sam said made a lot of sense. Maybe they could get Manny to work both sides and get the whole gang, all in one shot. "All right, Sam, let's do it your way. But if it looks hopeless, we take over."

"Fair enough, John. Let me get started then." Sam rose from his chair and had just opened the door to leave when in walked Colonel John Jones of the United States Army.

"Sam, I've had a lot of coincidental things happen to me in the past, but this one takes the prize. How'd you know I was about to open the door and come in? I declare, you have always had a knack for surprising people."

"Colonel, it was just being in the right place at the right time. It's great to see you again, Sir." Sam gave the colonel a big hug along with a strong handshake. After introducing the Captain and his crew to the colonel, they sat down, and Sam explained what was going on. Sam also told the colonel what they had found out since they last talked on the phone.

"Sam, this may be bigger than your Rhode Island job. Let me know if you need any backup. I might have some contacts who can help you."

"We might just take you up on your offer, Colonel. For now we'll just see what Manny may have for us. I think for now Captain Adams and his men are more than capable of handling this. However, if it ends up going deeper than we think, don't be surprised to hear from us."

"Captain Adams, you have a very good man here. Believe me when I say, if he gets certain gut feelings, don't ask questions. Just follow his instincts. He saved a lot of people during his last two missions. I just pray that when this is over all those missing girls can be found alive and well. Oh, Sam, I brought you twelve of those transmitters you asked for. After I told the General why you wanted them, he told me to give you as many as you needed. I also have three homing devises and twelve homing chips. My wife and I are staying at Harrah's, and if you need anything, please don't hesitate to find me."

Sam called Ivan, the cab driver. He was surprised to hear Sam's voice. "Ivan, would you by chance be working today?"

"Yes, I'm working, but not until two thirty. I may not be free tonight. I have orders to be available at one o'clock in the morning for a special job. You may have to call another cab driver. I'm sorry, but it's only ten in the morning, and I need my sleep for tonight." He said goodbye and hung up.

Sam flagged down another cab and headed toward Manny's apartment. He lived about fifteen minutes away from the strip. Sam instructed the cab driver to wait. He walked to the door and knocked. When the door opened, Sam had to look up. "Are you Manny?" he asked. The man stood at an impressive six feet six, weighed about three hundred seventy-five pounds, and was built almost like Walt Frazer, muscular arms and all.

"Who wants to know?"

"I understand you need some help. My name is Hurricane. I need to ask you a few questions, if you don't mind."

"Who sent you?"

"For his own protection I promised not to tell, but you can either talk to me or the police. From what I heard, you wouldn't want that. By the way, how's your family?"

Manny opened the door and let Sam in, looking nervously around outside before closing the door. He led Sam into the front room, offered him a seat, and asked if he would like something to drink. After refusing his gracious offer, Sam began the conversation.

"Manny, nobody in this town knows me yet, so I think you're safe for now. What did you slip in my drink last night?"

"Sorry about that. I was told to slip sleeping powder into your drink. It must have been pretty strong stuff. You passed out before half your glass of soda was gone. Your wife and Mr. Newman helped you up to your room."

"Who told you to drug me?"

"If I tell you, they'll kill my family."

"Manny, I know you're being framed. I promise you that if you tell me who these guys are, they will never bother you again."

"You may be able to stop one or two of them, but you'll never stop them all. The organization is too big, and if I tell you, I'm a dead man."

"How many are there, Manny?"

"I'm not really sure. I've never seen the big man on top, so I can't tell you. I only talk to him on the phone from time to time. I can tell you that every time I bring a girl to them, there are at least six guys on the docks and a few more inside. How many I don't really know."

"Could you find these docks?"

"No, I'm always blindfolded during the ride. All I know is I'm in a helicopter."

"How long is the flight?"

"I'd say around twenty or thirty minutes. I can't say for sure. I've never given it that much thought. I'm not sure how to tell since I have the blindfold on. I thought you were just a myth, Hurricane."

"No, Manny, I'm the real McCoy, and if you've read about my work, you know I always find a way to win. Can you give me anything I can check out on my own? If you work with us, we can guarantee you will not face any jail time, and I personally can guarantee you if you need help, I'm here for you."

"Tonight, I'll be visited at the bar by three body guards, and I will receive my next assignment. They normally arrive two days before the job is to be done, and two hours before my shift is over. Then before I go, I'll get a call explaining what will happen if I don't follow through with it."

"Thank you, Manny. You just act like yourself tonight, and don't get involved. I am going to start a fight and will make it look like an accident." Sam shook his big hand and told him not to worry. He knew for Manny that wasn't possible. Sam had to figure how to get Manny out of this and save his family as well.

Sam hopped into the cab and headed toward the Captain's office. After explaining his conversation with Manny, Captain Adams shook his head in disbelief, not wanting to face the fact that this was going on under his nose.

"Did Manny say how long this has been going on?"

"He never said, and I never asked. I figured he was under enough pressure. Why drop a fifty-pound weight on him as well."

"You're a very hard man to figure out, Sam. You have a rough exterior, but inside you're just a little pussy cat. What's our next step, my friend?"

"Tonight, I'm going to start a fight, and you're going to arrest us all, not just the bad guys."

"What time is this fight going to occur?"

"If Manny is right and they are on time, then somewhere around ten thirty or eleven tonight."

"I'll instruct my men on what to do. They will not harm you."

"Negative, John. They are not to treat me any different than the others, and they are to lock me up in the same cell."

"Sam, are you sure? That's like committing suicide. Think about this, will you?"

"Just do it, John. I know what I'm doing."

"All right, Sam. It's against my better judgment, but if that's what you want, don't hold it against me if you get hurt."

"One other thing, John, no matter what happens inside the cell nobody interferes. Understand?"

"Now, I know you've flipped. Is the desert heat getting to you?"

"John, I appreciate your concern, but I know what I'm doing."

"I hope you live long enough to regret this request, but if this is how you want to play this out, so be it. I just hope you survive the night, my friend."

Just as Sam was getting ready to leave, Janice walked into the police station and cornered Sam. "Are you trying to prove something here, or are you just this darn crazy, Sam?" she challenged.

"What are you talking about, Janice?"

"I just heard on the grapevine that you have a party going on tonight, and I wasn't invited. You need help to tackle these three guys, Sam. Please let me help you."

"Janice, I need you to stay back, just in case this doesn't work out as planned. I need someone on the outside I can rely on, and if this works, we can discuss something else I've been thinking about."

"What's that, Sam?"

"We'll talk later, baby. Right now I need a clear head so I can concentrate on what's coming up. I have to go and get ready for tonight's event." Sam exited the building and headed over to his room.

Janice knew he was as tough as they come, but she wondered if he was biting off more than he could chew. She decided that instead of sitting around waiting, she'd get a closer look at what was going to happen. Janice flagged down a taxi, and within a few minutes, she was doing some shopping of her own. She picked up a few throwing knives and some holders that she could strap around her leg and under her skirt. She also picked up a little .22 caliber handgun and a four-shot derringer, plus a couple boxes of shells.

When she returned to their room, she opened her suitcase and pulled out a pair of black nylons. As she was putting them on, Sam walked into the room. He stopped dead in his tracks, and whistled. Janice smiled and said, "See what you'll be missing when you're locked up in jail."

"That's not fair, and you know it. Will you wear those for me when I get out?" he asked with a big smile on his face.

"Only if you promise me you'll come back in one piece."

"Now that's the kind of motivation I need."

Sam went into the closet and returned to the bed with his duffle bag in hand. Janice was in disbelief as he started sorting out what he had. He took out another .357 magnum and two belt clips with additional ammo. He took out a leather coat and opened it up to reveal ninja throwing stars, and pockets inside the jacket that could hold six knives each. He removed the sleeves, opened up the material, and inserted one of his guns under his left arm. You couldn't even see a bulge in his coat. Then he laid it on the bed.

Janice tried to lift his jacket and said, "What kind of material is inside this jacket of yours?"

"Pure leather, sugar, with something extra added to increase protection in situations like this."

"I'll have to get me one of these."

"All in good time, baby. Now, where are those special knives I brought along? Here they are." He said as he loaded them in his bootstraps.

"Honey, just how did you get all those weapons past security at the airport?"

"I shipped them out Parcel Post two days before we left Wisconsin. I figured I'd need them."

"Very clever. You never cease to amaze me."

"I feel comfortable with my own equipment, that's all. I was hoping I wouldn't need them, but it seems lately like I always need them."

Sam gave Janice a big kiss and said, "I'll be seeing you, kid."

"Hey, that was a good Bogart imitation, Sam," Janice called as Sam closed the door.

She started preparing herself, and dressed for her part tonight. She knew Sam said no, but she just couldn't sit back wondering what was happening. Janice was dressed to kill as she exited the elevator and sat at a table by the bar. She had a clear view of where Sam was sitting. She ordered her drink and looked at her watch. It was almost ten thirty.

Just when she was beginning to think it was going to be a no show, three tough-looking guys walked into the casino. Janice glanced at her watch. Ten-forty. One guy stood about six feet two. He was tall and slinky, weighing almost two hundred pounds. The other two guys were about Sam's size, five ten or eleven. One of the guys may have been a bodybuilder. He had massive arms and appeared to be about two seventy. The other guy was maybe two ten. He had a get-out-of-my-way look on his face. He was average sized at best, but his shoulders were huge, and it looked like he didn't have a neck.

Janice was suddenly worried as she wondered if Sam really knew what he was doing. Maybe he would change his mind when he saw the size of these three guys. She saw the bartender shake his head toward Sam. He waited until they were at the bar and called Manny over.

"Hey, bartender, I need another drink," he bellowed.

When Manny started toward Sam to deliver his drink, one of the three men grabbed Manny by the shirt. Janice knew this was it as Sam slid off his stool and confronted them. "Hey, that was a very rude thing to do, pal. If you want a drink, wait your turn."

"Go mind your own business, little man," the tallest man ordered, and the others laughed.

"I may be smaller than you, but I'm not as ugly," Sam responded.

"Hey, funny man, what did you just say?"

"What do you know, you're not only ugly, you're ignorant as well."

"I'm going to crush you, little man," the giant spat at Sam.

Sam waited until he grabbed his shoulder, and then he landed a perfect blow right to his family jewels. The big man dropped like a rock. "What's wrong, big man? Now you're smaller than I am," Sam said with a laugh, as he turned to walk away.

"Hey, little man, we aren't through with you yet," another man yelled.

"What now, ladies? Do you want to dance?" Sam provoked.

Sam walked to a spot where he had more room to use his special weapon and waited for one of them to make the first move. Mister No-Neck came fast and hard. Sam side stepped him and hit him over the kidney. No-Neck stumbled, lost his balance, and crashed into the blackjack table.

The body builder made his play, walking slowly toward Sam. This giant stood toe to toe with Sam and took a swing. His arms were so big he couldn't swing fast enough to hit Sam. Sam just laughed and hit the big man with three sharp jabs. When the big guy shook his head, Sam said, "This will not take long." He hit the man in the solar plexus and came back with an uppercut, sending him to dream land.

Just when Sam thought it was over, Mister No-Neck grabbed him in a bear hug, catching Sam off guard. Sam brought both his big fists crashing into the man's ears, causing him intense pain. He released Sam instantly, but instead of being free at last, the giant was back at the attack. He hit Sam in the back of the head and sent him crashing to the floor.

"So, you like to hit people in the back, big man? Well, you just made a big mistake. Now you've made me mad." Sam acted like he was having trouble getting up. As the big man approached him, Sam spun and landed the heel of his foot to the giant's kneecap. It snapped, and he went down with a shriek. Just as Sam was going to finish the giant, he was pulled off the man and handcuffed.

"You boys just landed a night in the county jail. Maybe longer if you can afford your bail tomorrow morning," Captain Adams said as they hauled the four of them to jail.

"My leg is broken," the big man complained.

"Billy, go get the doctor and tell him what's going on. Tell him to bring enough stuff over to the jail to fix four big men," the captain ordered. By the time they arrived at the jail, Dr. Jenkins was waiting for them.

"You're a woman," the giant said as she walked over to check on his leg.

"Good observation. You have a dislocated kneecap, and I'm going to have to pop it into place. It's going to hurt, so just prepare yourself." She started to pull, and he tried to take a swing at her.

Sam grabbed his arm and hit him in the chin knocking him out. "Now you shouldn't have any trouble, Doc."

"Thank you, but that was totally unnecessary. I could have handled the situation by myself."

"I know, Doc, but it felt so good." They both laughed at Sam's comment.

After the doctor treated all the patients and was just about to leave, she heard Captain Adams say, "Well, I'm short a jail cell, so you will all have to be locked up together."

"Captain, you're not serious. They'll kill each other before morning," the doctor said.

"Sorry, Doc, but if I release one prisoner, I have to release all of them. That just isn't going to happen, not after the damage they did."

"Well, just the same, I'll stop in first thing tomorrow morning and see who needs more bandages." With that she was gone.

Reluctantly, Captain Adams put the first three guys into the cell. He looked toward Sam as if to say, are you sure about this? Sam entered the cell without any force. Captain Adams locked the door and walked out into the office area. He put the keys into his desk, told his men he was going out to get something to eat, and to call him if anything happened.

Meanwhile, inside the locked cell, the three men looked toward Sam with hate in their eyes. Sam just sat on the bench seat not even acknowledging they were there. He heard them talking to one another about jumping him while he was sleeping. Sam rolled over so his back was to them, coiled his right arm under his head, and pretended to be asleep.

One of the guys approached Sam. He must have bathed in his aftershave. Sam could smell him getting closer. Just as he was about to hit him in the side, Sam spun around and grabbed his neck, squeezing slowly. He was gasping and turning blue. "If I were you, I'd go back over by your friends before you have a bad accident."

When Sam released his grip, his cell mate was gasping for air. He must have thought for sure he was a dead man. He slowly went back to his buddies. They didn't seem as eager to try anything else right away. Then Sam overheard their conversation as he pretended to be asleep.

Steve, we have to make a delivery tonight, or we are in trouble."

"Shut up, Tyler. We don't know if that guy is asleep over there."

"I think he's sound asleep."

"Then why don't you go over and see, James. Maybe this time he'll kill you."

"Steve, we are supposed to deliver that girl tonight. We can't do it when we're in here."

"Tyler, I told you to shut up. I'll figure out something."

"Yes, you will, my good man," Sam said as he sat up.

"Hey, you're supposed to be sleeping."

"I'm looking for my sister, Brenda Barnes. She came here for a job, and now I'm told she's missing. Here's a picture of her. Maybe you've seen her?" Sam asked as he showed her picture to them.

James was the first to say he had never seen her, but Sam could tell by his facial expression that he was lying. "I'm only going to ask you this one more time before I start kicking some butt. Where is my sister?" Sam yelled.

"Do you really think we'd tell you, even if we knew?"

"So, it doesn't matter if I kill you or not, right?"

"You're bluffing. You can't kill us in jail," said Steve.

Tyler was the body builder, so he was Sam's first target. Sam walked over to the big man and said, "I don't need any weapons to kill you. I'll just do it with my bare hands."

"You're lying. There's no way you could kill..." Tyler didn't get to finish his statement. Sam hit him under the bridge of his nose, killing him instantly.

"Now, Steven and James, do I have your attention?" They both nodded their heads yes. Sam continued, "I don't like playing games, as you already know. Have you seen my sister?"

"Yes, we saw her a few days ago. We don't know where she is though," James said.

"Did you kidnap her?"

"You just killed Tyler here in the jail cell," Steve said in disbelief. "You'll never get out of here for doing that, and if you do, you're a dead man. They will see to that."

"Who'll see to that, Steven?" Sam asked.

"You'll find out soon enough, after the organization gets to you."

"Shut up, Steven," James said. "You talk too much."

"It's all right to talk to me, Steven. Is it the organization behind all these kidnappings?"

"Don't answer him, Steven, if you know what's good for you."

"James," Sam started, "if you interrupt us one more time, you'll be joining your friend down there on the floor. Now, Steven and I are having a nice conversation, so don't interrupt us again."

James started again telling Steven not to talk. Sam rose from his bench, walked over to James and, without warning, struck James with a powerful punch in his shoulder, causing his arm to sway helplessly at his side.

"You broke my arm, you bastard!" James howled in pain.

"Actually, James, I dislocated your shoulder. Now, if you're a good boy and let Steven and me finish our business, I'll fix it for you when we are done. If you think that is painful, interrupt us again, and I'll introduce you to some real pain."

"Sheriff, I need some help in here!" James shouted. Then he turned almost pure white as Sam rose from his stool once more.

"Now, James, did you really think it was coincidental that I was put into the same cell as you? I asked them to do this so I could find out what happened to my sister."

"That's just a bunch of bull. She's not your sister. You're a cop, just like them."

"No, James, I'm not like them at all. You see, they follow the law. I follow my own law, and if it means I have to torture, maul, or kill for information, it's done. I cause so much destruction getting what I want that I've been given the nickname 'Hurricane'."

Steven stood up and said, "We thought you were made up."

"No, Steven, they gave me this name because I don't like seeing innocent people get hurt, especially by scumbags like you types. I've been informed that many girls have disappeared from these casinos. I was called in special to help find the girls and arrest, or kill, those responsible. Now, either I get some cooperation from the two of you, or I kill you. The choice is yours. You have five minutes to make up your mind."

"One man against an army of men? What chance do you think you have of completing your mission? I think you better rethink this and leave while you're still alive," James said.

"James, I tried to explain it to you, but I guess some people just need a little more persuasion." Sam turned around bringing his left heel crashing into the side of James' right knee.

"You broke my leg! You're an animal!"

"I hope you now understand I mean business. I'm going to take you apart one limb at a time, until I get the answers I need."

Just as Sam was about to strike James again, the jail door opened.

"Sam, come with me," the captain ordered. When they were out of the cell, he continued, "Sam, something bad has happened. Janice is missing. And what have you been doing in there?"

"I'll tell you on the way to the casino. For now, don't let these guys out of that cell, no matter what. I still need some information from them."

When Sam and Captain Adams arrived at Harrah's, Wayne was being helped into an ambulance. Sam rushed over to find out what happened. Three men had dragged Janice away from Wayne's arms, assaulting him as they left. Wayne was able to call the police, and tore a patch off of one man's shirt. He handed the patch to Sam, and the ambulance pulled away. He was told that Wayne would be okay.

Sam was furious as he stormed out of the casino. He hopped into the police car and headed toward the jail. He wanted answers, and he wanted them now. Captain Adams was left without a car. He knew Hurricane was mighty upset and called a cab.

When Adams walked into the back of the jail, all he heard was, "This is just the beginning, you bastards. Where did they take my girl?" Then he heard a crash and a big cry for help echoing through the building. As the captain rounded the corner, he saw Sam inside the cell. He had James tied up in the corner, and Steve's arm was wrapped through the bars of the cell. His arm looked odd. "Sam, isn't his elbow supposed to be facing out instead of in?"

"Don't try and stop me, John. I need some answers fast."

43

"I wouldn't even think of stopping you, Sam. In fact, I think I'll join in the fun."

The men looked at each other, trying to figure out what to do. Hurricane grabbed Steve's arm one more time. He wrapped it through one bar and tied his hand to the upper bar. His elbow now faced out toward them. He then picked up a nightstick and brought it straight down onto his elbow. Steve's bone shattered as his elbow was disconnected from his upper arm.

Steve fell toward the floor. In shock, saw his wrist still tied up on the cage. Sam walked over to James and started tying him up to the cage bars. Instead of his arm, however, he picked James up with one arm and slipped his legs through the bars. James was now standing on his head, as Sam and John tied up his legs. When James saw Sam approach him with the nightstick, he started to sweat bullets.

"Hey, John, how many swings do you think it'll take to make James here two feet shorter?" Just as Sam raised the stick, James started to talk. "Please don't hit me. I'll talk. Just don't hit me."

"All right, James. Let's start with where they took my girl." Hurricane's voice grew louder with each word.

"We take them about thirty miles out of town to a place called Moapa River. I think it's by an Indian reservation. After that, I don't know where they are taken."

"Who would know if you don't?"

"I don't know his name."

Sam brought the stick down hard and fast, striking James' left knee. A definite pop was heard. James was crying, with tears running down his face, as he tried to plead his case.

"I'm telling you the truth, man. I don't know," James sobbed in pain.

"Then tell me who you answer to?"

"I can't do that. He'll kill me."

"That's what surprises me about you guys. You always worry about what the other guy will do. It's almost like I don't exist."

Sam delivered the stick across the knee one more time. "After my next strike, people will you call 'Stubby'." Sam was just about to bring the stick down one more time, and Steve spoke up.

"Wait! I'll tell you who it is."

"John, it looks like Steve's rejoined the party. All right, tough guy, who's the boss?"

"We call him Mr. Salvo. He usually stays at the Freemont Hotel when he does business.

"Is he there now? How many guards are protecting him?"

"He normally has anywhere from four to eight guards around him. It all depends if he's expecting any kind of trouble."

"What kind of trouble could he expect?"

"He says there's a new guy trying to take over his business. I don't know who he is or what he looks like. I've overheard Mr. Salvo talking about it a couple of times."

"Well, Mr. Salvo just added one more person after him, and if he thinks the other guy is trouble, wait until he meets the Hurricane. If he has my girl, what I did to you guys is nothing compared to what he's going to get."

"Wait, Mr. Hurricane. Could you help us down from these bars?"

"Please, Steve, would you slip your good arm through the bars?" After Steve did what Sam wanted, Sam grabbed his arm and pulled him forward fast and hard. Then he grabbed John's handcuffs and cuffed Steve's good arm above his head so he was almost standing up.

Then he went over by James and handcuffed his ankles together.

"You can't leave me hanging upside down like this, Captain," James pleaded. "The blood will drain to my brain."

"Impossible, if you had any kind of brains, you wouldn't be in this mess, now would you?" Sam asked. "You guys just hang in there. If I make it back alive and what you told me is true, I'll ease your pain and suffering. However, if you're lying to me, let's just say we will have more fun than you can imagine, and I'll introduce you to some serious pain."

John and Sam jumped into the patrol car and drove toward Harrah's. Sam had a few things he had to get. After getting to his suite, Sam went into the safe and pulled out a duffle bag. Captain Adams eyes' lit up as he took out his pair of .357 magnums. He then handed John a semi-automatic pistol with eight clips of ammo and put another into his vest, along with six throwing knives and about two dozen ninja stars. Then he grabbed his leather vest with body armor inside.

John just couldn't hold back any longer, "Not to be nosey, Sam, but how in the world did you get that arsenal of stuff past airport security?"

"I had a friend of mine ship it to me by Parcel Post. I received it yesterday before all of this went down."

"My friend, you must have some very good contacts is all I have to say."

"Better than any of these scumbags have. I have nothing against any organization, except the crime syndicate, of course, and how they treat people. You don't have to be a monster to make money if you treat people the right way."

I must say you have enough weapons to hold off an army, but what is with the vest?"

"I have two pieces of two-inch steel plates sewn into the chest of the vest. I might be crazy going after guys like this, but I'm not totally stupid."

"Isn't that kind of tough on the shoulders?"

"Let's just say you will not see me jumping over any walls or high fences, at least not very fast."

They both laughed at Sam's remark as they exited the hotel lobby. Neither one said a word until they were a block from the Freemont Hotel. Captain Adams asked, "All right, Hurricane, what's your game plan?"

"I'm going in first. You give me twenty seconds and then enter the hotel. I'm going to ask for Mr. Salvo's room and see what develops. If my hunch is right, I'll be met by three or four of his goons looking for trouble. When they grab my arm and start escorting me toward the back of the casino with the intention of inflicting pain on me, call in the troops, swoop in, and arrest them, but please don't take too long. I don't want to waste too much time dealing with these guys. We have the big man upstairs to see."

Captain Adams nodded his head and counted the seconds as soon as Sam entered the doors. He overheard Sam say to the desk clerk, "I'm here to see Mr. Salvo."

"I'm afraid you're at the wrong hotel. We don't have a person by that name listed here."

"Listen, you organ monkey, you call Mr. Salvo and tell him he has a visitor down in the lobby. I'll give you until the count of three, and if you're not dialing his room number, I'll tear those fingers off of your hand and stuff them down your throat. The choice is yours."

The desk clerk never took his eyes off of Hurricane as his fingers did the walking on the phone. Within a few minutes, three guys big enough to play lineman on any football team exited the elevator. Two of them had to be at least six-four and three-fifty easy. The other guy was about six-two. He was built more like a receiver or a tight end. As they walked over toward Sam, they were flexing their muscles. Their biceps must have been almost twenty inches around. They looked like giants until Hurricane flexed his arms. They looked like basketballs.

Slowly, Hurricane adjusted his vest. Captain Adams thought he would take it off, but then he remembered the steel plates inserted in the vest. He ventured closer to hear what would be said and stood behind a partitioning wall approximately thirty feet away from where Hurricane was sitting.

After the clerk pointed Sam out to the giants, they walked over. You could tell by their faces they weren't in the mood for talking. They circled Sam and asked, "Are you the little wimp that doesn't know what kind of trouble he's asking for?"

Sam stood up, and his nose came up to the men's chests. *It looks like Sam may have bitten off more than he can chew this time*, thought Captain Adams.

"I bet if I put all of your IQs together, it might just add up to one of your shoe sizes," Hurricane answered.

"For such a little pip squeak, you sure have a lot of guts talking to us that way. You are like a scrawny little maple tree surrounded by three big oaks," they laughed.

"Have you boys ever seen what a little hurricane can do to big oak trees?" Sam asked.

"Mister, if you've come here tonight to end up in a box, we might just oblige you. Let's go out back, shall we?" They grabbed Hurricane by the arm and started walking toward the back.

Captain Adams walked quickly out to the car and radioed for his backups who were standing by. He told them to enter in the back way. He then jumped into his car and waited for the first set of lights, so it wouldn't look too suspicious. Meanwhile, Sam was exiting the back doors with the three giants close behind.

"I have to give you a lot of credit, Mister. For someone who's about to feel some intense pain, you sure don't look too scared."

"If you boys were smart, you would give up now and save yourselves a lot of pain," Sam replied.

"Could we at least know your name before we kill you? I must admit you're the only person who's ever stayed for a beating. Most of the others turn tail and run."

"Just call me 'Hurricane.' "

"I hate to tell you this, Mister, but we're onto that joke. There's no real Hurricane. He's a comic book hero."

"Can I ask you something before we get started?" Sam reached into his pocket and took out a picture of Janice. "Have you seen this girl?"

"Hey, Barney, that's the one we got in this evening. Isn't she still here?"

"Shut up, you moron. Well, I guess it really doesn't matter. You're a dead man now anyway."

After Sam heard that, his temperature shot up to instant molten lava. "Gentlemen, prepare to meet the most powerful Hurricane known to man." Sam struck the shorter man in the throat. He went down holding his throat and gasping for breath. One of the bigger men came at Hurricane fast and took a big swing at his chest. Sam just stood there as the big man's fist hit the steel plate. Then he hit Hurricane with his other hand in the same place. He was holding his hands as Hurricane swept his legs from underneath him. Down he went, crashing the back of his head on the curbing.

The third guy came after Hurricane a little more carefully. He was looking for an opening. Sam slowly unbuttoned his vest. As he took it off, he swung it like a whip, hitting his enemy in the side of the head. The man stumbled but stayed on his feet.

Just as Sam was about to go in for the kill, Captain Adams and his troopers came speeding down the driveway. Sam held back as they jumped out of their cars and surrounded the men. They handcuffed and escorted the three giants to the backseats of three different squad cars. He might need these guys if Janice was not up in that hotel room.

When the goon squad was on their way to jail, Sam and Captain Adams went to ask the desk clerk a few more questions. They entered from the back of the casino and walked up to the counter. When the clerk finally looked up and saw the look in Sam's eyes, he knew he was in trouble. Sam raised his right hand, and with his index finger, motioned the clerk to come on down. When he moved toward the telephone, Sam rushed over to the cord and yanked it out of the wall. In one swift move, Sam jumped over the counter, grabbed the clerk by the collar and said, "You better tell me what room Mr. Salvo is in, or you will be permanently on the disabled list."

"I don't understand, sir. What did I do?"

Sam hit him on the back of the head and then talked so softly even the Captain couldn't hear what he said. Suddenly, the clerk was staring at Sam in fear.

"I guess you didn't hear the question I asked," Sam said. With one swift move he brought out his hunting knife and cut the clerk's hair above his ear. "I hope you can hear me now. What room is Mr. Salvo in? You have two choices: either you tell me in three seconds, or you lose an ear."

Sam started counting. By the time he reached the end of one, he heard, "Twenty fifty-six, but please don't tell him I told you!"

"I can only promise you one thing. If you call ahead of our little surprise, I'll come down here and finish what I started. And if you run, I'll find you and kill you."

The clerk was frozen in place. He could tell Hurricane meant every word he said. Sam was on a mission to find Janice, and when he learned who took her, hopefully the Lord would have mercy on him because Hurricane assuredly wouldn't.

The Captain and Sam took the elevator up to the nineteenth floor and walked up the next flight, just in case the clerk called ahead. They slowly opened the door and peered out. No one was observed. They entered the hallway and slowly started to walk toward room twenty fifty-six. When they arrived, they saw shadows from the light underneath the door. Somebody was definitely in there. As he knocked, Hurricane drew his weapon and stepped away from the peep hole.

"Nobody's here," a voice said. Sam knocked once more.

"Whoever that is better stop playing games, or I'll kill you."

Sam knocked again.

"If you want to die that much, here I come," the voice bellowed.

As fast as the man opened the door, he was flung back into the room. Three goons advanced on Hurricane, planning to assault him. He twirled around hitting two of them in the jaw with one kick. If not for the third guy ducking, he would have hit all three. Number three grabbed Hurricane by the collar, and Hurricane gave him a powerful uppercut. Blood gushed from the man's mouth. Sam advanced on the other two men. He kicked one in the leg, making a loud snapping sound. He walked over to number two, grabbed his arm, and threw him out the sliding doors, sending him over the outside balcony.

The man with the bloody mouth charged at Hurricane, but Sam twirled and gave him a round house kick in the back of the head, sending his head crashing into the television. He was the lucky one, until Hurricane jumped into the air bringing the heel of the boot down on the man's lower back, causing his spine to snap.

Sam was down to one man before getting to Salvo, but he wasn't going too far with his broken leg. Hurricane reached down and grabbed his bad leg and started twisting it, listening to the man scream for mercy.

"Where's the girl?" Hurricane asked.

"What girl?"

"That was the wrong answer," Hurricane scolded, and twisted his leg even more. Captain Adams couldn't believe how far his leg was being rotated. Was Sam trying to tear it off? *Which of these two men is the real bad guy*, Captain Adams had to ask himself.

"The girl who was brought up here is gone, if that's who you mean."

"Gone where?"

"Mr. Salvo sold her."

Just as he was about to tell Hurricane, a shot rang out, and the big man was dead. Sam looked over his shoulder, and just a few feet away stood a man about six feet tall, weighing about two hundred and ten pounds. He was dressed in an expensively tailored suit and pointing a gun at Sam.

"You must be Mr. Salvo."

"Well, since you know my name, may I inquire what yours might be?"

"My friends call me 'Sam,' but you can call me 'Hurricane.'"

"So you're the mighty Hurricane the papers write about. I thought that was a fabrication to sell newspapers. It'll be a shame to have to kill you in this manner, but you see, I have some unfinished business to take care of, and you're standing in my way."

"Mr. Salvo, you have two choices. Give up and tell me where the girl is, or don't and feel the agony when I torture you. Sooner or later, you'll tell me. I promise you that."

"I can't believe my ears. Here I stand pointing my gun at you. I could kill you right now, and there's nothing you can do about it. Yet, you are telling me to surrender? Do you think I've lost my mind?"

"Not yet, but if you don't drop your weapon now, I'll blow your head clean off your shoulders," Captain Adams spoke as he and three more men entered the room. "Hello, Sam. It looks like I'm late again, and you've had all the fun," Captain Adams said.

"Hello, John, you sure took your time getting involved here."

"Sorry, Sam, I was preoccupied trying to run the plates on a car I spotted downstairs previously. I figured you had everything well in hand up here."

Mr. Salvo had dropped his gun, and when he looked into the eyes of the Hurricane, he knew he was in a tight spot. *Who is this mystery girl he's looking for, or is this one of Sorrento's men sent to stop me,* Salvo wondered.

"You're not so tough without men to back you up. You're just a scared little man. Well ... Mr. Salvo, is it ... where is the girl you kidnapped from Harrah's tonight?" Sam asked.

"I don't know what you're talking about. We don't kidnap girls."

Sam smashed his gun down hard on Salvo's index finger. He wasn't in the mood for fun and games tonight. "You only have one more shot to answer my question before I smash every finger on your hands to the point where they will be of no use to you anymore. Now, where are all the girls you've kidnapped within the last six months?"

"Who hired you? I'll pay you ten times what he's paying." Hurricane smashed another finger on his hand without even answering his offer. Just as Sam was about to shatter another one of his fingers, Salvo cried out. "Okay! Okay! I'll tell you. I sent them out to the desert about twenty or thirty miles northwest of here. There's a building just outside of the Moapa River by the Indian reservation,"

"What happens to them after that?"

Normally, we leave the girls tied up and blindfolded. John Sorrento usually picks them up within an hour after we leave them. We go back later and pick up the money he leaves behind."

"You're selling them as slaves?"

"You wouldn't believe how much people will pay for beautiful young girls. Lately, however, Sorrento has been playing me for a fool. He tells us the last three shipments we sent somehow disappeared before he arrived."

"Well, what would you expect when it's one thief to another? How long ago did they leave?"

"You just missed them. They left about ten minutes ago."

"Was the girl you kidnapped from Harrah's with them?"

"Yes, but why is she so important?"

"Because she's my girlfriend, moron," Sam hissed at him, "and that's the biggest mistake of your life. If anything happens to her, so help me, I'll kill you slowly, so I can enjoy seeing you suffer."

Just as Salvo finished confessing, six officers came through the door, handcuffed him, and headed toward the jail.

Sam heard Captain Adams tell the men, "Whatever you do, do not release the others hanging in the cell." Then he turned to Sam and said, "Are you ready to go kick some butt, my friend?"

"Let's go. I just hope we aren't too late. I'd like to catch Sorrento as well. Besides, he has my girl, and he's going to pay dearly."

They drove back to the station and traded the squad car for the Hummer because they needed a vehicle that could travel fast in the sand. It was at minimum a thirty-minute drive, and the bad guys already had at least a twenty-minute lead. Their only hope was to make it before the next pickup was completed. Sam thought he drove fast, but Captain Adams had him beat. Unlike driving in the city, however, it was almost a straight shot through the desert. Besides, they had to make up time if they wanted to catch their prey.

Sam was hoping Janice was alive. If she had tried to fight her way out of anything, they might possibly have killed her. He smiled as he remembered the first time he had seen her fight. He had known at that moment that she was the type of girl he wanted. Sam also smiled remembering when Doug Stone had told him he'd find the right girl someday. Sam couldn't believe how much he really cared about Janice. Up until the time she was kidnapped, he had taken it for granted that she would be there for him. His adrenalin was pumping wildly. His memory brought back dreams about the time they had spent together. He finally snapped out of it as he heard Captain Adams calling his name.

"Sam! Sam! Are you all right?"

"Yes, John, I'm all right. My mind was drifting, thinking about Janice and how I really feel about her."

"Well, snap out of it, buddy. We are only five minutes away from the building. I think we may have beat Sorrento as well. I haven't seen any dust storms ahead of us, which means Salvo's guys haven't made it here yet."

"I can only hope you're right. We could wipe out all of these bums at one time. It sounds almost too good to be true. I only hope I brought enough fire power."

"Sam, you've brought enough fire power for a squad of soldiers. I just wonder how you're going to carry all those weapons."

"I have that covered, John. First, I unload with the big guns and then clean up with the small weapons."

"I knew I asked a dumb question, but I just had to hear your answer. Well, prepare yourself, Sam, we are here. But I don't see anybody around. I hope this wasn't a stall tactic by Salvo."

"If it was, I'll enjoy killing him all the more. Let's just hang loose for a few minutes and see what happens. If nothing happens soon, I'll go check inside the building."

Chapter Three

S am and Captain Adams were concentrating too much on the building to notice the shadows coming up behind them. Within seconds, two arms were thrust through the open windows, and a pair of hunting knives were resting on their throats.

"Give me your keys," a stern voice said. The Captain removed the Hummer keys and handed them out the window.

"Now, what brings you strangers into our territory?"

"We were told that many women have been brought out here and more were being sent out here today. We are trying to put a stop to what's happening to them," the Captain answered.

"How can we be sure you're not here to hurt these women like the other men have done?"

Slowly, Captain Adams reached for his badge and handed it out the window to the voice. They couldn't see who it was. The mirrors were all covered with dust. Hurricane also handed his badge out to his captor, and within a few seconds, they were asked, "What took you so long to find these men?"

Sam had figured it was Salvo's men, but now he heard the broken language and figured it out. "My friends, would you know what's happened to these girls?" Sam asked.

Suddenly Sam's pocket started to vibrate. He took out his phone, and a little green light was on. "John, the girls are here somewhere. That's Janice's code light going off in my pocket."

"You call us friends, but you don't yet know who we are," one of the men said.

"If you had wanted us dead, we wouldn't be talking to you right now. The only kind of people who could sneak up on us like you two did would be two brave warriors of a great Indian tribe."

"You talk as if you know who we are. How can you be so sure of yourself?"

"Because I am part Paiute. My mother was a Shoshone called 'Morning Star.' My father was called 'Arthur Rufus.' He was a lieutenant colonel with the Green Berets. He died shortly after I came home as a Green Beret, but as a youngster, I was lucky to have been taught how to search and hunt, both by my Shoshone people and in the white man's ways."

"Since we are both brothers of the same skin, we will take you to the women you search for. But if you are lying to us, you will not leave our camp alive."

"When I can turn and see you, I will become your blood brother. Blood brothers are always loyal and will not lie to one another. I will swear this by my warrior name, Screaming Eagle, which my mother gave me."

When Sam got out of the truck, he turned and saw a wise old warrior. He took the knife from his hand and cut the inside of the palm of his left hand. He gave back the knife, and the other warrior did the same. They clasped their hands together and hugged each other.

"I am called Running Bear, and this is my brother, Charging Buffalo."

After a few handshakes and a lot of talking, they jumped into the truck and were told where to go to find the women. They ended up on the Indian reservation, which brought back many memories to Sam. The warriors took Sam and Captain Adams to a secluded area where three big teepees stood. As the truck approached, about thirty girls came out to see who was coming. Getting out of the vehicle, Sam's eyes were busy searching. He was just about to give up when someone tapped his shoulder from behind.

Turning around, he found Janice standing behind him. Sam hugged her so tight she was gasping for air.

"I don't have to ask if you missed me, but I'm a bit surprised at the gigantic hug I just received. Not that I'm complaining, mind you, just a bit puzzled about your reaction."

"I'm awfully glad you're alive. I'm glad to see all of you. Running

Bear, are you and your brother responsible for all of this?"

"We could not sit back and see innocent people injured or killed. My brothers and I decided that we would hide all these women until help would come. What took you so long finding this place, my blood brother?"

"I was brought into this blind, but after, I was able to see the light. We have been on a very rocky journey, but with the help of Captain John Adams and you, brothers, we have been able to at least find the women. Now, I must continue until all those who have caused such misery are put to rest."

"When the sun is on top of the mountains, a group of men, fifteen or twenty, will show up by that building," Charging Buffalo explained. "And like the past three times, when they find nothing but empty space, again they will be angry. This time you and Captain Adams will be ready for them. These men are who you need to stop. Even though they are many, my brother and I are here to help you."

"Fifteen to twenty men are a lot to overcome, but not to the Hurricane," Captain Adams said.

"We have heard of such a man who has gone around and helped many people. Please tell us which one is the Hurricane?" Running Bear asked.

"I go by many names, my blood brothers, but not too many people know about my Paiute roots. I have made a good living helping people in need. Sometimes the travel is hard, but the rewards are good. It will be an honor to have you two brave warriors helping us today."

Captain Adams and the two Indian braves listened and helped as Sam made up a game plan. They couldn't wait to get their hands on Sorrento and his men. The two braves could not shoot them because of a law forbidding them from shooting anything except food. So they decided to steal their merchandise instead. Now, with Sam and the captain by their side, they would have a chance to even up the score.

After about forty-five minutes, a plan was set. As they exited the teepee, a voice interrupted the silence.

"Hurricane Sam Rufus, where have you been? I've been looking all over for you."

"Sorry, Janice, but we were setting up the game plan."

"Without me? Oh, boy, you have your nerve. Without me you would never have found us."

"Excuse me, Janice, but I did not receive your signal until these two braves, Running Bear and Charging Buffalo, almost beheaded us. If not for them, we would not have known about this place, let alone where to find you. It is to them that you owe a debt of gratitude."

"I'd like to thank you, Running Bear and Charging Buffalo, for allowing these two men to live, so I could get a shot at killing them myself," Janice said.

"Why on earth would you say that now?" Sam asked.

"You took too long finding us. We were almost slave bait," Janice said.

"Well, because of our two friends here, that's one thing we don't have to worry about. However, we still have to find the ring leader of this operation. We are far from done with this job. Just how many girls are still out there trapped as slaves?" Captain Adams asked.

"We did not know what was happening until we found the first girl. We don't know how many girls were already taken," answered Running Bear.

"You have a good game plan, Sam. However, with this territory being so flat, how are we going to find enough cover to surprise them? They will see us at least a mile away. Where is our element of surprise?" questioned Captain Adams.

"You'll have to excuse the white man, Running Bear, for he has never had a chance to see the way Indians hide. We will have to hurry now to get there before they arrive. I figure we have a little more than an hour, maybe less," Sam said.

The brothers asked the other braves to bring horses to them. They grabbed some shovels and rode down to the building. Six Indian braves came along to help dig holes in the sand for everyone to lie down in. They used buffalo hides to cover everyone in the holes, and then threw some sand over the top to make it look like the sandy ground. Janice was determined to go with them, so it was decided that the remaining braves would ride in to help when the fighting began. When the holes were covered, the braves rode back to the camp with the extra horses and waited for the hostilities to begin.

Captain Adams was getting nervous being buried beneath the sand. He was hoping Sorrento would get there soon. Now he knew what it felt like to be buried alive. Then he started thinking about what the others had gone through. He was just about ready to give up when he felt the ground tremble.

The roar of the engines indicated that Sorrento had arrived. He wasn't sure what the signal to attack would be. He figured he would find out soon enough.

He heard Sorrento enter the building and then start throwing things around. When he came out ready to explode, everybody heard Hurricane say, "Surrender, Sorrento. You're under arrest."

Sorrento stood in front of Hurricane, snickered, and asked, "Where did you take all the other girls, tough guy?"

"They are all in a very safe place, but I need to know where the others are that you kidnapped?"

"You're a pushy little man, aren't you? Before I tell you anything, may I ask what your name is?"

"Just call me 'Hurricane.' Now, save yourself some pain and tell me where the girls are."

"You stand before me, one man against twenty, and you want me to surrender. You've got a lot of guts, I'll give you that much. I hate to spoil this conversation, but I'm late for another appointment. So I'll just have my men kill you now."

When the others heard that, they all popped out of the ground.

"Well, what have we here, two lawmen, two Indians, and one of my hostages. Against all my guys? You are joking, right? You can't be serious. Nevertheless, you all die today."

Just as he finished, what appeared to be about eighty Indians came around the building on horseback and surrounded Sorrento's men. They all had guns pointed at the group.

Hurricane was as surprised at the sight as Sorrento and his men were, but he didn't complain at all. Acting as if this had been the plan all along, he said, "Now, Sorrento, as you can see, the odds are definitely in favor of the good guys. Order your men to drop their weapons, or we will drop them for you, and you'll be all alone."

Sorrento motioned for his men to drop their weapons, but one guy tried something stupid. Hurricane fired a shot before the fool's weapon was out, hitting him right between the eyes.

"Impressive, Mr. Hurricane. I thought you were a fictional character made up to sell newspapers. I guess I was wrong," Sorrento said.

"If I hear that one more time, I'll kill the person who says it. Now, as for you, Sorrento, if you've read those articles about me, then you know what I'm capable of doing. So I'm going to give you one more chance to answer my question before you start feeling what real pain is like. In case you've forgotten the question, where are the other girls?"

Sorrento made no move to say anything. Hurricane grabbed his .357 magnum from inside his vest. He held it to Sorrento's left hand and fired the gun. Sorrento turned a ghostly white. His left hand was almost gone. Hurricane had put a hole the size of a half dollar in the palm of Sorrento's hand. Sorrento was in shock. Just as Hurricane was about to shoot his left elbow, he said, "Wait, I'll tell you everything I know, just don't shoot me again." Sorrento looked around him and saw his twenty men being escorted toward the Indian reservation.

Sorrento was nervous as he tried to speak again.

"Hurricane, if I tell you what I know, you have to promise to protect me."

"Protect you from whom?"

"Quincy Sanders is the man you have to protect me from."

"Now who, pray tell, is Quincy Sanders?"

"He's the man on top. He calls the shots about who lives and who dies."

"Why does it always seem like whenever I'm on a job, it always ends up bigger than it starts out. I always end up chasing five or six people. Why can't I ever get lucky enough to find the top man right away? All right, Sorrento, you give up everything you have on this Quincy character and where I can find him. If everything checks out, I promise you won't have to worry about anything else ever again. I'll put you in a place where nobody will ever find you."

After Sorrento heard that, he opened up and poured out his heart. He told Hurricane that Quincy Sanders was the ring leader of a Colombian outfit he put together himself. He stood six feet three inches and weighed around three hundred pounds. He always wore patent leather shoes. He had a long scar running along the left side of his face from a fight with the last crime boss he faced. He's very heavy into drugs, including the new free-based stuff that was killing people. As long as he was making money, he didn't care what happened to others. He was also very active in the slave market, children and young women. Nobody was safe around him.

"You'll find him approximately fifty or sixty miles due north of here at a place called 'the Alamo.' He has a big ranch that's out in the open. He can see you coming from miles away due to the flat ground. That's how he gets away all the time. He has a helicopter in the back of his house, which he uses for his escape. He also has about forty or fifty men guarding his land all the time. It's impossible to get close enough before they kill you. Many men have tried and failed."

"Do you know the layout of his property?"

"It's useless. You'll never get past the guards. It'll be like committing suicide. How can you protect me if you're dead?"

"Let me put it this way, Sorrento. Either I get the layout, or I kill you right here. Then you won't have any more worries."

"All right, but I've only been out there twice. I didn't see everything, but I'll tell you what I have seen. He has a brick wall surrounding the premises. It reminds me of the western forts with a plank running along the wall, with lookout towers on all four corners. Three men are in each tower, and they walk the wall every hour on the hour. There are only two ways in, by the front doors or by helicopter, if you're lucky enough to get past the security. There's a three-story mansion, including a very deep basement you could drive a semi through. I think the basement is where he kills people. I've seen people go into the basement and never come out. There are at least twenty rooms per tier. I myself have never been past the first floor. However, I could see all the rooms from the hallway that extends straight up. You can see all the doors when you look up. If it extends past the doors I really don't know, I've never been upstairs. That's all I can tell you, Mr. Hurricane. Could I get something to stop the bleeding from my hand? I'm feeling a bit lightheaded."

Hurricane broke a table leg, found inside the shack, and inserted the shorter end into the hole in his hand. Then he asked Sorrento, "Before you pass out, how many men are inside that house?"

"I saw at least thirty men. If he has more, they must be scattered inside the house. I think I'll take a little nap." Sorrento's words drifted off as he passed out.

"He lasted longer than I thought he would. We were lucky to get as much out of him as we did. Running Bear and Charging Buffalo, could you escort our guests to your reservation, while John and I check on a few things before we go get Quincy?"

"We do not like babysitting. Besides, what are we to do with all the others we have already taken?"

"Brothers, I'm asking you to just hold them for a while. Whatever you do to them is totally up to you. After all, you also have a score to settle with these men. So let justice prevail."

"It is true what you say. We have been bothered by what these men have done to the women. We know what it is like to be taken away from our families. I thank you, my brother, for letting these men see the Indian justice. They have tried to make our people look bad. Now we have a chance to show them just how bad we can be."

"All we ask is that you leave Sorrento for us," Sam said.

"It will be done as you ask. We will mend his wound so he lives until you return."

Hurricane and Captain Adams shook hands with their Indian friends, loaded up the women, exited the reservation, and headed back to The Strip. They had a few questions for their captives before they ventured out to get Quincy Sanders. Hurricane wanted to check up on Wayne and see how he was doing. Besides, they had to make sure the girls were taken back to safety. Captain Adams put a couple of guards on them just for precautionary measures.

They took the girls over to the jail until they found an alternate place for them. Hurricane and the Captain went to the hospital to check on Wayne. They found out he had been released and had returned home. After finally finding out where he lived, they ventured over to his house. His yard was fenced in with a brick wall; they drove up to his front gate and rang the bell.

"Who is it?" a voice asked

"Tell Wayne its Sam and Captain Adams."

"I'm sorry, but Mr. Newman isn't in today. Please come back and try again tomorrow."

"Something smells fishy, Captain. I'll have to climb the wall. Let's find an easier access."

They drove around the back and found no other entrance. Sam had a feeling he had to move fast. There was no time to stall. He told Captain Adams to get as close to the wall as possible. When he was right next to it, Sam climbed on top of the truck and scaled over the wall. "So far so good," he said under his breath. He noticed two men in the upper window looking down at something. Figuring it was Wayne Newman himself, Sam cautiously headed for the house. Who were these men? Salvo was now locked up, and Sorrento was out of the picture.

Sam was getting a sinking feeling this went deeper than anyone had even imagined. He made it to the house in a matter of minutes. Looking through the window, he saw a woman sitting on the couch. When she looked toward the window, Sam saw a trace of blood on her lip and cheek. He crept over to the next window. It was slightly open and led into a bathroom. Slowly, he raised the window and slipped in. He was just about to enter the hallway when he heard a voice. "I'll be there in a few minutes. I have to use the bathroom." Sam slipped into the shower stall hoping to get the drop on this person.

When the man walked into the bathroom, he noticed the window was wide open. "Fools, I told them to leave these windows closed. You never know what kind of animal could get in."

Hurricane slipped out from behind the shower and walked up behind him. "Or in this case, what kind of Hurricane could get in."

"What the ..." was all the man could get out as Hurricane grabbed him by his throat and started to squeeze.

"How many men are in the house?" When he wouldn't answer, Sam asked one more time. Then he stuck one of his knives into the man's shoulder. "Show me a finger count before you pass out, or you'll never see anything again?" It worked as he open his hand twice then added another two fingers.

"Twelve, there are twelve including you?"

He shook his head, indicating it wasn't including himself. "Then there are thirteen instead of twelve. Since you lied to me, I'll make it right." Sam stuck him in the neck causing instant death. Then he tossed him out the window. Sam was cleaning up the mess when a knock came on the door.

"Ralph, come on man, did you die in there or what? Let's get out of here." Sam slowly unlocked the door and hid back in the shower. The door opened, and he heard, "Now, where in the heck did he go?" Then the lucky man walked away.

Sam knew he only had a few minutes before they found this Ralph guy, so he had to move fast. He noticed a dumb waiter in the hallway. Hoping it was big enough to hold his weight, he moved over to check it out. It was a little elevator, normally used to send food up and down. Sam opened it up. It looked big enough. He would soon find out if it would support his weight as he climbed in. When he was inside the cramped area, he took out his little flashlight and started to pull the rope until he was up to the second floor.

When he finally stopped, he heard a voice say, "It's about time you sent me up some food. I'm starving." As he opened the door, Hurricane smashed his fist into the jaw of the man. Down he went. Hurricane stuffed the man into the dumb waiter after snapping his neck. *Two down, eleven to go*, he thought to himself. He went slowly toward the light coming from the bottom of the door.

As Hurricane cautiously approached the door, he saw a shadow cross the threshold. Not knowing who or what was inside this room, Hurricane raised his hand and started turning the door handle slowly. Then he heard a familiar voice.

"Hey, how long are you going to keep me tied up in here?" Sam heard Wayne ask.

"Why, do you have some place important to go?" one of the bad guys asked him.

"As a matter of fact, if you don't allow me to go to the bathroom, I'm going to have an embarrassing moment," Wayne insisted.

"All right, Wayne, if you promise us you will not try anything funny, one of the boys will take you to the bathroom."

When Hurricane heard this, he went into the second floor bathroom and waited. He hid behind the door until Wayne came in. Once in the room, Wayne turned and said to his escort, "Do you mind if I have a little privacy? I'm not going anywhere or doing anything stupid, not while you're holding my family hostage."

Wayne closed the door and whispered, "Sam, I know you're in here. They have my wife and son in the dining room downstairs. I have four guys watching me inside that room, including my bodyguard. They have twelve or fifteen guys inside the house. As far as I know, they all have guns. I have to get back before I'm missed. Good luck, my friend."

"I'll get you and your family out of here safely," Sam answered.

Wayne opened the door and walked into the hallway. Sam waited until they had time to get back into the room before heading downstairs.

Suddenly, someone grabbed his shoulder and asked, "Hey, man, not so fast. Who are you?"

"Your worst nightmare," Hurricane answered, before he struck the man in his solar plexus. The man staggered back and briefly lost his balance. While he was gasping for air, a powerful right hand smashed into his neck. He dropped like a rock. Hurricane knew he was dead as he picked him up and deposited him in the shower stall.

When Sam finally made it down to the first floor, he couldn't believe his eyes. He was looking at four doors, two on the left and two on the right. Hurricane took a quarter from his pocket and flipped it into the air. *Heads its right, tails left*, he said to himself. He turned right toward the first door. It was a closet. *I wonder what's behind door number two*, he thought to himself. After opening it he found three more doors down a long hallway. *This just isn't my lucky day.*

Then he noticed the first door on his right was slightly ajar. He stepped over and looked in. It was dark. He advanced inside and approached the desk in the corner. The hallway light gave him enough illumination to see what he was doing. Just as he found a crumpled up piece of paper with writing on it, he heard two voices in the hallway. Hurricane moved quickly behind the open door. He carried a compact mirror for just such occasions. Holding it in his palm, he extended his hand out past the door. Two men were standing in the hallway. They talked freely, not knowing Hurricane was inches away from them.

"What happens if this guy doesn't know anything, Dave?"

"I guess we have to kill them."

"Why? They are no threat to us."

"They know our faces, and they'll call the cops."

"I don't like killing innocent people, especially when they are unarmed."

"Quit acting like a big cry baby, Jim. This is why we get paid the big bucks, my man."

Hurricane couldn't believe his ears. Were these men mercenaries or paid assassins? *What have I stumbled into this time? All right, let's just see how good they are.* He checked his guns, making sure they were loaded. Then he thought of something different. Hoping it would work, Sam took out some clear fishing line he had in his pocket. He wrapped it around a bullet and tossed it out the door.

"What was that?" Jim asked, startled.

"I don't know, maybe a rat. Just settle down, will you, Jim?"

"No, it looks like a bullet on the floor. Where did that come from?"

"Maybe it fell out of your pocket."

"I'm going to check it out just the same."

"Jim, you're paranoid. There's nobody is here except you, me, and the other three guys in the room. If anyone came inside these doors, we would have heard them. But if it will calm you down, go and check. I'll stay here."

Jim walked over, and as he bent down to get the bullet, Sam pulled the string. It rolled toward the open door. Just as Jim was bending down again, the toe of his shoe nudged the bullet. Sam pulled it into the middle of the room. Interested to find out if that was truly his bullet, Jim entered the room and picked up the bullet. Sam was standing right in front of him, smiling.

"Hey, how did you get in here?"

That was the last thing Jim would say as Hurricane broke his neck and pulled him behind the desk. Just as he had hoped, Dave was on his way toward the room.

"Jim, what in the heck happened to you? Man, you know we were given orders to stay out of this room. No unnecessary fingerprints in the house. If he finds out you went in here, he'll kill you." When Dave saw Jim's shoes behind the desk, he walked into the room, trying to get Jim out of there. When he turned around, Hurricane was behind him.

"I guess I'll save your boss a little work." Before Dave could say anything, Sam hit him under the bridge of his nose, causing instant death.

Meanwhile, outside the house, Captain John Adams was a busy man himself. He devised a bogus arrest occurring just outside the front gate. He had a plan set up to allow his guys to enter the yard over the back wall. He was worried about finding enough guys to help out, but after they found out the Hurricane was involved, they all volunteered, even a few retirees, hoping to become famous for helping this legend they had only read about. Even though it was a dangerous mission, his men were willing to help out.

It was a pretty set up. As they were taking their time, the enemy became impatient and opened the front gate. They came out yelling at the officers on the scene because they were blocking the driveway. When the bad guys started to reach for their guns, a dozen plain-clothes policemen surrounded them with their guns drawn. Within ten minutes, they were escorted to jail.

Captain Adams was hoping he had enough jail space for all of these criminals. He had the occasional drunk or thief, but never a full jail. He hurried up and staged a few of his men around the gates just in case someone was watching the cameras.

Within ten minutes the bad guys on the outside were no longer an issue. Captain Adams was getting set to enter the house. He gave all of his men a stern warning that if they encountered a man who looked mean as hell, they should call out his name and let him know who they were.

After Captain Adams had instructed his men, he took five volunteers into the house with him. They headed for the opposite door from the one Hurricane had used. Captain Adams knew if any shooting started, his men would charge into the house.

Hurricane had no idea what was going on outside the house. All he knew was that he had to get Wayne's family out of there to safety. Slowly, he headed for that closed door. He still wasn't sure what he was going to do. Maybe he should not have killed Dave and Jim until he found out what the layout was inside. Hurricane hated going into enemy territory unless he knew the score first. He was getting ready to crash through the door, when a cook pushing a tray of food walked in the room.

Hurricane put his finger up to his lips as he whispered, "Who are you?"

"My name is Connie. I am Mr. Newman's cook."

"Is there anything beneath that table skirt?"

She shook her head no, and Hurricane climbed onto the lower shelf surrounded by the table skirt. Maybe he could surprise them like the Trojan horse set up. Connie knocked on the door.

Immediately, Hurricane heard, "It's about time. I'm starving. Look at this spread, won't you!" Connie pushed the cart inside the room. "There's chicken, corn on the cob, ham, and some dinner rolls."

"Yes, Johnny, it almost looks too good to eat, but we are hungry."

"You two can keep talking, but I'm going to eat," a third man spoke.

As they were picking their food, Hurricane slid back the skirt and looked around. He didn't see Wayne's wife or son. He wondered at first if David lied to him until Johnny said, "Hey, Phil, what about the two we have tied up in the bedroom?"

"So, what about them, John?"

"They have to eat, too. We can't let them starve."

"Since you're so worried about them, take this cart into the bedroom and see what they want."

Johnny grabbed the cart and went into the bedroom. *What a break,* Hurricane thought to himself. When Johnny stopped the cart, Hurricane slipped out from underneath the skirt. He was grateful the bed was high enough to fit him as he rolled underneath.

"Hey, Johnny, did you forget about us? Bring that cart back here."

Johnny left the two tied up in the bedroom as he took the tray of food back. Sam knew he had to move fast. He slid from underneath the bed, untied them, and asked, "Are you two all right? Did they hurt you at all?"

Startled, they asked, "Who are you, and where did you come from?"

"I'm a friend of Wayne's. I'm going to try and get you out of this. Only problem is, I'm not sure how just yet."

"I know a way out," Mrs. Newman said. "Behind that desk is a hollow wall that leads to the hallway. Wayne had it installed in case of a fire inside the bedroom."

"Sounds good to me. Why haven't you used it before now?"

"They were watching our every move. Then they tied us up when it became an inconvenience."

"Well, they are more worried about their stomachs right now and have temporarily forgotten about you. Now is your chance."

"Are you coming with us, mister?"

"Just call me 'Hurricane,' and no. I need to stay here and teach these guys some manners."

"Thank you. They all have guns, so be careful."

Hurricane nodded his head as a gesture of thanks and watched them slip through the wall opening. Then he went to work setting up his plan of attack. Figuring it wouldn't take these guys long to find out the hostages were missing, Hurricane was setting up a little surprise party of his own. He took out the fishing line and strung it around the leg of the bed post, then stretched it across the floor and tied it to the dresser drawer handle.

He checked both his magnums to make sure they were fully loaded. He was hoping to take them quietly, but just to be on the safe side, he then slid a chair into the path of a possible falling victim, hoping that when he fell he'd hit his forehead in the process. Just as he was trying to set up something else, Sam heard the big question and slipped inside the closet.

"Where are our prisoners, Johnny?"

"They can't get away. They're tied to the bed."

"Take a look, you idiot! They are gone! We have to find them."

When the bad guys came running into the bedroom, the front two tripped on the spread wire. Johnny hit his head on the way down just as planned. The other guy was bleeding as the wire cut into his ankle. When he tried to stand, blood was gushing from his leg. He yelled a profanity and sat back down.

Two down, and one to go, Hurricane thought, as the third guy very cautiously checked the closets. When he opened Hurricane's door, he came face to face with one of Sam's Magnums aimed right between his eyes. Sam threw a knife hitting him in the head. *Two dead and one barely alive, after all the blood he's lost.*

Hurricane walked to him and asked, "Who are you working for?"

"John Baxter."

"Where can I find this Baxter character?"

"You won't have to. He'll find you. You're a dead man walking."

"Who is John Baxter?"

"He is death," the man said with his dying breath.

What have we stumbled into? We now have Salvo, Sorrento, Quincy Sanders, and now this John Baxter character. Why doesn't this surprise me? Now we need to find out some information about this Baxter guy, but first, I must save Wayne.

Hurricane wondered if all the rooms had those secret walls inside them. He found the kitchen, but the cook was gone. Maybe she made it out with Wayne's family. Hurricane saw one door on each wall for the dumb waiters. Wondering, he opened each door, curious as to where each waiter went. He climbed into one that had more space than the first one, and went down into the basement. Being very careful, he opened the door and found a whole arsenal of weapons. It was like hitting the jackpot for Hurricane. He stuffed his pockets with extra ammunition and other needed weapons. Turning on his flashlight, he started to explore. Maybe he could find something else he could use. He was by the furnace when he heard voices coming through the registers.

He could pick up four other voices besides Wayne's. He listened for a while until he heard, "I figure we'll soon hear from Mr. Newman's friends."

"You'd better hope my friends are in a good mood," Wayne said.

"Why, Mr. Newman, are you saying your friends will try to save you? Before they do, you and your family will all be dead."

"What is it with you guys. Is this really worth your life?"

"It isn't a matter of what we want, but of who we want. You see, I'm the new kingpin in Vegas. We want Salvo out of jail so we can kill him. I want full control of the organization in this area."

"I hate to be the bearer of bad news, but you have messed with the wrong guy today. You should have waited until he was gone."

"He's only one man, and I have a whole army. Why should I be worried about him?"

"He's as fast as a hurricane and twice as deadly."

"How could he be worse than a hurricane?"

"Real hurricanes leave survivors. This Hurricane destroys everything that is evil. He doesn't stop until everyone is dead. You may have just sealed your fate, friend."

"For the last time, I'm not your friend. Now shut up. I'm getting tired of hearing your famous voice."

"Allow me to say one more thing. He's so quiet you never know when he'll strike. He may be listening to us right now as we speak and planning your fate."

"Hey, Stan, go on down to our other guests and give the guys a fifteen minute break. Then report back here."

Hurricane headed back up to the room he had just left and waited for his guest. The door opened, and Stan walked in, "What the hell?"

"Now, son, you shouldn't use that vulgar language."

"Who the hell are you?" Stan asked, reaching for his gun. Hurricane swept Stan's legs from underneath him. As he went crashing to the ground, his gun slid across the floor.

"Hello, Stan."

"Who are you, and how do you know my name?"

"I'm the person who's going to take your soul, Stan."

"I don't know who you are, but I will not go down easily."

"Stan, Stan, I could already have killed you. I just wanted you to meet the Hurricane face to face before you left this world."

"You're the guy Mr. Newman was talking about. What have you done with my friends?"

"Don't worry, Stan. You'll be seeing them again soon."

"You go to hell whoever you are."

"I'll see you down there soon, but for now, say hello to your friends for me." Sam turned quickly, snapping Stan's neck as he fell to the floor.

Sam decided he would head straight up the stairs and take his chances. He was surprised to see the corridor empty as he approached the stairway. When he was heading toward the bedroom door, one guy came out of the bathroom and met Sam face to face. Hurricane threw him over the railing, and he went crashing down. It happened so fast he never even screamed before he hit the ground.

Just as Sam reached the bedroom, Captain Adams and his men entered the hallway. Sam smiled, and nodded toward the men, and then he proceeded to kick in the door. They caught the bad guys completely off guard as they surrounded them. Hurricane looked at the head guy and said, "Captain, he's mine."

"He's all yours, my friend."

Standing in the corner was a young guy about twenty-five years old. He was maybe six-feet tall with a slender build. He gave himself away with the expensive cigar he had dangling from his mouth.

"So, you're the fellow they call John Baxter?"

"That's unfair. You know my name, but I don't know yours."

"In time, but for now, you're the guy who wants to take over this beautiful area in Nevada."

"Everybody has to make a living, so why not me?"

"But you kidnap young girls and sell them as slaves."

"Hey, pal, business is business. I don't care what I have to do to make a buck."

"You also force people to pay you for protection against their will."

"Everybody needs protection from time to time."

"What about protection against you? If they don't pay, you destroy their property."

"Sometimes, I have to educate people the hard way. After all, they need to be taught a lesson. Besides, what business is it of yours? "

"When you put my friend and his family in jeopardy, you made it my business, and I think it's about time someone taught you a lesson."

"Like you?" Baxter said with a smirk on his face. Baxter soon found out that was the wrong thing to say. Hurricane struck Baxter's right shoulder blade with his fist, causing it to pop out of its socket. He almost swallowed his cigar as the pain shot through his body.

"You bastard, you broke my arm. This is excessive use of force. I'll sue this place. I'll sue …"

Before he could complete his statement, Hurricane spun around and kicked his left knee cap. He kicked with such force it totally bent his knee backwards. After hearing a loud crack and seeing Baxter fall fast onto the floor, Hurricane asked, "Now that I have your complete attention, is there anyone else in your organization I need to talk to, or are you it?"

"Why should I tell you anything? You're just going to kill me anyway. Look at the pain you've already put me through?"

"Tell you what, Baxter, buddy, if you tell me what I want to know, I'll ease your pain and suffering. What do you say?"

"How can you do that, my arm and knee are completely out of their sockets?"

"I can snap them back, and they will be as good as new. I've done it numerous times without any complaints.

"Now, why would you do that for me?"

"Because after you're done signing a confession that you kidnapped, tortured, and killed these girls, you will also sign an agreement to leave this state and never return."

"What about my jail time?"

"Even though I totally disagree with the captain, you'll be a free man as soon as you sign the agreements."

"Let me get this straight one more time, if I rat out my partners and sign these statements, I'll be free to take my business elsewhere?"

Sam bit his lip as he said, "That's the captain's agreement."

"I supplied Salvo and Sorrento with the girls. What they did with them after delivery I never knew until now. Not that it would have mattered. I was trying to squeeze Salvo out of business and take it over myself. I guess now he can have it all for himself. I'll start over somewhere else. Let me make out those statements, so I can get out of here," Baxter replied.

After he was through writing out the statements and signing them, Hurricane walked over to him and popped his shoulder back in place.

Baxter almost passed out from the pain. Then he snapped his knee back in place as well. "In a while, you'll be able to stand on your knee again. By the way, were you serious when you said you would start up this same business somewhere else?"

Baxter made the cardinal mistake of saying yes.

Hurricane couldn't stomach another bunch of girls going through this hell. He advanced toward Baxter and extended his hand to help him up. But as he raised him up, he quickly spun him around breaking his neck.

"I was wondering how long you were going to wait, my friend," Captain Adams said.

"Well, Captain, I had to make sure he was one of the final four. Now, let's go talk to Salvo, shall we?"

Chapter Four

J ust as Sam and Captain Adams got into the car, Janice walked up to them and asked, "Now, just where are you gentlemen going without me?"

"I figured you had enough of these guys, and after what you've just been through, I thought you needed some time to rest up," Sam answered.

"Samuel Rufus! If you think for one minute I'd be able to rest after what he put us girls through, you really don't know me that well at all. You've seen how I can protect myself, and yet you want to leave me behind. You need help, and I can be a help to you."

"Janice, this isn't just seriously beating someone, this is survival of the fittest. Let me ask you a serious question. If it came down to it, could you actually kill somebody without even blinking an eye?"

"I think I could."

"Janice, these are cold-blooded killers. They don't care who you are or what they have to do to kill you. Now, if you're uncertain you could kill someone, I'd feel better with you here in the casino. These men will not hesitate to put you away. If you so much as blink, you're dead."

"Sam, can I at least go with you and think it over. If my decision is that I can't kill, let me at least stay in the car until it's over. I just have to be there when this goes down."

Even though Sam was against it, he knew she would just follow him anyway. Besides, he knew she would be a lot safer in the car than at the casino. "All right, I'll let you go on one condition. If anything goes wrong and I don't make it out of there in thirty minutes, you are to drive off and keep driving. Don't look back or stop until you're back on the airplane headed for home."

"Agreed, but I won't be heading home. You two are going to make it out without a doubt."

"I hope you're right, kitten. John, when we make it back to the station, could I make a couple of phone calls."

"Yes, by all means, but who are you planning to call?"

"Janice might be right about needing some help, and I need to see if an old Marine buddy is still in town."

When they arrived at the station, Sam walked over and picked up the phone. He remembered that Colonel Jones would be staying at Harrah's. Sam talked to the desk clerk who told him the colonel was out but was expected back in about two hours. Sam left a message to be called back as soon as possible. When he hung up, he suggested that the captain should release Salvo tonight.

"Are you out of your mind, Sam? We spent too many man hours busting this guy, and now you want us to let him go? Why?"

"Remember those transmitters Colonel Jones brought us?"

The captain nodded yes.

"We plant one on Salvo and let him lead us to Quincy Sanders."

"How on earth will you plant that on Salvo? He doesn't have a coat or hat. Are you going to make him swallow it?"

"Not a bad idea, Captain," Sam chuckled. "No, go get his shoes. I have an idea."

After the captain returned with Salvo's shoes, Sam pulled apart the heels of both shoes. There was a hollow spot between the heels and the soles. He inserted one transmitter into each shoe, just in case they found one of them. Nobody would expect there to be two. Now they had to devise an escape plan that wouldn't be so obvious.

"Sam, why not let him trick my men and take the key?"

"Too much of a gamble, Captain, and I don't want anyone getting hurt or killed for Sanders. It isn't worth a good man's life. There has to be another way."

Janice had an idea. "Sam, what if a key just happened to show up on his dinner plate tonight? You could have it brought in by a different person, with a message of it being a present from Quincy."

"That's why I love this girl, John. She's always thinking smart. Is there anyone we could send that Salvo will not recognize?"

"There's a new girl over at Harrah's singing with Wayne tonight. Let's go see if we can talk her into it," the Captain said.

"Good idea, John. Why don't you and Janice go talk to the girl?"

"You're not going, honey?" Janice asked.

Sam was a little stunned and speechless before he answered. "No, I'm going to see Colonel Jones and find out about possibly borrowing a few gifts we can take along for our surprise party."

"What could you possibly need that you haven't already brought along on this trip? A tiger tank maybe?"

"Well, for one thing we need some night-vision glasses and some jackets. It gets a bit cold in the desert at night. I also need a few odds and ends I couldn't fit into my duffle bag. I shouldn't be long. I'll meet you at Harrah's, and then we'll work on our attack plan."

After they all agreed, Sam went to see the colonel. He was happy to see Sam. He was even more excited about helping them out. He called the commander at the military base and was granted permission to look at their stuff. The colonel drove his car. For some reason, he knew Sam wasn't going back with him.

Sam was like a kid in a candy store when he saw what they had to offer him. There, in the dark corner, was a halftrack, which has a truck front and track wheels in the back. The only difference was this vehicle had two machine guns on top, one in front and one in back, instead of one in the middle. His face lit up when the soldier who was on duty told him it could travel ninety miles per hour on the flat desert surface. The guns were nickel plated so they wouldn't rust, and they carried thirty-millimeter shells. There was enough ammo on board to wipe out China. He just smiled because deep down in his mind he knew he might just need all of that ammo. He was impressed to find out these guns could go through almost eighty rounds a minute.

The colonel informed Sam that this weapon had never been tested for accuracy. This was a test model that never made it out the door. Sam's motto was "nothing ventured, nothing gained," so he said he would give it a test run. The only difference was this was not a test run. This was a real and very dangerous mission. Sam loaded up the halftrack with all the weapons he needed, including a few grenade launchers, night-vision glasses, flares, and enough M-16 rifles for a little army of his own. Sam also found some lightweight flannel underwear to try out. These were supposed to keep you warm when cold and cool when it was hot. He almost felt like a guinea pig. Then again, if it worked, it would be worth the effort.

While Hurricane was having fun shopping, Captain Adams and Janice were busy talking to the new girl in town. They found out the girl's name was Jennifer Stills, and Janice was a little envious of her. She had the prettiest complexion Janice had ever seen. Her skin looked velvety soft to the touch. Janice noticed how the Captain was having trouble concentrating on why they were there. Janice broke him out of his trance as she said, "Jennifer, we need you to do something for us. It could be dangerous, so if you decide not to do it, we'll understand."

Jennifer seemed a little confused until Captain Adams said, "Jennifer, we need you to deliver a basket of food to the jail for a certain prisoner. You will tell him Quincy Sanders sends his regards and wants to meet him at their usual place."

"That doesn't sound so dangerous to me," Jennifer responded.

"After you deliver the message, please leave as fast as you can. If you stay until he escapes, he may take you as a hostage. We'll have enough trouble trying to follow him without having to save you as well."

"What's this man done that is so bad?"

"Jennifer," Janice butted in, "I was one of his hostages. That was until Captain Adams and Hurricane rescued me. I would have been headed to who knows where. He sells beautiful girls as slaves. We need to find the head man and stop him, and that's why we need you. You're kind of like the hunter setting the trap."

"What happens if he grabs me?"

"I can't lie to you, Jennifer," Captain said. "You have to get out of that building fast. You'll have two minutes tops after you deliver the message. If he gets hold of you, we'll have to abort the mission and save you first. If you don't think you can do this and get out safe, let us know now, and we'll think of something else."

"No, Captain, that will not be necessary. I'll do my best not to disappoint you. When do you want me to do this?"

"Hurricane should be back shortly, and as soon as he returns, we'll come find you, so don't travel too far."

"I'll be playing blackjack until you need me," she said and then disappeared just like that.

When Hurricane arrived back at Harrah's, Captain Adams and Janice filled him in on the game plan.

"Why would a young woman, a perfect stranger, accept such a dangerous request?" Hurricane asked. "She's unaware of the danger she'll be in. This guy is so evil-minded he doesn't care who he hurts." Hurricane felt uneasy, but he set aside his intuition for the moment.

"I just hope you're wrong, Sam."

"It's just a gut feeling, Captain."

When everything was in place, Sam, Janice, Captain Adams, and two men were sitting in their cars across the street from the Police Station. In a few minutes they would find out if Sam's prediction was right.

"This is boring just sitting here," complained Janice.

"Janice, we've only been here fifteen minutes. You should be with us when we stake a place out for hours or days at a time."

"No, thank you, Captain. This is more than enough for me."

"Quiet, you two, I think this is our girl walking down the street," Hurricane said.

They all stopped and watched as Jennifer entered the building holding the basket of food she was given to deliver. Almost ten minutes went by before the captain said, "Something is wrong. She should have been out of there at least five minutes ago."

Hurricane ran across the street to check it out. He looked in the window and couldn't believe what he saw. John Silvers and Charlie Watts were slumped over their desks. Sam knew they were dead, but what were they doing there? It was supposed to be empty. The building looked deserted, so Sam motioned for the other two to come across. Just as they started crossing the street, a car sped around the corner directly toward them. Hurricane squatted down, took close aim and fired toward the cars. He hit one of the rear tires. The car sped out of control, crashed into another parked car, and flipped over.

Captain Adams and Sam cautiously ran over to find out who they were. They were disappointed to find both men dead.

"Friends of yours, Captain?"

"I've never seen them before now."

Sam pulled them out of the car and began to search them. He was aware that something about them was familiar, but he couldn't place where he had seen them. Their facial injuries and the blood prevented him getting a good look at them. He pulled out a piece of paper from one pocket with a phone number on it. He found a five dollar bill rolled up between the folded papers, with a little note attached that read: Call this number only in an emergency. Sam continued his search and found a similar note and money on the second guy. He was looking for a name he could use. They had no driver's licenses or any other identification on them. The Captain rolled one of the men over, and Sam spotted a tattoo with the name Carlos on the back of his neck.

"I hope this is his name and not a close friend of his."

"Why's that, Sam?"

"Because one of us will be calling this number in a few minutes. First, let's see what went wrong inside."

Before they went inside, Sam warned Captain Adams about what he had seen through the window. When Captain Adams saw his men slumped over their desks, he became very distraught. "What were Charlie and John doing here? They were supposed to be out of the office. Why did they have to kill them? Sam, I want those bastards, and I want them dead!"

"We'll get those guys, John. You can count on that," Sam reassured him. "Right now, let's find out what happened."

Sam began to explain his observations. "Apparently, Charlie and John were in the middle of doing some paperwork. They must have lost track of time. Jennifer walked in on them, if that indeed was her name. She dropped her skirt by Charlie's desk, causing him to lose his concentration just long enough for her to stab him in the neck. When John turned to see what was going on, she threw a knife, hitting him in the heart. She turned them around to make it look like they fell asleep, but she left a blood trail on the desk drawer and the chair. She also left behind the skirt she was wearing when she entered the building. What I can't understand is why John didn't turn around when she walked in."

"Charlie was a single guy. He always had women walking in on him when he was working. John may have turned and glanced her way at first, but when she approached Charlie, he didn't give it a second thought. John, on the other hand, has a wife and two little ones. How do I break the news to them?" the Captain exclaimed. His deep pain was obvious.

"That's the hardest part of this job, buddy. There is no easy way to tell anyone about the death of a loved one, especially when it's a ruthless, unforeseen killing such as this. We were trying to set up Salvo, and we end up with a double cross. They think they're so smart, but there was one thing they never counted on."

"What's that, Sam?"

"They've made this a personal war now. Do you know what happens when you corner a mad dog? He gets meaner and will do anything to get free. I promise you one thing. I'll stop at nothing until all of these men are dead and buried."

"I'm with you all the way, Sam. We still have one thing on our side."

"Sorrento!" they both yelled at the same time.

First, I want to stop and ask our two friendly bartenders a few questions," said Sam.

"You better fill me in on this, Sam. I don't think I've met these two men."

Janice spoke up, wiping her tears for the two fallen police officers, "Sam, I was with you for that meeting."

The three of them hopped into the Hummer and headed toward Harrah's to see the two bartenders. When Sam asked for them by name, he was told both of them had called in sick. Sam was now beginning to get a handle on what had really happened when he suddenly realized who the two men in the car had been.

Manny and Danny must have seen Sam and Captain Adams talking to Jennifer at the casino. They questioned her to find out what the plan was and offered her more money, not telling her she'd be involved in murder as well. Manny and Danny were waiting in the back of the jail with the prisoners when Jennifer walked in. Both officers turned to look at her when she entered. When they did, the bartenders charged into the office, stabbing both the officers. Jennifer tried to run, and they caught her skirt, ripping it off of her body. They left the skirt on the floor by Charlie, making it look like she had killed them. Then they tried to kill Janice and Captain Adams with the car, hoping Sam was with them. They gambled and lost their lives. But they are the lucky ones. They won't be there when this Hurricane catches up to Salvo and company.

When Sam explained his version to Captain Adams, he knew he was grasping at straws. However, even the captain had to admit it sounded reasonable. The only question on his mind was why Charlie and John were inside the jail at that time? Maybe he would find the answer as the investigation proceeded, or maybe it was better not knowing the truth. But Captain John Adams was the kind of man who only wanted the truth, no matter what the consequences would be.

Sam walked over to the hotel phone and dialed the number from the paper he found on the body. After six rings, a rugged voice answered, "Who's this?"

"Carlos. We had a little trouble with that Hurricane guy. He seems to pop up everywhere when you least expect him. Manny and I barely escaped after he shot out our rear tire and we crashed," Sam said.

"If you crashed, how did you get away?"

"We killed two of the cops inside the jail, and put them in our car, making it look like we bought the farm. Watch the news tonight, it should be breaking news. I'll call you back tomorrow after you've seen it to confirm our story." Sam hung up the phone, and then he contacted the news room and told them how to report the story as rehearsed. Maybe they could find out where they were and put a stop to this once and for all.

Janice decided, since they were at the hotel, that she would go on up to their room and get some much-needed rest. Sam agreed and instructed her to put the extra lock on the door, just in case.

Captain Adams and Hurricane went to talk to John Silvers' family and let them know the truth about what had happened. When they approached John's home they couldn't believe their eyes. There was a moving truck in front of his house with some furniture packed inside. They parked the car and walked toward the house. Just as they walked up to the front door, John Silvers came walking out carrying a box and loaded it on the truck.

"What the hell is going on here, John? You're supposed to be dead. We saw your body back at the station."

"Sorry, Captain, but we were ordered not to tell you anything about what was going on."

"Who's the jackass that gave you such an order?"

"That jackass would be me, Captain Adams." Sam and Captain Adams turned to find two men standing behind them.

"Who the hell are you?"

"I'm agent Jack Lawrence, and this is my partner, Barry Simmons. We're taking over this case."

"Who were those two men inside the jail, if it wasn't John and Charlie?"

"They were extra bodies we had on ice from another job, just in case we needed them. We had it set up that Salvo would escape from prison and take us to Sorrento."

"Where's Charlie?" Captain Adams demanded.

"We've been instructed to tell no one. They are being put into protective custody until this is over."

"What about Jennifer?" Sam asked.

"Who's Jennifer?"

"That's the girl you and your agency probably just killed. We had the same plan for her to slip him a key and then get out of there. She never came out, and two other men are dead," Sam replied.

"Why didn't you check in with us and find out what we were doing?" Captain Adams asked.

"We don't have to tell you squat, buddy. We are the FBI. We *give* orders, we don't *take* them!"

"Why don't we work together instead of butting heads?" Sam asked. "We could help each other and maybe solve this case faster."

"Just who the hell are you, mister?" Barry Simmons asked.

"Well, my friends call me 'Sam,' but you can call me 'Hurricane.' "

"Hey, look at this, Jack. We have a Hurricane here in Las Vegas."

Jack came over and shook his hand. "Mr. Hurricane, forgive my partner here. I've read some of your cases. They sound like total bull to me. There is no way one guy could have accomplished all of that."

"Well, first of all, if you could read, that would really be scary. Second, if you had read those stories, you would have known I had help from different agencies, and other people as well. I suggest, gentlemen, instead of fighting each other, let's work together and save the rest of the victims involved."

"What other victims? We were never told of any victims in this case. We were sent here to get Sorrento, and that's all."

"Well, it seems like your boy has been causing a lot of trouble around here. He's kidnapped almost two dozen girls and sold them to a man named Quincy Sanders. We are after both of these men. Salvo knew where Sanders was, and now we've lost him as well. We need your help to find them both."

"Mr. Hurricane, is it? We don't care about those girls. Our mission is to get Sorrento and that's all."

Sam exploded with a quick, straight jab to his mouth.

"You bastard, you broke my tooth." Jack cried.

"You're lucky. I was trying for the front four."

"You're relieved of this mission. If either of you get in our way, we'll kill you, if necessary."

"Well, we gave you a chance to join us, and you turned us down. Let me tell you something that you should know. If you try to carry out your threat, you may not be going back home."

Sam instructed Captain Adams to head back to Harrah's. He needed to talk to Colonel Jones. Arriving at the casino, Sam called his room. When the colonel heard his voice, he invited both men up to his room. They explained what they had just gone through with the FBI agents. After about an hour of phone calls and talks, the colonel told both men what they had to do and where to go. He told them to follow his instructions as close to the letter as possible and not to worry because help was on the way. He gave Sam and the captain a two-way radio that he happened to bring along just in case. They were directed to call Colonel Jones when they were ready to advance against the enemy. The only problem for them now was trying to decide who the enemy was. In addition to Salvo, Sorrento, and Quincy, they also had to deal with a couple of hot-headed FBI men.

Chapter Five

When Sam and the captain exited the casino, the sun was up, and the temperature had to be at least a hundred degrees. They headed toward the captain's car and noticed two men across the street who were following them, trying not to be spotted.

"Well, one thing is for sure, these two are not pros."

"Sam, let's head down toward the valet parking area and find out just who these guys are."

"I like your thinking, Captain. Besides, I'm getting a little tired of all these surprises lately. It's time we gave them a few bombshells of our own."

When they walked around a huge pillar briefly, they lost the guard dogs. Sam sidestepped toward the back as the captain sat down on the bench outside the casino. The two men approached the captain and asked, "Where's your friend?"

"Which one of my friends are you talking about, sir?"

"Don't sir me, mister. Now where is the other guy you came out of the casino with?"

"Oh, that guy isn't my friend."

"Whoever he is, where is he? Don't make me ask you again!"

"Well, in that case, he's right behind you."

"Oh, right, you expect us to fall for that old trick."

Just as he finished, Sam tapped him on the shoulder. He took no notice until Sam hit him full force. When they turned around all they saw was the barrel of his .357 magnum staring them in the face.

"Who are you?" Sam asked.

"FBI agents, John…"

Before he finished, Sam hit him on the head with his left hand causing him to stumble a little. "You're not FBI agents! You're too dumb to be the FBI. Who are you working for?"

"I'm telling you the truth, mister. We are the …"

Sam stopped him and then said, "If you say the FBI one more time, I'll shoot you in the knee cap."

"You're one crazy bastard! You can't shoot me. You're a cop."

Sam lowered his weapon and shot him in the knee cap as promised. "I am not a cop, I'm the devil himself sent down to claim your souls. If you don't tell us who you're working for, this will be the last thing on this earth you will see." He aimed his gun back into their faces.

"All right, you win. Just don't shoot us. Salvo sent us here to stop you."

"Where's the girl who was inside the jail with you?"

"What girl?"

Sam shot the other guy in his knee cap. If you don't spill the beans, you're both going to end up dead. Now, where's the girl?"

"Last time we saw her Salvo had her. He said he could make a lot of money selling her.

"Where was he going?"

"Honest, mister, if we tell you, he'll kill us. Sam shot the bigger guy in the chest. He turned to the shorter guy and said "He isn't dead yet. You have one more chance to save your friend and yourself. Where is Salvo hiding?"

"He was headed to the Frontier Hotel. He was going to hold up there until Friday, and then he'd go find Quincy Sanders. That's all we know, cross my heart. He didn't tell us anything else but that. Can we go now?"

"One more question, then I'll relieve your pain. Did he send you here to kill us?"

"Yes, we were supposed to follow you for a while and then kill you. Since we didn't shoot at you, I guess we aren't a real threat anymore."

"Wrong," Sam said as he unloaded his gun into both men killing them on the spot.

"Sam, you said you would relieve his pain. I guess he doesn't feel anything now," the captain said.

"Captain, let's get out of here before someone else sees us."

They went back to the jail house to compose themselves. Sam could see in his face that Captain Adams was worried about what they had stumbled into and tried to calm him down. "Captain, we're going to win this war. You must believe in me."

"It's not that I don't believe in you, Sam. It's just that I'm worried about how many more men have to die before it's over."

"As many as it takes, Captain. As many as it takes." Sam hesitated a minute and said, "We need to get some rest before we go on our next mission. We haven't had enough sleep these past three days."

"You have a point there, Sam. I've been working on pure adrenalin, nothing else. If we have to go up against all those men, we are definitely going to need some rest. I'll come by and pick you up in four hours."

"Perfect, Captain. We need to make a couple of stops before we hit the mother lode."

"Sam, why does it seem like when we take a step forward, something comes up and sends us two steps backward?"

"This time, it'll be different, Captain. When we hit them this time, we take no prisoners."

With that said, Sam walked out into the blazing heat of Vegas. There was a taxi already waiting. Within ten minutes he was back at their room. Sam knocked his usual knock, and Janice unlocked the door. As they settled into bed, Janice said, "Sam, this is scary and exciting all at once. I am so wound up I don't think I'll be able to get any sleep."

"Janice, you have to try. We have to be at our best with this one. These guys don't mess around. If you hesitate one second, you're dead, no questions asked. They play hardball. It's taken me thirty-two years to find someone like you. I sure don't want to lose you today." Sam rolled over on his side and closed his eyes. Janice closed her eyes with a wide smile on her face and somehow managed to fall asleep.

When Janice woke up, Sam was sitting across the room watching her. "What time is it?" she asked.

"Almost six o'clock. The captain will be here shortly."

"Sam, why didn't you wake me up instead of sitting there watching me sleep?"

"I was just wondering what you were dreaming about"

"Now, why would you say something like that?

"I've never seen someone sleep with a smile before. What were you dreaming about?"

"Never mind, and besides, how long have you been up?"

"Almost an hour now, why do you ask?"

"Sam, you only had three hours of sleep, and you need more than that, darling."

It took a couple seconds before his brain registered what Janice had just said. "We'll be all right. We can take them," he said, but deep down inside, he wasn't as confident. These men played with totally different rules than what he was accustomed to. Even though they used the same basic technique—when in doubt, kill—they were more ruthless than he was. Sam knew he was up against some powerful and vicious men. Compared to these people, Sam was a pussy cat. He knew they would have to have the element of surprise on their side. The question was if that was even possible. He was hoping by show time, he would have something planned."

Sam looked at the clock and realized it was six o'clock. At the same time there was a knock at their door. He grabbed his gun, and slowly opened the door just in case. Captain Adams was standing in the hallway smiling at Sam.

"Well, children, shall we go out and play?"

"Yes, Father, can we go and shoot some bad men tonight?"

"I never knew you were a mind reader as well, Sam."

They all laughed as they went down into the lobby. When the elevator doors opened up, three men charged into the elevator with long, sharp knives. Sam jumped out of the elevator, along with one of the men, before the doors closed. Janice and Captain Adams were still inside with two of the attackers. The man lunged at Sam with the knife extended. Sam kicked his arm, and the knife flew into the air. When he grabbed the intruder's arms and pulled him forward, the knife came straight down and stuck in his left shoulder blade. Sam knew lady luck was on his side today. As Sam extracted the knife, he twisted his enemy around until he had the knife against his throat.

"Who sent you to kill us?"

When he didn't answer, Sam cut off his right ear. "Maybe you can hear me better now; who sent you here?"

Just as Sam snapped the man's right knee, the hotel manager came running up.

"Hey, mister, what is going on? If you don't release this man, I'll call the police."

Just as Sam was going to say something, the elevator doors opened. Captain Adams and Janice walked out covered in blood. "Captain Adams, this gentleman has a complaint he'd like to make."

The hotel manager walked away saying some foul words under his breath. Sam noticed the blood on their clothes. "Is any of that yours?"

"No, we're all right, but there are two guys taking up space on the roof."

"I was worried about you two! What happened?"

"Well, Captain Adams was a bit faster with his thirty-eight than the other man with the knife. I just taught his associate a lesson about messing with a woman who has PMS," Janice said.

"I was just asking this fellow who sent him, but I've been unsuccessful so far."

"No problem, babe. It was Salvo. The other guy sang like a canary."

"Is that so? Well, tough guy, guess what? You lose," Sam said as he stuck the knife into his throat and watched him tumble to the floor. "Now we go and see Running Bear and Charging Buffalo."

Before they traveled out toward the reservation, Sam asked Captain Adams to help him with some luggage. Captain Adams was amazed how heavy the duffle bags were. He knew better than to ask what Sam had inside. He'd find out soon enough. After everything was loaded and all weapons were accounted for, they headed out to the Indian reservation.

It would take at least a half hour before they would reach their destination. Janice noticed how Sam was motionless and staring into the wilderness, almost like his mind was in a different place. When he finally shook his head and his eyes cleared, she said, "Welcome back, darling. A penny for your thoughts."

"Just planning what we'll do once we get there."

"Bull!" she said. "You were so far out in left field I was afraid to shake you. What is it that troubles you so much? You can open up to me, if you need to get something off your chest."

"Just some flashbacks from old days in the service, that's all."

"Something else is eating you up inside, Sam. Please talk to me, and let go of what is haunting you. Let the demon go. Clear your mind."

"It was almost fifteen years ago, and we were on a secret mission in Cambodia. Our mission was to get civilians out fast. Peace talks were breaking down, and trouble was brewing. They put me in charge of the mission. I was barely eighteen years old and green as grass. I had been in a few skirmishes, but this was my first squad: Charlie Smoltz, Johnny Beal, Emilio Sanchez, Barry Wilson, and myself. I was so excited I never bothered to study what we were up against. I just took it for granted we were the best and couldn't be beat. We had no trouble getting into the building that held the civilians, but I never thought about it being a trap. When we tried to exit the building, bullets started flying in from all directions. Whatever peace talks were being discussed, they obviously were not successful. We took the first attack with ease and arrived at our pickup spot."

"Just as we were getting into the helicopter, they opened up on us so hard that the helicopter had to leave with the civilians, leaving us behind. We were stuck until we found our other extraction site. We were like sitting ducks out in the open with no place to hide. Fortunately, we reached the high grass as we crawled out toward the east. Just when we thought we were safe, three commies came out of nowhere. Barry took a bayonet in the shoulder. Johnny caught a bullet in the leg. And I almost took a bullet in the head, if not for it glancing off my helmet."

"When the shooting finally stopped, we figured they were surrounding us for the final kill. When Charlie slowly lifted his head to take a look, everyone was gone. We didn't know if this was another trap or not. With Johnny and Barry hurt, we couldn't afford to sit around and wait to find out, so I picked up Johnny and carried him out to a new extraction point. When we were finally getting onto the helicopter, they started shooting at us again. However, this time we were already onboard and lifting off. I was just about to say we all made it when I looked over and saw Johnny slumped over. He had been hit by a bullet in the chest. Because of my ignorance a good man died. I made myself a promise that I would never take anything for granted again.

"Here I am once again, going into something half blind. I don't know the layout of the building, I don't know how many men we are facing, and I have no clue even who our enemy is. How will we know if we get the right guy? Before, I had nothing to lose, but now I have you. I worry that we might not make it out of this alive."

"Remember why we are here, Sam—all those innocent girls being sold as slaves. If I have to die to set them free, it will be worth it," Janice said.

"Are you sure you were never a Green Beret?" Sam asked with a big grin on his face. All right, if you're so gung ho to do this, just promise me you'll stay close beside me."

Just her smile alone told Sam he had nothing to worry about. He couldn't figure it out. He had never had a problem with any mission before. Why now? It finally dawned on him that he must truly be in love with Janice. But now he had to stay focused. He had to shake this feeling before the fight.

When they finally arrived at the reservation, Sorrento was strapped up between two trees. Both of his arms were strung out from his sides and stretched to the max. His ankles were tied together in a way that prevented him from falling. His shoes were off and his feet were bloody as the red ants were having a picnic on his bare skin. He looked thirsty due to the hot sun beating down on his bare chest; he looked like he was on fire.

Running Bear came out of his house and walked over toward Sam. They shook hands and Running Bear said, "I told you he'd live to regret this day."

"Running Bear, is he in any shape to answer questions?"

"Let's see," Running Bear answered. Then stood up and walked over to Sorrento with a glass of water. He put the glass up to his mouth. Sorrento started to drink it down fast, causing instant pain in his stomach. "I still think he will talk just fine."

"Sorrento, you should know better than to drink anything cold so fast when you're so hot, it just ties your stomach up in knots. I need a few questions answered by you. If you refuse to answer, my friends will show you the true meaning of pain."

"When I get out of here, you're a dead man, whoever you are."

"You're a very funny man, Sorrento. Instead of thinking about what shape you'll be in, if you get out of here, you would rather threaten me, thinking that I'd kill you fast and save you the suffering of real pain. Well, that just isn't going to happen." Sam hesitated as he grabbed a shotgun out of the truck and walked back. "You see, Sorrento, we need some answers, and one way or another you will talk." Sam slammed the end of the gun onto Sorrento's bare foot breaking open his skin. The ants looked like vultures that hadn't eaten in weeks. Sorrento was in shear agony, he tried to shake the ants away from his foot. He fell forward almost tearing his arms off of his shoulders.

"Sorrento, Sorrento, Sorrento, why put yourself through all this torture? All you have to do is tell us where we can find Salvo and Quincy Sanders, and I'll ease your pain. You can feel what happens when these red ants smell blood; they will eat up your entire body, bones and all."

"If I tell you, I'm a dead man."

"Sorrento, that's what amazes me so much about your little operation. You guys would rather deal with your own pain and suffering than to rat on your people. There is only one way of ending this torture, tell us where they are. Now, if you don't tell us, I'll slice you up to your belly then sit back and watch these ants feast on you. The best part about it is you'll be alive through the whole thing. You see, they are so small it'll take you two to three hours to die. When I slice you I'll only break the skin so they can smell the blood. You'll even feel your bones being devoured by these amazing creatures. Now, ask yourself, are Salvo and Sanders worth all this pain and suffering you're about to go through?"

When Sorrento stood there and smiled, Hurricane reached for his knife and started to slowly break the skin on his leg from the ankle to his knee cap. When Sorrento saw how many more ants piled out of the ant hill and climbed up his leg, he turned a pale white. Within seconds all you could see is red up and down his leg. He was screaming in agony so loudly that Janice had to leave the scene. She knew she shouldn't, but she couldn't help feeling sorry for Sorrento.

Within a few minutes, after the shock wore off, Sorrento cried out, "You win! You win! I'll tell you everything I know, just get these ants off me."

Running Bear and Charging Buffalo brought out two big buckets of water, and threw them on his leg. All the ants scampered back in the hill for safety, but it wouldn't take long for them to be back in this Nevada heat.

"All right, Sorrento, you can start talking. But heed my warning, if we so much as get an indication that you're lying to save your skin, you'll be tied down and spread over the ant hill. Honey will be poured over your body and the blood and honey will attract every ant around, along with a few vultures. You'll die in a very painful, slow, deserving way, and you'll be begging someone to take your life."

"Sanders' place is about two miles west of Alamo, Nevada. It's built like an old western fort, complete with a crow's nest in each corner of the building. He could have anywhere between twenty to fifty men surrounding the place, more if he's expecting trouble. By now Salvo has made it to his place and warned him about you, unless …"

"Unless what, Sorrento? I'm warning you, come clean or these will be the last words you'll ever say."

"Relax, Hurricane," said Sorrento. "Maybe he's still on the strip, hoping you take out Quincy. That way he becomes the kingpin without losing any of his men. He normally stays in one of three places downtown: the Golden Nugget, Fitzgerald's or the Freemont Hotel. He might figure neither one of you will come out of this alive, so he'll be in the clear to do as he pleases.".

"Which one of the two sells the girls?"

"That would be Quincy. He normally holds them for a couple of weeks. He trains them to be obedient by torturing them. If they are still a problem after the two weeks, he will kill them and bury the remains out in the desert somewhere."

"Who does he sell them to?"

"Whoever offers him the most money. It doesn't matter if it's the Chinese, Koreans, Vietnamese, or any other nationality, as long as they want American women. It does not matter who or what the girls are. As long as they are Americans, the customers don't care."

"What's the easiest way to get into that fort?"

"You'll never make it going straight toward them. It's all flat land, and very easy to see within a good ten miles, unless, of course, a sandstorm pops up as a shield for you. Now, if you brought him a truck load of girls, he might let you in, then again maybe not."

"Yes, he might not let me in, but I might get close enough to launch a surprise attack, just like when the Greeks surprised the Trojans with the wooden horse."

"Brother Hurricane," Running Bear said, "I and my young warriors would like to help you stop this man who tortures people for his own pleasure."

"I appreciate your offer, my brother, and I would like nothing better than to have you help us. It's just that I have no game plan at this time. I need to see what we are up against before we proceed with a plan. From what Sorrento's told me already, the fort sounds almost impossible to sneak up on."

"Samuel Hurricane Rufus, I'm surprised at you!" Janice bellowed out. "Why don't you call that colonel friend of yours and see if he could get some aerial pictures for you?"

That put a big smile on Sam's face as he called from his untraceable phone. After several minutes of explaining just what he needed and why, Sam came back and gave Janice such a big kiss on her lips that she was breathless for a few seconds.

"Wow! I do not know what that was for, so I will just enjoy it."

"Colonel Jones will have all the gear we need as soon as we get back to our hotel. Thanks to you we may have just what the doctor ordered."

"What's that, my friend?" Captain Adams asked.

"Much needed help. It seems the Air Force and Marines are training not too far from where we are going. The colonel is going to contact the officer in charge and ask them to help us. Unfortunately, we have to go back before we go forward."

"How much time do you think we have, Sam? Will the girls still be there by the time we arrive?"

"I asked Colonel Jones the same questions. Seems he's going to send helicopters over every ten minutes, making it look like training maneuvers. He told them if they see anything suspicious, take them out and make it look like an accident."

"Now I know who must have trained you in the service, Sam."

"Very funny, Janice. Now let's head back to The Strip. We have somebody else we need to see as well there. My brothers, we will be back for you soon," he told the Indian warriors. "Get your weapons ready, and prepare for war."

"We will be ready, and we will not let you down. It will feel good to be able to ride like the wind again," Running Bear said.

Just before they headed out, they heard a voice say, "Hey, what about me? I told you everything I know about Salvo and Quincy Sanders. You said you would let me go."

"I said I would ease your pain, not let you go. Then again, you do have to answer for all those girls you tortured yourself, right?"

"Hey! That's not fair. I told you what I knew. I kept my end of the bargain. Now you have to keep yours."

"You know, Sorrento, I wonder how many of those girls were told the same thing. How many of those girls were released thinking they were going back to their homes. But instead of going home, you killed them, thinking they would talk. Now, I'm faced with the same problem. If I let you go, you'll go tell Salvo and Sanders I'm coming for them."

"You're wrong, Hurricane! I won't talk to anyone. I promise."

"Please forgive me, Sorrento, but for some reason I have a hard time believing you. Brothers Running Bear and Charging Buffalo, feel free to treat this prisoner any way you want to. We will be back before the sun sets beyond the hills two times. Make him feel the horror others felt when he killed them."

"Don't worry, Brother Hurricane, he will regret he was even born," Running Bear said. Charging Buffalo made a gesture with his hand. Six braves staked Sorrento over the ant hill, then they proceeded to pour honey over his whole body, including around his eyes. Being very careful not to drop any into his eyes, they wanted him to be able to look to the heavens and know that death was close.

Before they left the reservation, Janice looked back just in time to see blood from a goat being poured over his body. Then she heard the shrill screams, as the ants and other insects started to eat his flesh. She turned away briefly, and when she turned back again, she could no longer see his body, only a mass of ants, lizards and vultures tearing him apart. She felt sorry for him again as she heard his screams of pain. *What an awful way to die,* she thought. *Maybe its poetic justice after all those others he had beat up or killed.* That would be the last time she turned to look at Sorrento.

Chapter Six

Whon they arrived at The Strip, Hurricane, Captain Adams, and Janice headed over to see Colonel Jones. After going over details about the military stepping in and giving the trio some much needed help, Hurricane decided to go after Salvo by himself. He figured he would be able to move faster without the others around, at least for now.

"Hey, Janice, while you and Captain Adams discuss the details with the colonel, I'm going out to find Salvo. If I'm not back in an hour, I'm either captured or dead. Since Salvo doesn't know anything about the two of you, you might have to continue this mission without me. They'll never expect either of you were a part of this."

"Where are you going to be in case we have to come and save you?" Janice asked.

"If Sorrento was right, it will be either the Golden Nugget, Fitzgerald's, or the Freemont Hotel. Besides, you have to go and save those girls. Don't waste your time looking for me."

"All right, Sam, I promise," Janice said, crossing her fingers behind her. Captain Adams agreed, against his better judgment.

"Sam, the last time you surprised them. This time they'll be waiting for you."

"I know, Captain. I need to find another way in."

"Just remember, my friend, if it seems too easy, it's a trap. Get out of there. Don't try to play hero with these guys. They would like nothing more than to bury you, and they don't even care if you're alive or dead."

"Thanks for the vote of confidence. It's good to know I have friends who really care. Besides, I have a tracking device inside my ear. The control is on the bed."

With that said, Hurricane turned and exited the building. He hailed a cab and headed for downtown Vegas. He checked all his weapons in his vest and around his belt. He instructed the cab driver to drive around the hotels first. After checking out which one had the most guards around it, he had the cab pull to a stop two blocks away from the Fitzgerald Casino. Hurricane paid the man and exited the cab. The temperature gauge on the taxi said eighty-two degrees outside. Sam was glad he only wore his vest instead of his full length coat. He noticed quite a few people walking up and down the streets. *How many of them work for Salvo?* Sam wondered, as he walked toward the hotel.

Hurricane walked into the lobby, headed toward the counter, and asked for Salvo's room. He noticed when the clerk quickly shifted his eyes toward a couple of guys over by the fountain. Acting like he didn't see the look, Sam smiled and walked toward the elevators. One of the two men was medium built, five feet eight, with a tailor-made suit and a pair of Italian shoes that would shine in the dark. The other guy was at least six feet tall, and he had the biggest hands Sam had ever seen. Sam swore the man could wrap his fingers around a basketball. He also had on an expensive suit and Italian shoes.

When the elevator was finally down, Sam stepped in toward the back wall. He turned around just in time to see the big guy stop a few people from getting into the elevator.

"That was kind of rude, friend," Sam said.

"Mind your own business, punk," the big guy snapped back.

"Now, there's no need to talk back to me like that."

"Shut up before I flatten you to the wall, stupid."

"Well, Salvo sure knows how to pick his help—big and dumb."

Both men turned to look at Hurricane. The shorter one asked, "What makes you think we work for that Salvo guy you mentioned?"

"Well, it isn't everyone who gets an escort up in the elevator. You two are so obvious, you couldn't even sneak up on a deaf and blind person."

"After the boss gets done talking to you, mister, we are going to bust you up good."

"Who says I came up here to talk to Salvo?"

"Then why are you headed up to his room?"

"I'm here to kill him." Hurricane kicked the big man's knees, sending him crashing to the floor. He grabbed the little man, and just before he hit him, the elevator door opened. Hurricane faced three men with guns drawn on him.

"Let him go, mister," one of the guys said.

Hurricane, with a grin, watched the three men. Just as the one guy was starting to say let him go one more time. Hurricane hit him in the face, breaking his nose. It was so quick his captors looked startled. His nose was broken before he completed his demand. As Hurricane exited the elevator, one of the men tried to hit him. Hurricane ducked and elbowed him in the neck, killing him.

Hurricane was hit from behind. When he woke up, he found himself tied to a chair in the middle of a big room. After his eyes cleared up, he noticed a desk in the far corner. When he canvassed the room, he noticed red carpeting on the walls and figured this was a sound-proof room. He saw a silver cart in the farthest corner with a battery charger standing behind the cart. Then it dawned on him. Quincy Sanders wasn't torturing those girls. Salvo was. This was the room he used. Hurricane was so busy studying the room that it took a few minutes to finally occur to him that he still had his vest on. He wondered if they had checked it for weapons, and put it back on just to confuse him. He saw the camera in the upper corner of the room. They were watching, and that was a sure bet.

Sam wanted to put on a show and make it look good, even though he was tied up. He was able to bounce the chair off the floor. This wasn't only for show, however. Rebounding on the floor also gave him a chance to check the lower back lining of his vest. He discovered that they had found the weapons on the outside of his vest, but they missed the weapons hidden inside. Hurricane found the hidden zipper. He slowly unzipped it and out popped a little knife. He bounced around until he was certain they couldn't see his hands and slowly started cutting the ropes that bound him to the chair.

The door opened suddenly and in walked Salvo. "So, you're this super crime fighter, Hurricane, who can't be stopped. Your reputation precedes you. But now you're in no position for us to worry about it. By the time my men are done working you over, you'll be begging us to kill you. First, we're going to make you suffer for all the money you've cost me so far, not to mention tarnishing my reputation in the syndicate. My only regret is that you haven't killed Quincy Sanders like I was hoping."

"I'll kill him after I'm done with you, fat man," Hurricane retorted.

"I must say, Mr. Hurricane, I like your spunk." Salvo clapped his hands and in walked four guys, looking like they meant business.

"Unfortunately, I don't think you'll be in any shape to do anything after my men are finished with you. I must leave now, but I'll tell everyone you died like a little girl, kicking and screaming. I'll squash your reputation of being called a tough guy, and laugh while I explain how stupid you were to land in my trap."

"Before you leave, Salvo, tell me where you're going?"

"I don't see how that really matters to you now, but if you must know, I'm going to see Quincy Sanders at the Alamo. You see, while you were busy trying to find Quincy, I've collected about twelve more girls. Since I have no more worries about you interrupting my business, I'm personally going to deliver these fair maidens to Sanders. I'm sure my men here will keep you entertained while I'm gone. I just wish I could stay and watch. However, since you spoiled my last delivery I must complete this one myself. Who knows, maybe I'll see you in your next life." Salvo laughed as he walked out the door.

Hurricane studied his opponents as he waited for somebody to say something. One of the men stood about six-five with a slim build, weighing in at about two hundred pounds at best. Hurricane noticed a slight limp in his right knee when he walked. He had short black hair and a scar behind his left ear. One of the other guys walked over to the desk in the far left corner. He stood almost six feet, with broad shoulders. He was almost the same weight as the taller guy. In fact his arms looked as if he was definitely a weight lifter, not all that muscular, but very tight skin. Then he saw the ten-pound sledge hammer and bolt cutter that he took out of the dresser drawer. His other two guests walked over to retrieve the battery charger and the silver cart. As they came closer into the light he noticed they were both of Asian descent. Both men were very small, a little over five feet. Both men looked to be a good hundred and fifty pounds and very muscular. Sam figured they were into martial arts, and they moved with confidence.

They wore lose fitting clothes, so they could move freely. When he finally saw the tray, he realized it had surgical tools on top of it—scalpels, rib spreaders, and various other tools used for extracting parts of the body.

The tallest guy finally asked, "Is there anything you would like to say before we begin?" Then he back-handed Hurricane, cutting his cheek. Hurricane spotted the razor sharp points sticking out at the top of his gloves.

"Yes. If you guys give up now and let me go, I'll spare your lives. If not, I'll kill all of you."

They all laughed. Then one of the Asian men asked, "Why would we be worried about you, when you're tied up?" He decided to get into the fray as well, striking Hurricane in the nose with his fist. Sam felt the sting as the Asian man said, "I told you guys I could break his nose with one shot. Now pay up." The others each took out a ten dollar bill and paid the man.

"When you decided to put my vest back on, you forgot a couple of things," stated Sam.

"You're crazy, man. We took all the weapons out of your vest. We just put it back on you to insult you." He waved a pair of brass knuckles in front of Sam, and then struck him in the forehead. "Hey, man, did that hurt? I didn't feel a thing." They all laughed.

After Hurricane regained his wits, he asked. "How sure are you that you found all my weapons?"

"Man, you're just stalling for time. I wonder how long it'll take you to start crying like a baby."

"If you're so sure you found all of my weapons, then how can my hands be free behind my back?"

"No way, man. If your hands were free, you would have killed Salvo right here. However, if it will make you happy to have us play your game before we kill you, Johnny would be happy to check it out for you."

When Johnny squatted down to take a look, Hurricane grabbed him by his throat and spun him around until he was on his lap. Sam's knife was securely positioned at his neck, capable of causing fatal injury. Johnny's body was shielding Hurricane.

"As I was saying, gentlemen, drop your weapons, exit that door, and your lives will be spared. However, if you decide to stay, you'll end up dead."

"I'm curious to find out just how good you are, mister. I've heard all the rumors. I just have to know if they are true.

"Dying isn't a very good way of finding out, friend."

"This is bull. He's only one man. Let's take him out," one of the Asian men said.

"Besides, his legs are still tied to the bottom of that chair," the other Asian man spoke.

"Well, junior, it's your call. Make your move and die."

Just as Hurricane was getting ready for the attack, Captain Adams, Janice, and about five deputies came charging into the room. When the captives looked away, Hurricane made a swift move and threw Johnny to the floor. At the same time, he flipped over, bringing his legs down on Johnny's body, breaking the chair, and freeing his legs. Then Sam charged the big man and dropping down, sweeping his legs from underneath him and sending him crashing backward hard on the floor. Hurricane looked toward Janice. She was taking out one of the Asian guys. Captain Adams and his men were handcuffing the other Asian guy, and he wasn't putting up much of a fight.

Hurricane sensed someone coming up behind him. Just before his attacker was in striking distance, Hurricane spun around and thrust his fingers into the guy's throat. His eyes nearly popped out of their sockets as he dropped to the floor.

"Sam, your face is swelling and is already black and blue," Janice said.

Hurricane did not comment as he picked up the charged ends of the battery charger. He slowly walked over toward the lone survivor who was handcuffed and sitting on a couch. Before he said anything, he swung his mighty fist striking his captive in the nose. Blood started streaking out. "I owed you that, little man. Now let's see just how tough you are."

Sam ripped open his shirt baring his chest. Since his arms were secured behind his back with the handcuffs, he attached one end of the cables to his bare arm.

"Hey, little man, now just where did you put my weapons? Not talking yet?" Sam said as he took the other cable and touched the man's stomach. All you could smell was burning flesh. Hurricane made a path of burnt flesh, that traveled up his stomach between his ribs. The little guy surprised Hurricane with his toughness. When the searing pain was close to his heart, then you heard his screams.

"In the back closet," he said in a faint voice.

"What was that? I didn't hear you."

"It's in the kitchen in the big closet. Please, have mercy, I just can't take any more of this."

Hurricane came back with his weapons intact. Looking down at his captive, he said, "One more question before this can end. Which room is Salvo in?"

"I can't tell you that. If I do Salvo will kill me."

"If you don't tell me, I'll kill you." Sam proceeded to take off the man's shoes and socks. "Better yet, let's see how long it'll take to burn off your toes, shall we?"

"You're bluffing, man. You don't understand. I can't …"

Just before he finished, Hurricane clamped the cable across his toes. Flesh started to melt off the foot at once. It didn't take long before the little toe was completely gone.

Hurricane decided to turn up the heat a little, so he turned the power on all the way. Instantly the flesh started to smoke. Just before the second toe was completely gone, Hurricane heard, "I'll tell you anything you want, just release my toes."

Hurricane did as he was asked, turned to his captive, and said, "If you don't talk, next time it stays on until the job is done."

"He's on the twenty-seventh floor. He has a helicopter pad on the roof."

"How many men are there?"

"He normally has anywhere between five to fifteen men. Five if there are no problems, and up to fifteen if he is expecting trouble."

"What kind of weapons do they have?"

"They have mostly automatic weapons and machine guns."

"How did he know I was coming after him?"

"He never said. I guess he just knew somehow you were alive. Maybe someone he knows saw you in town. He has everyone in town scared to death of him. He may have given them no choice but to call if they saw you."

"Is there a fire escape in back of the building?"

"Yes, but that's twenty-seven stories up. It will take less time if you take the elevator."

"He'll never expect me to go up the back way, and his stooges will be waiting for me if I use the elevator."

"You're nuts, man, if you plan on taking these guys all by yourself.

They'll cut your heart out and feed it to the fish."

"Is there anything else you can tell me about Salvo?"

"No, I don't know anything else. Please don't tell Salvo what I told you. He'll kill me for sure."

"If you're that afraid of dying, I'll release you from your fear." Hurricane turned, bringing his left foot around, and striking the little man in the neck. He slumped over dead as his head hung loose.

"Hurricane, you should go and let the doctor check you out."

"I'll do that later, Captain. I now have an appointment with death."

"Sam! I can't allow you to go up there alone. Let me call for backup before you go up. They will be here in less than ten minutes."

"Good, that'll give me a ten-minute head start. But heed my warning: if you're not up there before I make it to the top, I'm going in without you. However, you're welcome to join me later, if you would like."

Captain Adams went out to his car and radioed for some help. He saw Hurricane heading around the back of the building. He didn't panic. Not even a man like Hurricane could climb twenty seven floors in ten minutes.

Hurricane walked behind the building and discovered the fire escape that extended the entire height of the building. He felt a little shaky because of the broken nose he got during the fight. His legs were still a little stiff from being tied up in the chair. Surveying the back alley, he saw a few dumpsters and a couple of cats looking for food. Other than that it was empty. He didn't need any more surprises tonight. Looking at the bottom of the ladder he knew he had to jump to reach it. He started thinking of the women Salvo sold or killed. His adrenalin started pumping, and his strength returned as he made the jump.

Hurricane started climbing up the ladder. As he thought about all the women he had saved just a few hours ago, his speed picked up. Then he started to think of the women who were killed and sold already and the group Salvo had up in his room now. Before he knew it, Sam was standing on top of the building.

According to his watch he still had three minutes before the cavalry would appear. Hurricane wanted to make sure the ladies were safe before the big conflict. When he walked around the big air conditioner on top of the roof, he saw a helicopter waiting on the launch pad. Hurricane walked over to the unguarded machine, took out his hunting knife, and proceeded to punch a hole in the gas tank.

He was within three steps of the exit when the door opened up. Hurricane grinned as he looked at the three startled men before him.

"Who the hell are you, mister? You don't belong up here."

Hurricane's only answer was a swift, straight kick under his jaw, dropping him where he stood. One of the other guys charged and was flipped onto his back. Number three tried to sneak up from behind, but Hurricane powered a straight kick into his kneecap. After a loud snap, he was out of commission, unable to cause any more trouble. The other two tried to rush Hurricane at the same time. Spotting a knife in the bigger man's hand, Hurricane charged the assailant and grabbed the arm that held the knife. As they were testing each other's strength, Hurricane was totally aware of the other thug coming up behind him. Hurricane swung under the arm that held the knife, and swung the arm backward in a circular motion, catching the rushing enemy in the stomach with his partner's weapon.

"Looks like your buddy got the point," Hurricane said with a little snicker. Then he proceeded to pop the man's arm out of its socket, causing him to drop the knife. Hurricane was in no mood to play games. "How many men does Salvo have downstairs?"

When he didn't answer, Hurricane picked him up by the bad arm, and hoisted him up over his head, and heaved him over the side of the building. He then walked over to number three.

"I hope you are smarter than the last guy down there. How many men are guarding Salvo?"

"There are fifteen in the room and five in the hallway."

"Including the three of you?"

He nodded yes, and then added, "I promise you, I won't tell them you're coming."

Suddenly, a voice came out of the man's pocket.

Hurricane reached down and tore his jacket as he listened to the radio.

"Roger, where are you? Are Fred and Sam with you? Why doesn't anyone answer me?"

Hurricane pointed his big gun at the man's head "You better make this good, or you're dead where you stand," as Roger answered the call.

"Fred and Sam went to the bathroom, I'm getting everything ready. I can barely hear. It must be the metal in the roof. We'll call you back when we're done."

"Make it fast. Mr. Salvo's talking about going to see Mr. Sanders when you get back."

The little radio went silent. Hurricane looked at Roger, then said, "I'm very disappointed in you, Roger. I thought you and I had an understanding. I guess I was wrong and that's too bad. You never told me about your two-way radios, and I have to believe you would have told Salvo and the others I was coming. Because of this I hope you will understand my position. I was going to kill you last, but, Roger, I'll have to kill you now.

Hurricane moved so fast that Roger never screamed out when Hurricane stuck a pair of carving knives right through his ears. It happened so quick Roger never felt a thing. As he slumped over dead, his eyes almost burst out of their sockets.

Hurricane took their guns. *Why not use up their ammo first?* he figured. Cautiously, he entered the hallway, slowly opening the door. It seemed empty. As he started to step out, he saw a shadow on the floor of a man holding a gun. He closed the door and made sure it was shut.

"Hey, Roger, is that you? Stop fooling around. Mr. Salvo is not in a joking mood today. You fool, let's get going!" Hurricane heard the voice getting closer. He positioned himself to strike. When the door opened "Who the …" was all that was said as Hurricane struck him in the throat, causing him to gag and lose the handle of the door as it closed behind him. Hurricane sprung on him like a mountain lion.

"All right, pal, what room number is Salvo's? I realize you can't talk right now and I'm sorry about that. Just indicate what number with your right hand." With that said, Hurricane grabbed a knife and stuck his left hand onto the wall.

He just hung there in shock, but as soon as Hurricane grabbed his other hand, he quickly signed the number 2740 with his fingers.

"Chester, where are you? Where the heck did he go? Hey, Chester, stop playing games and get out here now." Hurricane quickly stuck Chester's right hand to the wall. He waited until he heard footsteps outside the door. He pounded on the door and then went halfway down the stairway and waited for his prey.

The hallway door opened up. When he saw Chester hanging on the wall, without even thinking about looking around, he started to release him.

"How did you get hung up like this, Chester?"

"He met the Hurricane," a voice behind him said. Before the man knew what was going on, Hurricane had him against the wall hitting him with a thunderous blow in the stomach. Just before he doubled up and started coughing he was stuck into the wall just like Chester.

"Who are you? Are you crazy? Do you know who lives up here? Let us go and I promise nobody will know anything."

"Not that it's any of your business, but call me 'Hurricane.' Yes, I'm the craziest person you'll ever meet. Yes, I know who lives up here. As far as telling anyone, let's just say after I'm done with Salvo, I want you to let people know that whoever tortures and sells people, sooner or later will face swift and unexpected justice when the Hurricane arrives.

"He has twenty men inside that room. You'll never make it out alive. Think about what you're doing. They will skin you alive."

Hurricane took a roll of duct tape out of his pocket, tearing off two pieces as he turned to his two captives. "Just be thankful I let you live to talk about this." Then he taped their mouths shut. "I'll see you boys in a few minutes." He opened the door and stepped out into the hallway.

Hearing the elevators approaching, he knew his help was closing in. He took out his two big cannons and kicked in the door. Shots were echoing through the room. Hurricane saw Salvo surrounded by five shooters in the far corner. Three others were trying to circle around him. Hurricane shot through the furniture. He heard some grunting and knew he hit one of them. Just as his clips emptied, two men ran toward him. Sam pulled out two of the four guns he collected on the roof and fired two shots, killing both of them. After rapidly reloading his cannons, he noticed Salvo's men weren't too anxious to charge anymore.

"Hey, Salvo, give yourself up now, and maybe you'll live. Put up a fight, and I'll skin you alive.

"I don't understand you, Mr. Hurricane. Why do you fight for all of these women? Why do they mean so much to you?"

"This is the United States of America. We don't have slavery in this country. When I fight these battles, I fight for everyone. I don't care if you're black, white, Hispanic, Chinese, or whatever ethnic group you belong to. I don't care what religion you are. I only know we all fall under one category, we are Americans. Unfortunately, we have scumbags like you who get a thrill out of using people to get what they want. Because of people like you, they need people like me to balance the justice."

"You surprise me, Hurricane. I thought we were alike, but you have a heart and a conscience after all. I don't."

"Don't let my heart fool you, Salvo. When I get my hands on you, you'll change your tune. You don't have a chance of getting away. Why don't you make this easy on yourself and your men and give up.

"You underestimate me, Hurricane. Do you really expect me to give up when I have twenty-five men against you?"

"Actually, it is twenty-five minus seven already. Let's see, that makes it more like eighteen left, plus yourself. I've a feeling the odds are going to get a little better for the side of justice in a few minutes."

After Hurricane answered Salvo's question, the door burst open and in swarmed several police officers along with Captain Adams and Janice.

"About time. It took you long enough to get here," Sam said.

"We must have stopped on every floor on the way up in that elevator, and then there was a power glitch. We were stuck on the fourteenth floor and had to wait for the power to be turned back on," Captain Adam's said.

"That's why I take the stairs, Captain." Hurricane smiled as the captain looked over toward him.

"Salvo, I think the odds are just about even now, so throw out your weapons and come out with your hands over your heads.

"This time, Hurricane, I'll make sure you stay dead." With that said, Salvos men started shooting up the place. Bullets were flying all over the room. Two young police officers made the fundamental mistake of standing up; they were both killed. Hurricane crawled toward the end of the big couch he was hiding behind. He peeked around the armrest and saw three of Salvo's men loading their weapons. He raised his two Magnums, took careful aim, and squeezed the triggers. He sent six direct shots toward the three men. Two died instantly. The third slowly slumped down. He would die a slow and painful way.

Shots were suddenly coming in from behind them. Salvo's men must have slipped through different doors leading out into the hallway. Hurricane noticed the sun was starting to rise, so he shot out the lights in the room. The street lights were so bright they could still see the silhouettes of the men standing up.

"Aim for the shadows!" Hurricane said.

Everyone started shooting, and just like pins on a bowling alley, three more guys fell to the ground. However, Hurricane and company were now caught dangerously in the middle of the room, until the sun finally poked out from behind the clouds. The four guys near the door were instantly blinded. Sam stood up and fired six more shots, dropping two of them.

Captain Adams and Janice were shooting back and forth with the five surrounding Salvo. Janice noticed a red dot on Hurricane's back. Turning quickly, she let out a burst from her machine gun. Hurricane turned and saw an unidentified man dancing as the bullets ripped through him. After smiling at each other a brief moment, they returned to action. Hurricane saw a flash of light from his side vision; he turned just in time to see Salvo and two of his goons heading up to the roof.

"Sam, Salvo's getting away!" Janice said.

"Relax, baby, he's not going anywhere for a while," Hurricane said, as he smiled back at her.

Sam took a dummy hand grenade out of his vest pocket, pulled the pin, and threw it into the kitchen. As the last five bad guys came running out it looked like a carnival duck shoot. The only difference was men were falling down dead. Hurricane stood up and went into the kitchen and retrieved his grenade.

"Are you two all right?" Hurricane asked. Janice and the captain shook their heads yes.

Hurricane headed up to the roof. Janice and Captain Adams ran right behind him. When the door opened, they saw Salvo in the helicopter smiling back at them. Captain Adams raised his gun toward Salvo.

"Don't shoot at him, Captain," Hurricane said.

Captain Adams looked back at Hurricane with a very puzzled look on his face.

"Aim for the big wet spot on the ground underneath the helicopter," Sam explained.

Captain Adams smiled and let two shots land where Hurricane had mentioned. There was a fast flash and then fire, which followed the path of the leak right up into the gas tank of the helicopter. Salvo's grin turned to fear as the helicopter burst into flames.

The recently abducted girls were found, a little undernourished but relatively unharmed, inside one of the adjacent rooms. They were all giving high fives when Captain Adams noticed Hurricane favoring his left arm.

"Sam, what's wrong with your left arm?"

"I just bumped it on the door. It'll be fine in a few minutes."

"Since when do bumps bleed?"

Sam was so focused on the fight he never felt the bullet penetrate his left arm. He took off his vest and shirt. There was a chunk of skin missing where the bullet hit his arm. It was a flesh wound, but deeper than most. This one was only a sixteenth of an inch from doing some permanent damage.

After wrapping up the arm, Sam was ready to go again. He knew it was only a matter of time before word reached Quinton Sanders about Salvo. He would run if he got scared, and they had already had a hard enough time finding him. Besides, they still had a few young ladies to rescue.

Chapter Seven

Hurricane couldn't believe how hot it was as they exited the hotel. Captain Adams was driving them back to the jail to gather up more weapons and ammo. Hurricane asked the captain to stop at Harrah's first, so he could get some things from their hotel room. Janice and Captain Adams waited in the car while Hurricane went inside. Within fifteen minutes, Hurricane came out carrying his big duffle bag. Climbing into the back seat of the car, he held the bag on his lap like it was a dog going for a ride.

Janice was a little concerned about Sam. He seemed to stare into space. She couldn't remember ever seeing him like this. *How badly had they beaten him at Salvo's place? Were we too late this time to save him? Look how swollen his face has become. I wonder if they gave him a concussion?* she wondered to herself as he just gazed out the window.

"Sam," she called out. "Sam! Honey, can you hear me?"

Sam shook his head like he was clearing out some cobwebs and answered, "Yes, Janice. I can hear you. I'm just remembering what I have gone through so far these past few days. We've been so busy looking for the bad guys that I never realized how beautiful Las Vegas really is. I was soaking up some of the sights before our fight. Who knows, we may never have a chance to see this city again once this is over."

When they reached the jail, more weapons and ammunition were loaded into the truck. After Salvo was finally finished and the twelve girls he had kidnapped were saved, they had found that four of the girls were in

111

law enforcement from various parts of the United States. They offered their assistance after finding out what was going on. Three of the girls were about the same height as Janice, standing at almost five feet eight inches. Crystal Smith was a blonde, Joann Fisher was a brunette, and Roxanne Redford was black haired. Crystal and Joann were from different areas of New York. Crystal was from Brooklyn while Joann was from the Bronx. Roxanne was from Green Bay, Wisconsin.

Then there was Diane Carter. Diane stood six-four and was the most gorgeous African-American woman Sam had ever seen. Her skin was flawless, and she had exquisite facial features. There was something special about Diane. Her smile was so warm it almost melted your heart. Diane hailed from Chicago.

After all the introductions were made, Sam sat down with everyone to go over his plan.

"Hello, ladies and gentlemen. I've come up with a plan. If it works, we could be inside this fort. If not, we'll be sitting ducks."

"Well, spill it then. We'll put in our two cents and let you know what we think," Crystal said.

"All right. I was thinking of putting a few girls inside this truck as a lure to get into the fort. After we're in, I'll ditch the truck, give the girls guns and tell them to wait until the cavalry arrives before making their move. I'll sneak around and eliminate the guards in the towers, so they don't see you coming."

"What girls were you planning on taking for this mission?" Diane asked.

"Well, until you girls arrived, I was going to ask a few locals, unless you would be interested in going along."

"Count me in," Joann said. "I owe that bastard for what he put us through."

"Include me, too," Roxanne said as she stood up. "He has to pay for his crime, and I'd love to be there to help."

Diane and Crystal both stood up and Crystal said, "Include us. We want to kill this dirt bag."

"Make it five girls, Sam," Janice said. "I also owe this scumbag for a few embarrassing moments of my own."

"As long as you all understand how risky this maneuver will be. I can't promise you anything except, if this works, I'll leave Quinton Sanders alive for your own pleasure."

All five ladies agreed, but Crystal made a good suggestion.

"Sam, we'll need different clothes than what we have on, in case Quincy wants to see us, right?"

"Good suggestion, Crystal. You're right. We'll get new clothes before we go."

"I have a few leftover clothes from other prisoners who, after they found out how it was to be in jail, changed their minds about what they were doing. If they fit, you're welcome to them." Captain Adams said.

He left and returned shortly with a big box of clothes.

The girls picked through the box and then headed for the bathrooms to change. After twenty minutes, they all came out. The men stared with their mouths hanging open.

"Well, boys, what do you think?" Diane asked.

"I think I'm in love," Deputy Billy Connors said out loud.

The girls laughed, "I guess we're a hit, ladies," Janice said.

Sam was speechless as he thought to himself, *I thought these girls were beautiful before, but now they are gorgeous.* Once again, Janice found Sam in a trance, but this time she knew why.

Sam called everyone together and started passing out the weapons. When the girls had their guns, they all raised their skirts and strapped them to their thighs. Everyone whistled as they put on a marvelous show for the boys. The skirts were long enough to hide the guns, but short enough to stop traffic. All five women were total knockouts, more beautiful than any magazine models Sam had ever seen. These women had natural beauty. They didn't need makeup. Sam wondered why they were all still single.

Then he remembered when he first met Janice. He couldn't believe there were still more women out there just as beautiful as she is.

"Ladies, I must say this is by far the most dangerous mission I've ever been on, especially since we don't know what we're getting into. However, this will go down as one of my most memorable missions as well. Thanks to you lovely women, I don't think we'll have any problems entering that fort, unless Quinton is totally blind. When he looks at you, he will not hesitate to open his doors."

"Glad to help out, Sam. Not that we don't appreciate what's going on here, but we're burning daylight. Don't you think it's time we headed toward our destination?" Roxanne said.

"You're right, Roxanne. Let's load up and get going. We have one stop to make at the reservation before we get there."

Within fifteen minutes they were heading out. Sam was leading the way with the big truck and listening to beautiful music as the ladies started singing in the back. He had a good feeling that this was going to work. If Sanders passed on this truckload of women, he just wasn't right in the head.

Since Captain Adams knew the way, he pulled directly ahead of the truck and took the lead. It was nearly two in the afternoon, and the sun was dreadfully hot. Captain Adams looked at the little thermometer on his truck window. It read a hundred and five degrees. This wasn't even the hottest part of the day. It could easily rise another ten degrees before it reached its peak. Hurricane was worried the truck wouldn't make the long trip through the desert, but he knew people's lives depended on him. He was determined to make it, one way or another. He would find out quickly if lady luck was still on his side.

By the time they reached the Indian reservation, Running Bear and Charging Buffalo were waiting for them.

"Hurricane, my brother, we thought something bad had happened to you. We were getting ready to come and save you."

"We ran into a little trouble, Running Bear, but my friends and I took care of one big problem. I thank you for your concern. However, now we could use your help with the second half of our journey."

Forty or fifty Indians on horseback surrounded Sam. "Our young and old warriors are at your service, brother Hurricane. We are grateful you trust us to help out."

"Colonel Jones cleared it with Washington for you to help us. I explained how you helped the other girls by bringing them here for safety. He wants to repay your kindness by giving you the freedom to use your weapons, so you can help put this barbarian away forever."

"It is an honor to ride by your side, Hurricane," Charging Buffalo said.

"Sam, we have a lot of ground to cover and not a lot of daylight left."

"You're right, Janice. Running Bear and Charging Buffalo, we'll meet you on the outskirts of Alamo. When we get there, we'll plan our attack. Just in case something goes haywire, let's make sure we have enough water. It gets awfully hot out in that desert, and besides, if it's my time to die, I'd rather go down fighting."

"Hurricane, you can make it there much faster and be less noisy if you ride with us."

"I know you speak the truth, Charging Buffalo, but I need this truck for our plan of attack. Let's get going, my brothers, and don't start anything before we get there."

Without saying another word, everyone scattered. Hurricane and his posse went toward Highway 168, hoping the map they had was accurate and would lead into Highway 93, straight to their destination. Running Bear and Charging Buffalo headed toward the rugged open country. Unless they encountered problems, they would be there before the others.

Captain Adams and his five deputies were in the Hummer ahead of Sam, who continued to enjoy the singing in the back of the truck and thinking of his plan of attack. That was until his radio interrupted his thoughts.

"Sam, Sam, can you hear me?"

"Yes, Captain, what's on your mind?"

"Do you really think your Indian friends will beat us there?"

"If I was a betting man, Captain, I'd say yes, it's a very good possibility. Even though they are on horseback and we are driving, they will ride straight through without stopping. They also have a straight path, and we have a few boulders and rocks to drive around. Besides, the Indians know this territory better than we do. Remember, this was all their land at one time."

"It's hard to believe that once they owned this whole territory and now they have such a small piece of land. I wonder why we couldn't just live together back then."

"Just like today, Captain, the greed for money determines who's boss."

"You're right, Sam. Even I complain from time to time about what I'm paid to do my job. We'll have to finish this conversation later. Right now we need to save our batteries. You never know how much we'll need them after we get there."

They had been driving almost an hour when Sam called Captain Adams on the radio. The truck was starting to overheat with the hot temperatures, and they had to let it cool down for a while. It was a good thing they had brought plenty of water. They rested up almost fifteen minutes before heading out again. If Sam was right, they were only about half an hour away from the Alamo. He noticed the farther out into the desert they drove the warmer it became. It had to be a good ten to fifteen degrees warmer than back on The Strip. It was so hot he started to wonder if he could fry an egg on the ground.

"I wonder if Running Bear had to stop," Janice said.

"Chances are, they stopped just long enough to water the horses. I wouldn't be surprised if they're waiting for us as we speak."

"It's hard to believe they can travel that fast on horseback without getting exhausted from the heat."

"Remember that they are accustomed to this heat. They learned how to survive through the hot and cold spells out here. When you live in this climate, your body adapts to the changes. They can travel for days without stopping if they have to. You see, we would have to find water, but they know where it is and how to retrieve it."

"What cold weather? It must be a hundred and twenty degrees here. How could it possibly get cold out here?" Crystal asked.

"Believe it or not, ladies, when the sun goes down and the stars come out, it can get as cold as forty below at times. That's the greatest mystery of the desert—how a place that gets so hot during the day can get so freezing cold at night. However, if it is a clear night, the stars are like a gigantic flashlight in the sky. You can actually see for a great distance, and the view is like millions of angels looking down on you. It's amazing how many stars are up in the sky. You can't help thinking that maybe someone is looking down on us as we're looking up at them."

"I think the heat is getting to you, Sam," Janice said.

"I just hope we get into the fort before the sun sinks in the west. We didn't bring enough equipment for a night in the desert. Well, at least not for all of us. Captain Adams and his men will have to spend the night camping out, or maybe he'll sneak up on the place at night. Whatever he prefers to do is fine with me. I just hope my plan works, and we get in without any difficulty."

"How will the captain know if we get inside or not?"

"There is a very small microphone sewn into the collar of my shirt. Captain Adams will be able to hear me, but he can't communicate back."

"What if something happens to him? How will he let you know?"

"That's where my friends from the Indian tribe come in. They will send me a signal."

"I've always been impressed how you plan things out, Sam."

"Janice, we've been together for some time now. You must know me well enough by now."

"Just when I think I know you, something like this comes up, and I realize just how much I really don't know about you. Not that I'm complaining, mind you. At least, I can say you're not boring."

They both laughed, and Sam said, "All right, ladies, we're almost there. You all know what to do. Once we get inside, we split up in pairs. Those earrings you are wearing have little transmitters inserted in them. We will be able to hear each other. If someone gets in trouble, pick out a landmark and let us know where you are. We'll come get you. Good luck, ladies. I must say, I've always had very good teams to work with in the past, but you are by far the most gorgeous bunch of teammates I've ever had the privilege of working with." The ladies all smiled at Sam and each other.

"Our main goal is to take out the men in the towers first, to give the others an easy passage into the fort. Try not to throw any of the men over the tower. Set them up as if they are alive. Since there are only six of us and four towers, we need as much time as possible before they realize something's wrong. We'll take out the two towers in the front and the back left tower. They can't see over the house from the far right tower, so we might just be safe for a few minutes before they realize something is wrong. Hopefully, by then, we'll be there to give them an early morning wake up call."

Everyone was quiet during the last five minutes of the ride up to the fort. Captain Adams had fallen back to stay out of sight. Hurricane surveyed the fort as they journeyed up to the gate. Whispering, he relayed what he was seeing to the captain and his men, who in turn sent it to Running Bear.

They spotted an exit hole with a grate over it toward the back of the fort. Maybe Sanders figured nobody could sneak up on them, so why worry.

There were two men stationed at each tower, but it seemed like they walked back and forth from tower to tower—something Sam never figured on. "Well, maybe this is a better set up. Let them come to us instead of us going to them," Sam spoke out. Sam knew the girls were also listening in, so it wasn't a surprise to them. When Hurricane was finally at the front gate, he noticed a camera focused down on him.

"Whoever you are, you're trespassing. Please turn around and leave, or we will kill you."

"Mr. Salvo sent me with some girls for Mr. Sanders."

"We are not expecting a delivery. Why this surprise visit?"

"That Hurricane guy is back in town. Mr. Salvo wanted to make sure he didn't mess up this delivery. He sent me as soon as he was certain Hurricane was indeed in town."

"Hurricane, huh? Hey, I'm going to send a few of my men into town to get rid of him once and forever. Have you ever seen him? Do you know what he looks like?" asked Sanders.

"I've only heard of him. I was told that if you encounter him, you end up dead."

"How many girls do you have with you?"

"I brought you five of the most beautiful girls you've ever seen, Mr. Sanders."

"Bring them out and let me see them before I let you in."

Hurricane got out of the truck and walked to the back, grinning. He opened the tailgate and escorted the women around to the camera. Slowly, the camera went from one to the other, and a voice bellowed from the intercom. "You're right. I've never seen such beauty in one truckload of girls. You're welcome to enter. Just pick a cabin, and we will check everything out in the morning. It's getting a little late today. Besides, I have a meeting with a very important client in five minutes, which can't be interrupted."

Hurricane's plan was successful, thanks to these lovely ladies. After the women were loaded back into the truck, he drove the truck toward the back of the buildings. It was darker and gave them a better chance to set up their plan of attack.

They were unpacking the truck when a man started walking toward them. The women picked up a few things and took them into their room. Hurricane waited until his guest was upon him.

"Hello. We saw you drive in. I was sent to make sure things were all right for you."

"Yes, everything is just perfect, thank you," Sam responded.

"You have a lot of stuff for leaving in such a hurry. I might have to report this."

"What's the trouble, Sam? You said you would bring in the rest of our things. Well, hello there," Crystal said trying to act surprised at finding the guest by the truck. "Maybe your friend could help me pop my trunk, as long as you're in no hurry."

"Yes, ma'am. I'll be happy to help pop your trunk." He left Sam and headed into the room.

Within a few minutes, Crystal and the girls were standing in the doorway smiling. "I guess it was too much excitement for him, the poor man. He had an accident and died right on the spot. It must have been a heart attack or a severe blow to the head." They all laughed. They went back into the cabin, dressed in their dark outfits, and waited for their assignments.

Hurricane knocked on the door and walked inside. "This is even better than I imagined. We can do our elimination job without any worry. After we take out the guards, we'll meet back here and plan for tomorrow. Let's pick partners and get going."

"Doesn't really bother me who we partner up with," Diane said. "Why don't we split up Crystal and Joann for one, Roxanne and me for two, leaving Janice with you, Sam?"

"That sounds good to me, Diane. Why don't you and Roxanne take out the left front tower, Crystal and Joann will eliminate the back left tower, and Janice and I will take out the right front. Remember, they travel from one tower to the other, so be careful, and be prepared to help each other."

"Don't worry," Diane said. "I know just how to get their attention."

"Just have fun and try not to get hurt, ladies. We'll meet you back here shortly. Remember, if you need help, speak into your transmitter, and someone will come to help you. Now, let's go have fun," Sam said.

Hurricane watched as the four girls headed toward their appointed towers. The suits they had on were perfect, and it was hard to see any movement at all through the dark night. Bringing along the night-vision glasses was the right call. They discovered ladders attached to the walls for climbing up into the towers. They scaled up the ladders, peered over the sides, and saw that the men were asleep inside the towers. *This was just too easy,* Hurricane thought as they tapped their shoulders and then slashed their throats. Janice noticed a schedule on the table and pointed it out to Hurricane. Apparently, the guards changed towers every two hours, not all the time as they thought. That gave them a little time between towers. Sam gave Janice a big hug for finding the schedule.

They saw a flash of light, and looking over toward the tower where Diane and Roxanne were heading, they saw silhouettes that looked like they were kissing the guards. Then one of the girls moved in a more sexual way. Within a few minutes, two more people were in the tower. Shortly, the other two people were being dragged toward the back tower. When he looked back to see what Crystal and Joann were doing, he witnessed both girls kicking the crap out of some guy. He was glad he brought the night-vision glasses, so they could check on each other.

Hurricane found out one thing for sure—these girls could fight. He knew he had one heck of a good team. For a brief moment, he almost felt sorry for the guys in the fort, but then a sinister smile stretched across his face.

Somehow, he had to find a way up to Sanders' room to find out who he was talking to. While the girls positioned the men in the towers, Hurricane went to check on which lights were on in the house. He spotted a glow from the first floor. "What a break," he quietly said to himself. He was about ten feet from the back patio when he heard some voices. He ducked back into the darkness. Two men with machine guns walked right past him. Hurricane wondered who they were protecting.

Gradually, Hurricane crept up to the sliding doors. They were already cracked open for a little night air. He had no problem listening to the conversation going on inside.

"As I've stated, President Salvantez, we have five of the most beautiful girls I've ever seen. We just have to get them trained, and they can be yours for the small price of one hundred thousand dollars."

"When I see them, I'll give you my answer."

"Well, here they are, Mr. President. You can see them right now," Sanders said, turning on his computer. He must have taped the girls at the entrance of the fort. Even though Sam was with them, he couldn't believe how nice they looked on camera.

"Who's that man with them?" the president asked.

"He's the guy Salvo sent to deliver the girls."

"I've never seen him before. Did you check him out?"

"He seemed innocent to us. Look how he reacts when he's pushed by one of my men, hiding his face and afraid to get hit. I guarantee you he's no threat to us, Mr. President."

"I hope you're right, for your sake, Quinton. I'd sure hate to make you an example in front of your own men if you happen to make a mistake."

Hurricane was so involved in wanting to know what the mystery man looked like that he forgot about the guards. He heard the voices coming up fast. He slithered back slowly into the darkness behind the furniture on the patio. Finding a planter box next to him, he smeared dirt all over his face to avoid being seen himself.

Sam was hoping the guards would walk on by again. He wanted to get a look at that president's face. But the two guys decided to stand and talk for a short time before they continued walking. Hurricane wasn't sure, but he could have sworn he saw a tattoo on one of the men's arm, a tattoo that was only applied to experienced soldiers in the services.

Could these guys be mercenaries? he wondered. If so the girls may be in a much tougher spot than they figured. It was too late to turn back now, and he was just hoping the others would be here faster than planned. When Hurricane turned back to look into the room, all he saw was darkness. He sneaked around to the front of the house, using the bushes as camouflage. He froze as he heard the front door open. "Well, Mr. President, you have a safe journey back, and we'll see you in two weeks."

"You make sure those girls are ready to leave. I can make a lot of money off of those beautiful women. If they are not ready by then, you will lose your position here. My patience is growing thin with you."

Oh, great! Just when I thought it ended here, Hurricane said to himself.

The president turned as he reached his limousine driver saying, "Remember, Quinton, you have two weeks and only two weeks." Then he sat down inside the car.

Hurricane had a tiny camera with him. After he took a few pictures of the president, he figured he'd better hightail it back to the cabin before the girls decided to come looking for him. Then he could develop the film in his camera, so they could see just who it was they'd be going up against. Besides, it was starting to get very cold outside. These suits were warm, but wearing even the warmest suit, you will get cold if you are out for an extended period.

Looking around before he exited the bushes, Sam noticed two guys sitting down in the general area where he had to travel. *Great, I'll probable freeze to death waiting for these guys to leave,* Hurricane thought to himself, frustrated.

Within a couple of minutes, four of his ladies came walking around the corner. They stopped and asked the men, "Would you strong men kindly show us where the bathrooms are?"

There was no hesitation at all. Sam couldn't blame the men for jumping up at the suggestion of helping these lovely ladies. Sam noticed as Diane looked his way and gave him a wink. That's twice now that these women saved the day. Hopefully, Sam would be able to pay them back in full.

Hurricane made it back to his cabin, and just when he thought the coast was clear to re-enter it, he heard a stern voice ask, "Hey, boy, what are you doing out of your cabin?"

"Well, sir, I had to use the bathroom, so I was out looking for it."

"Why didn't you just go in the trees over there?"

"What I had to do … I needed something to wipe with."

"I think you've been traveling with these women too long. You're already acting like them. All you had to do is use some of the tree leaves. You're not one of those flaky guys are you?"

"Listen, I've been trying to be a gentleman, and all you're trying to do is make me mad."

"Gentleman? You mean an impostor trying to act like a man, but …"

Before he could finish his statement, Hurricane grabbed him by the throat. "Now, listen, I've been trying to be real nice to you, but it seems like instead of being my friend you would rather try to bully me." Hurricane squeezed his throat a little more, and his face started to turn blue. "I'm going to release you now, but heed my warning. If you so much as try anything with me, I'll kill you right on this spot. Do you understand that?"

When the guy shook his head yes, Hurricane released his grip. The man gasped for air for almost five minutes. When he finally recovered from the strangle hold, his eyebrows folded down, and his mean stare told Hurricane all he needed to know. He waited until his guest made the first move. When he raised his hand to strike, Hurricane twisted the man's arm around his back and hammered his own massive fist down onto his foe's shoulder. There was a sharp crack, and his guest stood frozen in shock as his arm just hung free, blowing in the wind.

"You bastard! You broke my arm. I'm going to kill you." He charged again. This time, Hurricane thrust his fingers into the guy's neck and tore out his throat. Looking into the man's eyes, he saw a surprised expression. Then just before he slumped down to the ground, Hurricane picked him up and put his body in the closet of his cabin.

As he was closing the closet door, a knock interrupted his train of thought. He wondered who could be at his cabin door. Cautiously, Hurricane opened the door. There, looking back at him smiling, stood five angels. Without saying a word, Sam motioned for them to enter. When the door was closed, they lit the candles that were provided and started to talk. Sam stood up and started to search the place, thinking maybe the rooms were wired. Not wanting to sound as if they knew anything, the girls started talking about anything and laughing. They joined in and helped search the place. Sam found a wire under the phone. Diane found one behind the picture on the wall. Crystal found one up in the drop ceiling tile in the bedroom. Sam was surprised when Roxanne discovered one in the candle itself.

Janice retrieved some chewing gum from her bag and they used the foil, wrapping it around the little microphones so it would cause interference.

Joann made a suggestion to remove it when they were done, in case they came in to check on them later when they weren't here. Sam smiled. He knew these girls weren't only beautiful, but they also had a lot of smarts and street knowledge as well.

Janice started out with the conversation. "Sam, we had to kill those two guards, but we also found out something you might want to know."

"Yes, Sam," Crystal said. "We have another guest to worry about, some president from Mexico. I think he's one of the three head men, including Quinton, and the other is a man who owns a casino on the Vegas Strip," Sam was frustrated.

"This gets more confusing with each move we make. How many more people are in on this? Where is it going to lead us? One thing is for certain, we have to take Quinton alive, if possible. We need to find out how deep this is going to take us."

"Whoever or whatever we are up against, I'm with you, Sam, all the way," Crystal said. "We must put a stop to this slave organization. Who knows how many girls have been sold or how long this has been going on."

All the other girls jumped on the band wagon as well, including Janice.

This caught Hurricane by surprise. He was frozen for a few seconds and then said, "I appreciate what you girls want to do, but what about your jobs back home? Who knows how long this could take? You could all lose your jobs."

"I don't know about all the other girls," Roxanne added, "but I have about six months of sick time coming. I'll gladly give that up to help out, not to mention my vacation time I have left."

"Good thinking, Roxanne," Diane said. "I think all of us may have a few extra weeks coming, if necessary. When we get back to The Strip, let's call our captains and explain what's going on. I'm sure they will allow us to use time off for this."

They all agreed and turned their attention back toward Hurricane. He was smiling as he said, "All right, girls. Do what your hearts tell you. For now, let's concentrate on why we are here. Maybe we can end it now and forever, but first we have to win this round."

He walked around the room gathering ash trays and other little items. He came back toward the bed and scattered them on top of the mattress. He was trying to build a map of the layout of this facility.

"Hurricane, can I ask how you know the layout of this place so well?"

"Good question, Joann. There was a replica of this place on Quinton's table when I was spying on him. I memorized the layout while listening to his conversation with President Salvantez. I took a picture of him and sent it back to Captain Adams to have him check it out. Hopefully, we'll know all about him when they get here tomorrow morning."

"So you already knew what we were talking about earlier?"

"About the President? Yes, Crystal, but not about the third guy. They never mentioned any other name. That's why we need Quinton alive."

"It looks like there are several barracks between the wall and the house. If they are all loaded … I don't know. However, I do know that we have taken out at least three of his guys already."

Sam pulled out his duffle bag, and without saying a word, he emptied it on top of the bed.

"Claymore mines! Where'd you get these?" Joann asked.

"Let's just say we are not alone here, girls. We have help on hold until we find something. Then all hell is going to break loose. Now, if we can set these mines by the barracks, this just might give us the edge we need for a surprise attack."

"How many barracks are we talking about, Sam?" Crystal asked.

"If I counted right we have ten barracks."

"We only have eight mines," Diane said.

"That's why I brought along a little grenade launcher, just in case, Diane. It only holds four, but it gives a big kick. Now, since that's clear, let's concentrate on setting these bombs. Again, we will be splitting up in three pairs of two, and these night vision glasses will help. If it gets too cold for you out there, head back and warm up. These suits are good for only two hours at the most in this freezing temperature. Set your watches to go off at least fifteen minutes before the two-hour deadline to give you enough time to get back here. Remember, put them close to the front entrance of each building. Good luck. We'll see you back here in two hours. Remember to turn on your tracking devices in your earrings, so we know where to find you in case you have problems."

Crystal and Joann exited first, then Diane and Roxanne, and finally, Sam and Janice. They couldn't believe how cold it was, but the sky was lit up with millions of stars. There wasn't a cloud in the sky, or so they assumed, because all they saw were stars. They had no trouble seeing where they were going, and because of the cold temperatures, nobody was on guard duty. Who in their right mind would go out in this weather, except for the Hurricane and company.

Diane and Roxanne were the first to arrive back at the cabin, followed by Sam and Janice. Just as Sam was going to look for the other two, they entered the door. Crystal was holding her hand, and Sam hurried over to find out what had happened. One of the levers of the bombs had frozen. Crystal had taken off her glove for a brief moment to flip the switch and was hit with frostbite. Sam immediately produced a hand warmer and a blanket and handed them to Crystal, hoping that her hand and fingers would be all right in the morning. He remembered the time when he ended up with frostbitten fingers. He never regained the feeling in two of his fingertips. Diane brought in a bucket of warm water for Crystal to soak her hand. When Crystal stuck her hand in the bucket, she felt the warmth of the water.

"That's a very good sign," Sam said. "You'll be back to normal by morning. Speaking about morning, it'll be daylight in about six hours. Let's try to get some much-needed sleep."

With that said Hurricane walked over to his cabin, leaving the girls to themselves. When he entered his door and turned on the light, three guys were standing in his cabin.

"Sorry, guys," he said, "but this cabin is taken. You'll have to find another one."

"You're a funny man, but we aren't guests here."

"You're not Rhodes scholars either. Just what is it you're doing here in my cabin?"

"Mr. Sanders wants you to leave when the sun comes up."

"All right, the girls and I will leave in the morning."

"No, just you leave, mister. The girls will be staying here."

"You go tell Mr. Sanders … No, wait, I'll go tell Mr. Sanders in the morning that the girls and I will be leaving. If he tries to stop us, they'll be scraping his carcass off the floor."

The three men started laughing out loud, and the one in the middle said, "You've got guts, I'll give you that much, mister. Who do you think you are, coming in here and threatening our boss?"

"Well, boys, what I just said wasn't a threat. That was a promise. If you knew me, you would know I always keep my promises," Hurricane said with a stern face.

"Mister, you just opened yourself up to a beat down, but before we beat you to a pulp, tell us your name so we know what to put on your tombstone when we bury you."

"My friends call me 'Sam.' My enemies call me 'Hurricane.' "

Their facial expressions said it all. They were frozen in their own tracks. The middle guy started to smile and said, "Well, boys, we have the so-called Hurricane in front of us. If we kill him, the boss will give us a big promotion."

"We know, Larry," the one on his left spoke. "He's only one guy, but what if the stories about him are true? What if he is as fast as they say? I don't feel like dying today, Larry."

"Fred, shut up. We can't let him just walk out of here."

"Fred, you sound like the smart one. If you help us, you will live. If you decide to join Larry, I will definitely kill you."

"Fred, don't be a fool. There's no way he can kill the three of us."

Before Larry could get another word out, Hurricane struck him in the neck. Larry's legs buckled underneath him, and he fell like a brick.

"Don't worry, Fred, he's not dead yet. I'm waiting for your answer. Are you with us or against us?"

"You hit him so fast I don't think he even felt it. I never did like this job anyway. I guess I'm with you," Fred answered just looking at Larry slumped over on the floor.

"What about your other friend here?"

"George, Mr. Hurricane would like to know if you're with us or against us?" Fred asked him.

George must have been in shock, as Fred shook him like a rag doll. "Did you hear what we asked you?"

George slowly shook his head yes, and then said, "I'm with you."

Larry was finally able to stand once again. He looked puzzled when he saw the other guys standing with Hurricane. "What's going on guys? There's no way he'll take the three of us."

"Larry, Larry, Larry. Right now you only have two choices. Either join us and live like your friends here, or die where you stand. The choice, as they say, is yours," Sam said.

"What? You turncoats decided to go with him? When did this happen?"

"When you were on the ground, laying there in front of us motionless," George answered.

"What do you mean? I've been standing here the whole time." Larry rubbed his neck.

"You were lying on the ground choking for almost ten minutes. He must have hit you so hard you don't remember what happened. Why do you think your throat hurts now?" Fred said.

Larry was wondering why his throat was hurting so much. It felt as if it was pushed back into his neck. Then he looked at his watch. Somewhere he lost a few minutes of his life. "How do we know that you won't kill us after this is all over?"

"I give you my word that if you help us now, you'll be free to go after it is over. I'll explain to them I planted you inside to help us, but if you have any ideas of setting us up, I promise you, you'll be as dead as your friends will be," Hurricane answered.

"What will we have to do?"

"Help us get into the house, tell us everything about what's inside, give us the location of the room Quinton Sanders is in, and help us take down this slave business once and for all. If you know who this President Salvantez is and where he comes from, we could squash this syndicate and what they stand for."

"Is that all?" Larry asked again.

"Wait. I also need to know who the man on the Vegas Strip would be."

"What man on The Strip? I thought it was Salvo. If it's someone big, Mr. Sanders will have it in his Rolodex or in his address book. He keeps stuff locked up tight in his vault.

"Where's the vault located?"

I've never seen it, but I was told it's in the wall behind his bookcase. How it opens I don't know. He has three bookcases in his room, and I have no idea which one hides the vault."

"Well, then, we take Quinton Sanders alive, so we can find these addresses you talk about. Who knows what other interesting names we might find in there as well?"

"We have to be getting back before they send someone out to look for us. Don't worry about us saying anything. We don't like what they're doing here any more than you, but up until now, nobody was willing to try and stop him. I have three sisters, and if they suddenly disappeared, I'd go crazy. He promised us as long as we work for him, they would be safe. I can just imagine what the other families must be going through.

"I know a few others who might be willing to help when this invasion starts up," George said. "I'll keep it quiet until it starts. That way, I'll know for sure whose side they are on."

"How many men do you have, Hurricane?" Fred asked.

"The five elegant women you've already met, the Las Vegas Police Department, our military friends, and about four dozen Shoshone warriors, all waiting for the signal to attack. We shall overcome."

"How do you plan on getting all those people here with all the outposts he has around the building?" George asked.

"If my calculations are correct, they should be entering this fort right about now."

There came a knock on the door. Fred opened it slowly, not knowing who it could be.

"Who are you? Where's Hurricane?"

Fred stood back, and Captain Adams and his six young officers came inside the cabin. Just as Fred was closing the door, Running Bear and Charging Buffalo pushed their way inside.

"Where do you want us, brother Hurricane?" Charging Buffalo asked.

"Come with us," George said. "We have two more vacant cabins you can use. There should be enough wood in the fireplace to keep you warm."

The warriors followed George to the cabins. It was so bright with all the stars in the sky that they had no problem following him in the dark.

Hurricane instructed them before they left to get some sleep, and he would be over to tell them the plan in a couple of hours. Right now, they all needed to get some rest and warm up a little. Captain Adams and his men stayed in Hurricane's cabin. Most of the cabins were two-story with four bedrooms that had two sets of bunkbeds per room. They had more than enough room for getting some sleep. Hurricane told Captain Adams and his men to use the bedrooms, and he would sleep on the couch in the front room. He instructed the captain to take the alarm clock and set it for three hours. Since there was only one clock, he would be in charge of waking everyone else.

While the others slept, Hurricane was up calling his long-time friend, Colonel Jones. He left a detailed message and was hoping he would get it in time to send the help he had requested. When he was finished, he tried to lie down to get some sleep, but he was too wound up from all that had happened since arriving at the fort. After taking four or five deep breaths and slowly letting the air out, Sam finally felt relaxed as he looked at the clock on the wall. Two-thirty in the morning was the last thing he would remember as he drifted off to sleep.

Chapter Eight

When the alarm clock went off in Captain Adams' room, he jumped up immediately. After waking three of his officers, they went around waking the rest of the team, giving them all fifteen minutes to get downstairs.

When Captain Adams went downstairs to wake up the Hurricane, he wasn't a bit surprised to see Sam standing up reading a map. Trying not to disturb him, the Captain stepped toward him as quietly as a mouse. When he was a couple of feet away, Sam turned fast, grabbing the captain, spinning him around, and sticking his big knife under his chin.

"I should have known better than to try and sneak up on you, but I just had to find out for myself if all those stories about you were true."

"What stories about me?"

"The ones that claim you have a unique radar instinct built into you that detects someone around you. I've often wondered if what they said was true."

"Did they also tell you how many people have been killed doing exactly what you just did? I would have felt bad if I had killed you, my friend."

"I wouldn't have been happy about that either, my friend. I'm sorry. I guess it gets a bit hard for you having people like me testing you all the time, like a human experiment, trying to get the best of you."

"If they would quit printing those stories about me, I wouldn't have to prove it to anyone. I'm good at what I do because of my military training. I bet there are at least three or four thousand solders or ex-military men in the United States just as good, if not better, than I am."

"You may be right, Sam, but the difference between them and you is simple. You're here because you love a good challenge. You enjoy the suspense and mystery in trying to find people. Besides, what other job will let you kick the heck out of people and get paid for it to boot?"

"I just have a hard time believing this has all happened because I helped an old friend back in New York," Hurricane said.

"It's hard to imagine us being here without you, Sam. I feel that some people are born in this world for a special reason. Yours just happens to be helping people in dire circumstances. You've been blessed with a certain gift for finding people, and you use it out of the goodness of your heart. You're a special type of person, Sam, and most of the people out there wish they were you. Some try to make a name for themselves by trying to take you on, and like it or not, my friend, with this kind of job, it simply goes with the territory."

"Thanks, Captain, I never thought about it that way before. The way you say it, maybe this is what I was meant to do with my life—help others."

"Hey, what have you guys been talking about down here?" Billy Conners asked as he walked into the room.

"Sam was just telling me how unimportant he is."

"Are you kidding us?" Sam Huston, one of Captain Adams' men, added. "What we've learned from you these past few days will now stay with us forever. We've learned how to find information by just acting out the scenes, or by looking for certain clues, not to mention how to track down people. I feel I've become a better police officer, thanks to you."

Hurricane nodded his thanks and spoke. "Men, today is 'free the captives' day. We don't stop fighting until the hostages are free."

"What's the plan, Hurricane?" Billy Conners asked.

"Last night, before you showed up, the girls and I set up a little surprise for our hosts. They have ten barracks set up in front of the house. Eight are full of men, and we've set some claymore mines by each of the entrances, except for the last two. We ran out of claymores, so we set up three rounds of C-four explosives for each of them. We have eight transmitters ready to blow each mine. It's important that we explode the front of each building as they exit them. The more of them we can take out, the better our odds of getting out of here alive.

"I have fourteen belts in the box here that have a radio inside the strap. We will know where everyone is at all times. If you get in trouble, we will be there as fast as we can. Remember, if we work as a team, we will survive. Some of us may get hurt, but I can promise you, if we help each other when needed, we'll all get out of here alive.

"Our job is to clean out the outside perimeter. The ladies will be our decoys for getting inside. They also have radios planted inside their earrings, and we will know when the time is right to invade the main building. It will be daylight soon. Let's all get into position to strike. Just remember to keep your head and help each other."

"Where are the hostages being held?" Sam Huston asked.

"Our sources told us they are in the middle bedroom on the second floor. If you get there before us, be careful. If it seems too easy, it could be a trap. Good luck, boys. We'll see you real soon."

They all exited in groups of two. Hurricane gave them all night-vision glasses. Within five minutes, they were all in position to strike. Hurricane noticed an orange glow in the west. "What the heck is that?"

"That's the sun, my friend," Captain Adams answered.

"Since when does the sun rise in the west and have smoke coming out of the back? Do you hear that windmill sound?"

Just then the sun rose over the mountains. Sam started laughing and said, "Remind me to buy that man a case of Scotch when this is over."

"Who are you talking about, Sam?" Adams asked.

"Take a look to the west, about ten miles out and closing fast. My colonel friend sent some Apache choppers to help us out. Let's get this show on the road!" Hurricane yelled.

Hurricane took a few shots into the barracks. They heard scuffling, and the windows opened. Hurricane unloaded, taking out several bad guys. They all scurried for the front entrance. As they rushed out the open door, BOOM! About twenty men were laid out on the ground. The majority of them were dead, but some were wounded. How badly they were wounded was unknown, but it was enough to keep them from fighting.

Suddenly, like the Fourth of July, bombs were exploding all over the place. Screams echoed into the desert air, and empty shell casings were flying all over the ground.

Suddenly Hurricane heard a familiar noise he remembered from when he was in the service. *No, it couldn't be*! he said to himself as he saw a tank circling around the corner.

"Sam," Captain Adams yelled, "we were never told anything about Sanders having tanks."

"I know, Captain, I know," Hurricane responded.

As Hurricane grabbed the grenade launcher, they saw a stream of light and heard a blast. The big tank was gone, just like that. Both Captain Adams and Hurricane looked up in the sky and waved. The pilot shook the plane from side to side waving back, and then sent several more Hellfire missiles streaking down. They took out one of the walls of the fort. Hurricane and Captain Adams heard screams. Looking to the left, they saw Running Bear and Charging Buffalo riding in with all their braves on horseback.

When Hurricane and Captain Adams stood up to charge the main building, all the others did the same. Nobody stopped firing their weapons until they were next to the house. The balcony doors flew open and several men stepped out. As they looked over the rail, arrows found their mark. They all fell over dead. Charging Buffalo and a few of his braves climbed up the side of the building and entered through the balcony doors. Hurricane and the rest of the cavalry entered through the front door.

When everyone was inside, they split up in packs of four. They had to find the women they hoped were still here. Hurricane told everyone to be on their toes. They received no resistance when they entered. Sam reminded everyone that it could be a trap, and to watch where they stepped. Suddenly there was a blast that came from the upstairs. Hurricane, Captain Adams, Janice, and Diane ran toward the stairway. Hurricane stopped them in their tracks before they headed up the stairs. With the sunlight coming through the window, Hurricane caught sight of a trip wire on the fourth step up. He followed it around the back of the stairs.

He found four sticks of dynamite taped together and fastened to the middle of the staircase. This definitely would have caused a lot of damage. Hurricane started to wonder how this could have been possible. *Was he set up to fail by someone? Where were all the guards? Why was the house so easy to enter?* he asked himself as he came out from under the staircase.

"What's wrong, Sam? You look confused?" Captain Adams asked.

"It just doesn't make sense, John. Why would they rig up the house for destruction? How did they know we were coming for them? I think we were set up, my friend. I don't know how or when it happened, but we were definitely set up. Running Bear and Charging Buffalo lost some good warriors because of this. They must have snuck out during the night while we were planning their defeat. They were two steps ahead of us. We look like the suckers now."

"Just the same, Sam, I think we should continue checking out the house. We might come up with something about where they went. Maybe the women are still here. We must go through this house no matter what."

Hurricane shook his head yes and said, "You're right, John. But let everyone know to be extra careful. This whole house could be booby trapped. I don't want anyone else getting hurt."

After everyone was told what might be going on, they all went their own way. Hurricane and his crew went to check on the second floor, being extra careful on the stairway. Once they were on the second floor, they noticed three doors on the left and two on the right. Figuring these were the bedrooms, they slowly walked down the hallway, checking the doorknobs. They didn't seem to be locked.

Janice and Diane went into the first room. It would have been totally dark if not for a little stream of light that entered through the slit in the curtain. Diane walked toward the window and pulled back one side of the curtains. When the bright sunlight entered the room, it revealed two twin beds, two night tables, two dressers, and a shiny earring glistening on the floor. As their eyes were sweeping around the room, Diane spotted a trash can turned over on its side. Diane went over and pulled off a piece of paper stuck on the inside. It was a folded piece of paper that read, "Taking us down to the basement tomorrow." It didn't seem important until they noticed yesterday's date on it. Diane folded it up and stuck it into her pocket. Maybe Hurricane could figure it out later.

Diane's hair was put up on top of her head. Janice thought a minute and asked Diane for a hairpin. Diane pulled a hairpin out from the back of her hair. As she handed it to Janice, Diane asked, "What do you need a hairpin for?"

Janice didn't say a word. She went behind the desk and tried to pick the lock on the top drawer with the hairpin. Then Diane walked over and inserted a screwdriver between the drawer and the top of the desk. Slowly, at first, she tried to pop the lock. When that failed, she nearly jumped on the screwdriver. When the drawer finally opened, and the other three side drawers opened with ease. They found folders inside the top drawer with numbers and dates scribbled on them.

Without saying a word, they gave each other a high five as they opened each of the drawers. They didn't know exactly what they were looking for, but they figured if it wasn't important, it wouldn't be locked up. Diane found a false bottom in one of the drawers. After slipping out the fake drawer bottom, she found a book underneath. She opened it and started reading.

"Oh, my God, Janice, take a look at this! Tell me it doesn't say what I think it says."

Janice rushed over to Diane and started reading the book. "How long has this operation been going on? Diane, there must be at least fifty pages of names in this book."

"Janice, one of the names on that list is my half-sister's. She was supposed to be home two weeks ago. When she never came home, I came here looking for her. I have to find her, Janice. I can't go back home without her."

Janice reached out to give her a hug. "We'll find her, Diane. I know Sam will not stop until this is over. If there's one thing Sam is good at, it is finding people." Janice was trying to comfort Diane, but in the back of her mind, she was hoping they weren't too late.

They found Hurricane and told him the story about Diane's half-sister as they passed the book to him. You could see Hurricane's eyes turn into molten lava. He was mad as hell now and even more determined to find these guys and stop them. Without saying a word, Hurricane walked into the room the girls just came from. He found a Rolodex filled with addresses and phone numbers hidden in the corner of the lower right desk drawer. He was going through the names and numbers, when he suddenly stopped. He ripped out a page and stuck it into his pocket. Then he continued his search. By the time he was finished, he had ten names and addresses he needed to check out.

Hurricane practically ripped that desk apart trying to find anything else. When he came up empty, he flipped the desk over on its side. He was almost ready to give up, when his eye caught something shiny underneath the middle drawer. Thanks to the sun's rays pointing in the right angle, he spotted the tape that was used to fasten it in place.

"The Lord is definitely on our side today, ladies," he said as he pulled the object from underneath the desk. It was a sealed envelope. Hurricane took his knife from his belt and slit the top open. Bingo! The paper inside listed the names of all of Quinton's customers, plus the names of the girls given to them. It must have been his private transaction notes. Now they finally had something to go on. He gave the list to Diane and said, "Diane, look at these and let me know if your half-sister is listed here.

Diane started looking through the names. When she was at the bottom of the fifth page, she said, "There it is, Louise Simon, that's her." Tears began rolling down her cheeks.

Hurricane took Diane in his arms, and told her in no uncertain terms that they would find her sister.

"Hey, gang, what's this other book I've found. Looks like code numbers of some kind," Janice said.

Hurricane rushed over to see if those code numbers jived with the marks in the book of names they found. Sam skimmed both books and said, "According to this, your sister is still somewhere on the docks waiting to be shipped out to China. We will have to find out which docks they are referring to and what building they are in." After a few minutes, Hurricane said, "Hey, they also have a number in parenthesis above the code number. I'll bet you it's a dock or door number where they have her. All we have to do is figure out which it is, unless we get lucky and find some billing information on them."

"Would it look something like this, Sam?" Janice asked, holding a manila envelope in her left hand and a bunch of what looked like invoices in her right hand.

After Sam examined them, he said, "Bingo, baby! Good job! Now we have to find which one of these is Louise's, and how many more girls are hopefully still here."

Captain Adams and Diane joined in looking at all the invoices. After several minutes, Captain Adams brought his knowledge into play.

"Hey, Sam, look at the top number in the book, then look at the invoice number on the ticket. There are no names, just numbers."

"Good work, Captain," Hurricane said. "If these are what we've been looking for, it seems like they are being held somewhere in Boulder City."

"Boulder City is by the Hoover Dam. They have to be holding them somewhere in or near the Black Mountains. That's the only place accessible that I can think of. But that dock isn't big enough for large vessels. So, how are they transporting them without being seen?" Captain Adams asked.

"Maybe they are being drugged and then hidden in the cabins of the boats. Then they are taken farther out to sea and loaded on a larger vessel awaiting delivery. But what would the numbers be then? If not dock doors, what?" Hurricane asked out loud.

"They've had some construction going on around there for quite a while, trying to redirect the road around by the dam. I wonder if this isn't a storage shed on one of the sites," Adams answered.

"How far is Boulder City from here, Captain?"

"I'd say around a hundred and twenty-five miles, give or take a mile or two."

"The only question I have is how do we know this isn't another stalling tactic, and was it planted in the desk for us to find to once again throw us off the trail?" Diane asked.

"Good point, Diane. I'll call Colonel Jones and see if they can do a couple of fly-bys and check it out for us. Meanwhile, let's get back to business. It might be possible that some of those girls are still here. Captain Adams, I'd like you to stay back here. See if you can make out some of the other names and possible places in this book."

"I'd like to do just that, but that means you'll be alone. Who's going to watch your back?"

"Just keep the volume up on your receiver. I'll talk to you every ten minutes and let you know where I am. If I happen to miss a call, turn on your transmitter and come get me."

Captain Adams shook his head, affirming that he understood. Hurricane quickly made the call to Colonel Jones. "We'll know what's going on in about twenty minutes, John. Until then, I'll be checking out the other rooms." Hurricane said as he exited the first room.

After Hurricane exited the room, he spotted a light coming from under the door of the room across the hall. At first, he thought it was the girls, until they came out of the room farther down. Hurricane motioned for them to follow as he pointed toward the door. Without saying a word, they nodded and headed his way. Hurricane pulled out his stethoscope and applied it to the door. He heard some scuffling before he heard a whispering voice say, "Let's go out the window, nobody is outside anymore."

Just as they were about to open the window, Hurricane and the girls crashed through the door. They had their guns drawn and pointed right at the two guys standing by the window.

"Don't move, boys, unless you want to be dead. My two partners here are just itching to kill someone. I have a few questions for you, and hopefully, you'll, have the correct answers, unless you would like to try my patience. But pay close attention to what I am saying. My patience is very thin right now. Where are the girls who were brought here yesterday?"

"You're a cop. You can't hurt us. We have rights, and we want our lawyer."

Before the wiseguy could get another word out, Hurricane drew his gun and shot the man's knee cap.

"As you can see, I can and will shoot you. The only right you have here is to stay alive, and you have that right only if I allow it. Now, if you don't answer my questions, I'll have fun finding out how much pain you can take. Stop screwing around and tell me where the girls are?"

"When I get out of here, I'm going to sue you, man. You just can't go around shooting people."

Before he uttered another word, Hurricane grabbed the leg he had just shot and started to twist it. The tough guy started screaming obscenities toward him. Hurricane smiled at his prey, took his gun, stuck it to the side of his leg, and squeezed the trigger. His .357 magnum took the man's leg clean off his body.

"Bob, just tell him what he wants. It's not worth dying over."

"Listen to your friend, Bobby, before you lose your other leg, then your arms, and if you're still around by then, we'll find something else to take off of your body. Be smart and die with dignity, not with stupidity. One last chance now, where are the girls?"

"They just took some of the girls with them."

"Where did they take them, Bobby?"

"I don't know, man. I'm just paid to watch this place."

"It wouldn't be Boulder City, would it?" Hurricane saw Bob's eyes widen and knew he had hit pay dirt.

"Nobody knows about that place. How'd you find out?"

139

"Just say it was a lucky guess. Now, where are they being held?"

"Honest, mister, I don't know."

"Now, Bobby, you know that I know you're lying. I can see it in your eyes. I'm done playing games with you. Time is running out, not only for those girls, but for you as well. Only difference is you'll feel more pain before they will when you die."

Hurricane went to grab Bob's right arm. He tried to fight back, but Hurricane was too strong for him. When his arm was stretched to the limit, a shot rang out and Bob fell backward minus a forearm. Hurricane never reneged on a promise. He was going to tear this guy apart just as he said. He walked over to where Bob was balled up in a corner and grabbed his left arm. Just as he was going to shoot, Bob's partner finally spoke.

"Bob, what's wrong with you, man? Tell him what he wants to know, or he'll tear you apart."

Hurricane looked his way and asked him, "We know Bobby's name, but what's yours?"

"Ralph, Ralph Sanchez. Please don't hurt him anymore."

"Well, Ralph, if you know what we want, now is the time to tell us, and I'll make sure your pain stops right here. But if you jerk me around like Bobby here, what I'm doing to him is nothing compared to what I have in store for you. I figure I have three more shots with Bobby before he's dead, so his life is now in your hands."

Ralph looked toward where Bob was sitting. Blood was running out like a river going down stream. Bob had one leg and an arm shot off already, and he was set to have his other arm taken off as well. "All right, I'll tell you everything. Just let Bob go."

Hurricane dropped Bob's left arm, turned toward Ralph and said, "Make it fast. I don't want Bobby dying before I'm finished with him."

"There are three big storage bins that Mr. Sanders rents out. I don't know if that's where they are, but it's possible."

"Which way does he travel to get there?"

"I've only been there once, and we traveled ninety-three to fifteen. Then he catches ninety-five and stops at a place called Cottonwood Cove. That's as far as they took me. I waited about twenty-five minutes before they came back."

"I know exactly where he's talking about, Hurricane."

Hurricane turned around and saw Captain Adams standing by the door listening. Before Hurricane could ask, Captain Adams said, "Your ten minutes were up, so I came to look for you."

Hurricane smiled and turned his attention back to his two captives and asked, "If he only took a few of the ladies, where are the rest being held?"

"There are three soundproof rooms in the basement, with a dozen or so guards in or around the rooms. You'll never make it to the girls in time, and those guards have orders to kill the girls if any rescue attempts are made."

"How do we get into the basement?"

"I only know of a trapdoor in the kitchen floor behind the counter, but I heard there is also a secret door in the big conference room downstairs. I've never seen it. I've only heard about it. I'm not even sure if it really exists. Maybe it was just talk."

"Well, thank you, Ralph. Now you see, Bob, all of this trouble could have been avoided. All you had to do was answer my questions instead of going through all that pain."

"Mister Hurricane, is it? You promised to end our torture."

"I've never gone back on my word, so let me do as I promised and relieve your pain." Hurricane raised his big gun and drilled Ralph with three slugs around his heart. Then he shot Bob once in the heart. "Your pain is now gone. All right, Captain, let's go see if that secret passage really exists. If we haven't found it in ten minutes, we'll go down the hard way."

Captain Adams nodded his head yes and off they ran. They called the troops together and explained what they were trying to find. They had four rooms and ten minutes to check them out.

Crystal and Joann went into room number one and started throwing books off the shelves. Hoping, like in the movies, one was a switch for a secret panel on the wall.

Roxanne and Diane searched room number two, taking all the pictures off the walls and checking all the light switches.

Billy and the captain went into room number three. They started looking underneath the beds, in the closets, and on window sills.

Hurricane and Janice entered the last room, which was almost in the center of the house. "What exactly are we looking for, Sam?"

"I'm not sure, Janice. It could be a switch on the wall or behind a book on one of the bookshelves. Maybe it's even mounted to a trip lever on the wall. It sounds crazy, honey, but they really had secret passages in some of the older houses."

Frantically, they searched the rooms. Just as Hurricane was getting ready to attack from the front, Janice called his name in an hysterical way. Hurricane saw the panel in back of the desk slide over. He radioed the others and then asked Janice, "How in the world did you find it?"

"I sat down in this chair to go through the drawers. When I moved the chair back, presto."

When Hurricane moved the rug from beneath the chair, there, looking right at him, was the button. Janice must have rolled over it. *There must be some truth to "dumb luck" after all*, Hurricane thought.

The others finally arrived, and Hurricane was already planning their next move.

"Captain Adams, you take the girls and head down this way. I'll go the front way."

"Hurricane, why not let one of us go with you?" Diane asked.

"I can move faster without having anyone else to worry about, not to sound ungrateful, mind you. I can think more clearly when I only have myself to worry about," answered Hurricane.

"Understood, but why not have one of us tag along after we give you a ten minute lead, just in case you need help?"

"Thanks for the concern, Diane. However, I'm hoping by the time any action starts down there, you'll be attacking from the rear, therefore having the element of surprise. Just remember, when you locate the girls, open up with everything you have. Don't let any of these bastards live."

"Janice, you're so lucky to have a man like that."

"Thank you, Diane. I hope someday you'll find a man just like Sam."

"I suppose I can always dream about it." They all laughed as they watched Hurricane running toward the kitchen.

"Well, ladies, I found four flashlights in the desk drawers," Captain said. "Shall we go get the others?"

They all nodded yes and headed for the secret passage. Just as they were inside, it closed. The only way out now was down the stairs. They slowly made their way toward the basement. On the way down, they found writing on the walls explaining what panel led where. There were many secret panels in this house. Maybe this is how they all escaped without being seen.

While Captain Adams and the girls were finding their way down the secret passageway, Hurricane found the kitchen and three guys standing guard as he entered the door. Hurricane was surprised when, instead of shooting, they walked over toward him. A big six-five, three-hundred-seventy-pound African American led the way.

When he finally spoke, he had a deep baritone voice and said, "My friends and I have decided instead of killing you fast we will make you suffer, like you did our friends back on The Strip."

Even though the other two guys were almost as big as their leader, Hurricane stood by the door smiling. He never figured on this, but if they don't make any noise, he just might be able to make it into the basement without any problems.

Hurricane took a stand as they approached him. One of the men grabbed Hurricane by the collar. Hurricane struck him in the bicep with a thunderous blow from his right fist. The man released his grip as his arm went limp. He was cursing Hurricane until a mighty blow from Hurricane's left fist struck him in the ribs. Sam hit him so hard that he flew a couple of feet backwards and landed on his backside.

The other two men looked surprised as their friend lay on his back spitting up blood. "Who do you think you are, doing that to our friend?" they said as they approached Hurricane.

The six-five guy thought that because Hurricane only stood five-ten he was an easy mark. That was until Hurricane struck the tall guy with a powerful shot right between his legs. Sometimes being smaller does have its advantages. The man stopped in his tracks and slowly sank to the floor, gasping for breath. Hurricane walked over toward him, grabbed a cast iron pan, and smashed it directly on top of his head.

The third guy was running for his gun. He was about to grab it when a pan struck him on his arm. Hurricane threw the pan so hard that the man's wrist snapped when it hit him. As the guy tried to grab the pan with his other hand, Hurricane grabbed him by the neck and picked him up off the ground. Then he asked him, "Where are the girls?"

"You're a dead man, mister."

Hurricane brought him down so his feet touched the ground. Then as fast as he could blink, he brought his foot up and broke his left knee at the joint. "Where are the girls?" When the man tried to play tough guy again, Hurricane snapped his right knee. "Tell you what, if you give me what I want, I'll kill you fast. If not, I'll torture you until you talk or die. Either way is fine by me."

"That's not fair. Either way, you'll kill me, so why should I tell you anything?"

Hurricane swung his mighty paw toward his open ribs. Hearing a big crack and seeing a little trace of blood ooze out of the man's mouth, Hurricane asked, "Do you want all this pain to go away? Just tell me where the girls are. You know, sooner or later, I'll find them anyway, so just make it easier on yourself. Besides, if you insist on acting tough, I'll kill you and work on your friends."

"My friends will never talk, copper. You'll have to kill us all."

Before he could say another word, Hurricane struck him in the throat, collapsing his Adam's apple. "Before you die, you need to know I'm not a cop. I'm the Hurricane."

His eyes rolled in back of his head as he gasped his last breath. Knowing that the giant would be out for a little while longer, he approached his first attacker.

"Hey, man, sorry for hitting you so hard, but you have to learn how to play better with others. Now, since your friend decided to put an end to his life, I was wondering if you would like to tell me where the girls are.

"Go screw yourself."

Before he could finish his statement, Hurricane hit him in back of the head, causing him to lose his balance and fall on his injured ribs.

"Didn't your mother ever tell you not to use foul language? Since you can't speak like an adult, I guess I'll have to train you. Now, if you could only see yourself. You're bleeding all over the place."

Hurricane noticed the giant was starting to stir. He would be conscious in a little bit. However, his attention was focused on the man in front of him. Hurricane noticed he was trying to stand once again, so he hit him on the right side of his rib cage. There was no way he'd try and get up now, as more blood started to run out of his mouth.

"Now that I have your attention once again, where are the girls?"

"Mister, I'm a dead man either way, so I'll take that to my grave."

"So be it. But before you die, take a look at yourself." With that said

Hurricane stuck two fingers in the man's left eye socket and pulled his eye out so he could look at himself.

"What kind of sick person are you, mister?"

"The giant awakens. All I want is to know where the girls are that you kidnapped, or you're all dead men."

"What did you do to Danny and Stewart? Why is Danny's eye dangling in front of him? I'm going to kill you myself."

"Now, now, before you go off half-cocked, think about what you've just said. You're in no position to make idle threats. Besides, if I don't get my answer soon, I'll go find them myself, and you'll slowly bleed to death."

"Wait until I get up! I'll squash you, little man."

Just as he was almost to his feet, Hurricane gave a roundhouse kick striking the exterior part of his left knee. The giant was back on the floor in excruciating pain.

"Well, Mr. Giant, seems like when I take your knees out from underneath you, you're not so big after all. I'm losing my patience now, so if you don't tell me what I want to know, you're a dead man."

"If you get by the fifteen guards down there, it's the second door on the right. I might die now, but you'll be close behind me if you go down there alone. Just remember, we'll have eternity to get acquainted with one another. What's your name so I know who to look for?"

"If you really want to know my name, think of the most dangerous storm in the world that has no sympathy for anything or anyone and not only takes lives but very seldom leaves any survivors. Those who think they can fight me and win are the ones who pay the biggest price."

"Don't tell me, you're the one they call 'Hurricane'."

Sam gave him an evil grin, then raised his gun and said, "Now that you know who I am, I can send your evil soul in the right direction." Hurricane pulled the trigger and shot all of them dead one at a time. Now he had to find that trapdoor.

Chapter Nine

When Hurricane finally found the trapdoor, he knew he was in for a good fight. I wonder if my friends will be there before I encounter trouble, he was thinking to himself. Slowly, Hurricane entered the unknown territory and carefully pulled a flashlight from his belt. Within a few feet, he found a torch against the wall, and returned his flashlight to his belt. Continuing on, he was hoping to find the entrance soon. Time definitely was not on his side today. Knowing a few of the girls were already taken out, he had to move as fast as possible to catch up to Quincy Sanders.

Hurricane's wish came true when he spotted a door about ten yards down on his right. When he was about five feet from the door, his heart started pounding as a warning to watch out. He spotted a little eye hole in the door. When he bent down to peek in, he saw four girls tied up with their arms stretched up to a ceiling beam. Then a shadow cascaded toward the left but stayed out of Hurricane's sight. Deciding to take a chance, Hurricane knocked on the door, hoping that whoever was inside would unlock the door. After all, they wouldn't be expecting company.

Just as he hoped, the bolt was unlocked, and the door slowly opened. Hurricane stood behind the back of the door. Just as the guard looked around the edge of the door, Hurricane hit him between the eyes, pushing his nose up into his brain with a powerful strike from a strong right hand. Carefully looking around inside the room, Hurricane noticed he was the only one in there besides the girls.

After pulling the guard inside and untying the girls, he let them rest while he tied up his enemy. Even though Sam was sure he was dead, he wanted to be sure nobody discovered him too soon. He pulled him up toward the backside of the beam. The pulley system they had rigged up worked great, as he hardly struggled tying up his victim.

The girls all hugged him and started talking fast. Hurricane made a motion with his finger to quiet down, as he reached for the torch on the wall inside the room. He gave the girls instructions on how to get out the way he came in, handed one of them the torch and said, "You girls go and find a room to hide in until we're done here. If I'm not back in forty-five minutes, get out of here quickly. My truck is around the back, and the keys are up on the visor. Get going and tell the local marshal where we are."

When he was finished, the girls gave him information on where the others were locked up, and how many guards he might face. He told them good luck and went for the others. Before leaving, the girls hugged him and told him to be careful.

"Nobody could fight all those guys and survive," one of them said. "Ladies, we owe our lives to that man, whoever he is." The others nodded in agreement as they headed for the trapdoor.

Now that he knew where the other women were, and as adrenalin flowed through his system, Hurricane moved a little faster. It still seemed like forever before he spotted a light glowing in the distance. He slowed his pace until he could see what he was up against.

Meanwhile, Captain Adams and the girls had found many secret panels between the walls that connected almost every room in the house. They decided to inspect every room on their way to the basement. In one of the rooms, they found some important information that Hurricane would want to see when they finally caught up to him.

Just as they were about to head to the basement, they heard voices coming toward them. Quickly, they ran back into the room they had just exited. Two of the girls took off their jackets and shirts. They fixed their hair and stood there in their bras. Just as they expected, the panel slid open and out came three guys. Two of them looked like twins except that one was almost a half head taller. They had curly brown hair, long legs, and average weight. The other one stood almost six feet tall with blonde hair and was a bit muscle bound.

"Hey, girls, we've been looking for you," the shorter of the twins said. "We were wondering if you would like to party with us?"

"Yes, we would. Could we bring a couple of friends along?" Diane answered.

"What friends?"

Before he could finish his question, the other girls tiptoed up behind them and whacked each guy in the head with a heavy object.

"We'll have to finish our party later, boys," Diane said chuckling.

After tying them up and getting dressed, they continued toward Hurricane. Figuring they were already late, they decided to move a little faster. Just before they were about to enter the basement, voices came through the walls. They stopped to hear what was going on. It sounded like female voices. Searching frantically, they finally found a peep hole. Captain Adams put his eye to the hole in the wall. "Bingo," he said, "it's the girls."

"Let's mark this spot and come back later," advised Janice. "We've spent too much time in here already. Remember, Hurricane needs our help."

They all shook their heads in agreement, and after marking the wall as a reminder, they continued going forward. When they finally found the end of the tunnel, there were two exits, one on each side of the corridor.

"Oh, that's just great!" Captain Adams whispered. "Which way do we go, left or right? Where does each door lead?"

"Well, there's only one way to find out," Diane answered. "There are six of us. Let's split up and try both doors. We still have our radios, so whoever finds the entrance can call the others."

Diane, Roxanne, and Joann went right, while Captain Adams, Crystal, and Janice went left. Before either party opened a door, they used their stethoscopes to listen for sounds.

Captain Adams' party heard nothing and continued searching. Next, they walked into a room and found several girls sitting on the floor chained to the walls. A dim lightbulb illuminated the room. When the girls saw them enter, they were excited and thankful that somebody had found them. Captain Adams, Crystal, and Janice tried to break the chains holding the girls, but without the keys, they needed a pry bar or a bolt cutter. Crystal found a cabinet on the opposite wall loaded with tools and torturing devices. The captain joined her and, searching through the contents, they discovered a big bolt cutter. The ladies would soon be free.

While Captain Adams, Crystal, and Janice were freeing the girls they had found, the other team, Diane, Roxanne, and Joann, walked into a torture chamber. The torch on the wall gave very little light, but they could see three girls strung up by their wrists. They could see shadows around the room but could not tell if they were alone or not. Diane and Joann decided to find out and slowly crept around the walls. After discovering nobody else was in the room, they went to the girls. When they got closer, they saw the girls were wearing only bras. Their shirts had been removed, and their backs were covered in welts. They had been whipped. Two of them were unconscious, but the third was able to speak.

"Where are the bastards who did this to you?" Roxanne asked.

"They ... they ... went on break," she said with difficulty. Joann found water and gave her some. "Thank you." She continued, "They took a break. They should be back in a few minutes. How did you find us? Are you going to rescue us?"

"That's the plan, but we'll need your help as well," Diane said.

"I'll do anything to get out of here. We can't take much more of this torture."

"What's your name?"

"Cheryl Larson. The other two are Brenda Simpson and Sandy Cruse. They have twelve more girls in another room somewhere. We don't know where they are. They keep moving us around from room to room to keep us confused."

"I'm Diane, this is Roxanne, and over there by the weapons is Joann. We need you to keep these guys busy while we sneak up on them."

"Not to sound ungrateful, but I hope you brought some help with you. These guys are pretty big, and I think they're on some kind of drug. They don't seem to feel pain."

"Is that so?" Diane said as she grabbed a few weapons of her own from the wall. "We'll see if this doesn't stop them in their tracks," she said as she grabbed a war club that had a few spikes poking out of it. Roxanne grabbed a war hammer, which is similar to an ax, except this was made of steel. Joann took a Dussack cutlass sword about two feet long. These swords were curved and could slice a person almost in half.

Just as they ducked down in the dark, they had company come through the door. These were three of the ugliest dudes the girls had ever seen. They were so deformed that, for a minute, the girls felt sorry for them, until one of them said, "Hey, Spike, look at this one. She's still awake."

"Yeah, she can sure take a lot of pain. Her friends are still out cold."

"Not true, ugly. I just can't stand to look at your faces," one of the other girls said.

"Well, now, we were going to save you for last, but since you like to insult us handsome guys, I think we'll kill you first. Spike, go bring over the swords, and let's cut her open real slow, so we can see the pain in her eyes as she dies."

"Where are the swords? They're gone."

"What do you mean, gone? I just put them back before we left the room."

The other two guys went over to look for their weapons.

"Hey, the hammer and club, they're gone, too."

"All right, what's going on here? The girls couldn't have taken them. Nobody's come in here since we left. I'm not sure what happen to them, but instead of using those, let's burn their flesh off instead."

The other goons seemed to like the sound of that more than the first plan, as they gave each other a high five. When one of them went over to pull the torch out of the wall, the three girls made their move.

They were all laughing as the other two guys were preparing to pour kerosene on the prisoners. Diane interrupted their laughing. "Now, didn't your mother ever tell you the proper way to treat a lady?" Diane asked.

As one of the men turned around, Joann thrust the long sword into his stomach. She was a bit startled when he continued to walk toward her. Thinking quickly she stuck the little knife into the side of his neck, and blood squirted out like an artesian well as she hit the carotid artery.

Before the other two were able to figure out what was going on Diane swung her mighty war club, smashing the skull of the next guy, and Roxanne hit the third guy in the legs with the war hammer. His knees buckled from underneath him as he fell to the ground while the kneecaps dangled from his legs. Before he could yell and warn the others, Roxanne swung the hammer hitting him on top of his head.

After searching the bodies and finding the keys for the chains, they released the three prisoners who hugged the girls as they were freed. Joann saw the concern in their eyes.

"Don't worry, ladies," Joann said. "We still have a little unfinished business, but we promise you will be free when this is over."

"We want to help," Sandy said.

"Believe it or not, ladies," Roxanne said, "this is what we are trained to do. You'll be more help if you go back through these walls to the spot we have marked and wait for us."

"How long will we be there? What if you don't come back? What do we do then?"

"With what you've already been through, we understand your concerns. You just have to believe us, we have to hook up with our other friends and take care of business. I give you my word that we'll be back sooner than you think. Please, just have patience and look for a secret panel or something while you're waiting for us. You'll know why when you find what we were looking for earlier."

"How can we be sure you will survive the battle?"

Joann took off her transmitter system and handed it to them. "Here, you can hear what's going on with this little transmitter. We all have one to help each other in case we get into trouble. You take it, and you'll know what happens to us. Don't worry about me, I'll just stay by one of my new friends here. We have to go find Hurricane and our friends."

"Hurricane really exists? I thought he was a comic book character," Cheryl said.

"No, he is real, and he's the reason we are here. You'll meet him as soon as we are done. Just watch each other's back and you'll be fine." After Roxanne said that, they were gone.

Ten minutes later, the girls caught up with the other group of three.

"Hey, where have the three of you been?" Captain Adams asked.

"Well, we found and released three of the prisoners."

After telling them what happened and where the girls were now, Janice and the others applauded their success. Captain Adams told their story about the girls they rescued. Now they stood ready, waiting for Hurricane to make his play.

Hurricane found not only one door but two, and they were spread out almost fifty feet apart from each other. He started getting a bad feeling in his stomach. Maybe this is where people were being tortured. When he was at the first door, he cautiously peeked through the little window. He was surprised to see three big bodies lying in pools of blood. Empty shackles were hanging from the ceiling. Figuring this was a good sign, he knew the others were waiting for him here somewhere.

Just before he made it to door number two, someone yelled, "Hey, you, what are you doing here? You're supposed to be getting the boss's car."

When Hurricane didn't answer him right away, the big guy came up to him, grabbed his shoulder, and flung him around fast. Hurricane spun around and stuck a knife in the man's stomach. Then he slowly twisted the knife as he said, "Yeah, I hear you loud and clear. Point me in the direction of Quincy Sanders." Before his eyes rolled back into his head, the man looked toward his left. Hurricane took that as his answer and headed that way.

It seemed like a long walk before he reached a solid door. There were no windows in the door and no doorknob on the outside. Hurricane took a few ninja stars out of his coat and said to himself, Well, here goes nothing, as he knocked on the door. It dawned on him that they might have a certain knock to enter, and then again who would they expect down here.

After a minute or so, Hurricane heard the handle turn and the door started to open out toward him. Stepping back a little to allow it to be opened all the way, he kept his head down until he had a clear path, and then he rushed into the room. Spotting two men to his right, he sent two stars, striking one in the head and the other in the neck, dropping them both.

"Hurricane! How can this be? How can you still be alive?"

"Hello, again, Quincy. Did you really think those three goons of yours could actually take me? I'm a little disappointed in you, Quincy. I figured you'd have a much bigger and tougher army."

"I must say, you are a very tough adversary, Mr. Hurricane. You surprise me how persistent you are. However, I never do anything without having a counter plan, just in case someone like you happens to sneak in here. If you want more competition, then your wish is granted." Quincy pulled a lever, and the desk he was sitting behind started to roll into the wall, chair and all. Then out from behind the wall, at least thirty men ran into the room trying to circle Hurricane. "Be very careful what you wish for, Hurricane," Quincy said with a laugh.

Hurricane backed up against the wall so they could not get behind him, and then he noticed a light from his left-side peripheral vision. It was Morse code from his partner, Captain Adams. His help was waiting for his cue to enter the fight.

"Quincy, you surprise me as well. I figured you'd have more guards than this. It almost seems unfair. You have what, thirty or so men? I might not even break a sweat with this bunch. This is just enough for me to get warmed up. Then I can be in tiptop shape when I come after you. Just hang around for a few minutes. This won't take long at all."

"You talk big for a man who is about to die, but if you insist on believing you can take out all of these men by yourself, who am I to doubt you. I'll just hang around here because, just before they finish you, I'll be the one to end your life. I'll be known as the man who killed the mighty Hurricane, and then nobody will ever mess with me again."

"Well, then, tell your men to make the first play, and let the killing begin," Hurricane said.

Just then one of the men in the middle made a move for his gun, but Hurricane drew his faster and put two holes in his heart. Then he tossed several stars into the group. Four men were hit, two in the arms, one in the neck, and the other in the leg.

"I don't need any weapons, Marine. I'll just kill you with my bare hands," one of them said as he charged toward Hurricane. Stepping aside as the man lunged at him, Hurricane hit him in the back of the neck. The man shook his head and charged again. He was quick with his hands. Hurricane finally swung low with his legs and caught the other man behind his knees. He went down. Hurricane knew he couldn't waste any more strength on this guy if he was going to survive the rest. When the man got up from the ground, Hurricane shoved his hand up under his nose, pushing with such force that he pushed the bone from his nose clear through the back of his skull.

Just as he hit the ground, Sam motioned toward the wall. Out came Captain Adams and the five girls, ready to fight.

"Why, Quincy, don't look so surprised," Captain Adams said. "You really didn't think I'd let my partner go into a building without any backup, did you?"

"As you now can see, Quincy," Hurricane said, "I have plenty of help this time around."

"Two men and five women, that doesn't exactly even the score Hurricane. The ball, as they say, is still in my court."

"Hey, man, if you're saying that just because we're women and you think you have the upper hand, you definitely don't know who you're dealing with," Diane said in an angry voice.

"Just who should I be afraid of then?" Quincy asked.

"That's easy, Quincy, my sisters and I are law enforcement women. We are very well skilled in martial arts and self-defense, and together with the mighty Hurricane and Captain Adams, we are going to put an end to your operation," Roxanne said with an evil look on her face.

"Now that we've made it quite clear who we are, Quincy, you have two choices and only two choices here. Number one, you can tell your men to drop their weapons and give yourselves up, or number two, try to fight us and die today. I sure hope you choose number two, so I know this racket you're running is out of service forever."

"Well, I guess I'll pick number three," Quincy said.

"And what is number three?" Hurricane asked.

"Why, it's my escape plan," Quincy said as he turned to exit the room.

The only thing he missed was Joann circling around him when they were talking. Just as fast as he went past the open wall, he came flying back landing on the floor.

"You're not leaving the party so soon, fat man," Joann said as she came walking from beyond the wall.

Hurricane quickly drew his two magnums and started shooting. Captain Adams and the girls started shooting from the other side of the room. Within a few short minutes the only one left, sitting in the middle of the room, was Quincy Sanders.

There he sat with a smug look on his face until Hurricane said, "Well, Quincy, I guess you think you're in the clear right? Well, let me just ask you a question. Have you ever seen what an angry woman can do to a man's face with her bare claws? Just think what a dozen angry females can do all at once. You see, Quincy, we've talked about what your fate should be if you somehow survived this war. We all agreed that you should be thrown into a closed room with the women that you've kidnapped, at least the ones still here, and let them take their frustrations out on you. They will give you back some of your own medicine, along with the pain that you've inflicted upon them. Joseph Joubert quoted it best when he said 'Revenge is an act of passion; vengeance is justice, injuries are revenged; crimes are avenged.' Now get up off the floor, and let's go get the girls, shall we?"

Quincy slowly stood up and led them toward the girls. He extracted the keys from the stone on the wall and opened the door. When the women saw Quincy standing there, they almost went into shock, until Janice said, "Don't worry, girls, we are here to rescue you. We've brought you a going-away present. Since this man took it upon himself to kidnap and torture you, we figured you may want to get even with him. By the way, he won't be able to hurt you or swing back, not with his arms handcuffed behind him."

With that said, Hurricane put Quincy's hands behind his back, using his handcuffs. Then he led Quincy to the middle of the room, and without warning, Hurricane thrust his heal into Quincy's knees. Quincy went straight down. He could no longer stand. He was as helpless as a baby. Hurricane heard a strange noise, and when he looked up, he saw three more women coming into the room.

"I found the secret lever," Janice said with a smile.

When the three women saw Quincy helpless on the floor, they went berserk and started clawing at his face, and the rest of them joined in. Three of the women even went back to the dungeon room and retrieved a few of the weapons that were used on them.

"Hurricane, the laugh is on you. Without me, you won't know who else is involved!"

Quincy started screaming.

"Do you mean like President Salvantez?" Hurricane asked and then added, "along with the shipment of girls in the next couple of days over by the Hoover Dam?"

"How'd you know that? Who talked? I demand my rights?"

"All right, Quincy Sanders, you have the right to scream as loud as you can because nobody will hear you."

Hurricane and his rescue team were laughing as the ladies continued their assault on Quincy Sanders. They grabbed Quincy and strung him on a table facing up, so he could see what was coming. First they attached dungeon balls to his arms and legs, and hung them over the table. These were leg irons that had a twenty pound steel ball attached to the end. When they let the balls roll off of the table four loud pops were heard. Quincy's arms and legs snapped from the sockets. His screams of pain were like music to the girls' ears. They took the war hammer and struck Sanders in the rib cage, being careful not to hit him hard enough to kill him right away. It was pay-back time, and Quincy was getting everything that he dished out to these girls.

Hurricane couldn't believe how they knew exactly where to hit without killing him. He started to almost feel sympathy for Quincy Sanders, but that only lasted a brief moment.

When just about every bone in his body was smashed, one of the girls brought in a small bucket with a lid on top. When she pulled off the lid, Hurricane spotted a good size rat sleeping inside the bucket.

"Do you remember Sara, Mr. Sanders?" she asked with tears welling up inside her eyes, then continued, "Do you remember how you forced us to watch as a rat ate out her stomach." Sanders' eyes almost popped out of the sockets when he saw the size of the rat she had. "I think, in Sara's honor, the same punishment should be done to you."

With that, she made a small incision in his stomach to start the blood flowing. Then she flipped the bucket over on his stomach with the rat trapped inside the bucket. When the rat smelled the blood, it started eating through Sander's stomach to get free. It wouldn't stop until it was free, and Sanders would still be alive through the whole thing.

Hurricane couldn't think of a better ending for this deranged killer. Curiosity overcame Hurricane as he finally asked, "How did you girls know where to strike Quincy without killing him?"

"Betty, Phyllis, and I are registered nurses, and we know everything there is to know about human anatomy."

"Janice, remind me never to get these girls mad at me," Hurricane said, and they all laughed as they exited the building.

When they finally made it outside, the girls had trouble adjusting to the sun. It was then that Diane spotted her stepsister. "Louise!" she yelled as they ran toward each other and hugged. After everyone had introduced themselves, they climbed into the two Army trucks waiting for them.

Hurricane's phone was ringing in the truck, and when he picked it up he said, "Hurricane here, Colonel."

"Just checking in on you, Sam, and wanted to let you know your brother, Running Bear, and a few of the braves are heading to the Army hospital at the base. That blast put them out of commission for a while," Colonel Jones said.

"How's Charging Buffalo?" Hurricane asked. "I saw him go in just before the blast."

"I'm sorry Sam. He caught the full impact of the blast and never made it out," Colonel Jones said.

Hurricane was quiet for a moment. "Thank you for your honesty, Colonel. His death will not be in vain. We have to finish this now, for Charging Buffalo. Thanks for the Apache helicopter you sent to help out here, sir." The colonel could hear the sorrow in Hurricane's voice and knew he was grieving.

"You're welcome, Sam. I had to call him back here to transport these men to the hospital at the base, after I was sure he was through helping you. Call me again if you need any help," Colonel Jones said.

Hurricane ended the call and sat quietly thinking about his warrior brothers. Charging Buffalo had been a great man and would be missed. He hoped Running Bear and the others would be well soon. These people had sacrificed a lot to help him rescue the girls and bring down Sanders.

Sam was happy all these girls were safe, but the battle was only three quarters over. He still had one more round to settle the score with President Salvantez. He knew when and where he was going to meet him, but now he had to have a solid game plan.

Turning to Captain Adams, he said, "When we get back, John, let's go check out those docks at Boulder City, shall we? I'd like to get an idea of what we are going up against."

Captain Adams nodded and laid his head back to rest. The girls were all busy getting acquainted with one another.

A little over two hours later, Hurricane and the girls finally stopped in front of the Police Station. One by one the girls exited. They were hungry and dehydrated.

"Do you want me to go find a doctor?" Crystal asked Hurricane.

"Good idea, Crystal. Look in the phone book and find out where to go," Sam said.

"No need to do that, you two. I know just the man to call," Captain

Adams said as he headed for the phone. When he was finished with his conversation, he said, "The doctor will be here in about fifteen minutes."

"John, could you call that helicopter pilot we used before, and see if he can take us to scout the drop zone, so we can plan our welcome party for this President Salvantes?"

"I've already called him. He will be here after he fuels up his chopper," Captain Adams answered.

Hurricane shook his head to signal his approval, and then he pulled out his map to study the area. Ten minutes later, he was interrupted by a knock on the door. He walked over to the door with his gun in hand. Cocking it in case of trouble, he opened the door. Standing on the porch was a man about Sam's height wearing a suit coat and tie. He had small wire-rimmed glasses and carried a black bag.

"May I ask who you are, sir?" Hurricane asked.

"I'm Doctor Henry Adams, John's brother, young man. Captain Adams called me about ten minutes ago to check on a prisoner."

"All right, come on in," Sam said, "but they aren't prisoners. They were hostages until earlier today."

The doctor shook his head yes and followed Sam to the back. When he saw the girls, he was shocked.

"These girls need food and something to drink. I can see that without even examining them. They are so skinny and pale. Where have they been?"

Just then Captain Adams came in the room. "Henry, Sam and I found these girls being held hostage out in the desert. We just returned with them before I called you."

"How long were they there?"

"Well, Doc, what's the date today?" Cheryl Larson asked back.

"Today is the twenty-fifth of June."

"Most of us have been there almost two months, and some of the girls were there before us," Brenda Simpson answered in a fragile voice. "Our parents must think we're dead. We've had no contact with anybody since they took us."

"We'll solve that problem for you, ladies," Captain Adams said. "After the doctor checks you out and you get some good food in your stomachs, you can all call your parents to let them know you're safe and you'll be home very soon."

"Thank you, Captain," all the ladies said in unison. Some of them started to cry, thinking about what their parents must have been going through. They couldn't believe they had been captives that long.

Doctor Adams was kept busy for quite some time tending to the wounds the girls had received while being held captive. Some of the girls had bones broken that hadn't healed right. The doctor couldn't believe these girls had survived their long ordeal.

While the doctor tended to the girls, Captain Adams called Wayne Newman to tell him about the rescue. After about forty-five minutes, Captain Adams said, "Ladies and gentlemen, after we are done here, we've been invited to eat at the buffet restaurant at Harrah's. Mr. Wayne Newman has offered to pay for your meals."

"Who's Wayne Newman?" Cheryl asked.

"He's my old boss," Sandy Cruse said. "I was working in his show when I was abducted. He's the best man I've ever worked for. He really cares about his employees."

"He's the reason Hurricane and Janice are here as well," Captain Adams added.

Not long after the captain finished talking to Wayne Newman, his phone rang again. Being a bit hesitant, Captain Adams answered the phone. It was the helicopter pilot trying to find out where they were. The doctor agreed that if they didn't make it back before he was finished, he would take the girls to Harrah's to eat.

When Hurricane and the captain finally arrived at the take-off site, the pilot was sitting in the chopper waiting. It only took a few minutes to fly to Boulder City. Hurricane brought his binoculars along to help see things more clearly. When they were above Hoover Dam, Hurricane steered the pilot in the direction he wanted to check out first. Trees and bushes blocked their view when they flew over going east, but when they flew back to the west the sun's bright beams were shining off the top of four storage bins.

"Those aren't supposed to be there. What are they for?" the pilot asked.

"That's what we're going to find out, my friend," Hurricane answered. "Can we go around one more time, partner?"

"Yeah, that's no problem, Sam. What are you looking for?"

"I'm interested in knowing if anyone is down there, so when we come back we know what to expect," Hurricane answered.

Hurricane took his binoculars and spotted the area while the pilot hovered over the target. His glasses were so strong he could see the footprints in the sand. He followed them and bingo. There, hidden under the bushes, he could see four pairs of shoes poking out.

"I see shoes but no legs," Sam said just as they started to pull away. "Now I see them, those little maggots. There are four guys in the trees holding rifles. All right, that's all I need to know. Thanks for your help, buddy."

"Captain, if this is anything dangerous and you need some help, I'm only a phone call away. My name is Buck Stone."

"We might just take you up on that, Buck. My name is Hurricane," he said as they shook hands.

"Wow, you really do exist. No offense, man, but you sounded too good to be true. I'd like to see you in action, that is if you don't mind."

"Tell you what, Buck. When I call, you bring a camera with you," Hurricane said.

"Yes, sir. Thank you. I'll be waiting for your call," Buck said. He couldn't stop grinning all the while they were up in the air. He was still grinning as he dropped them off by their cars.

When Hurricane and Captain Adams got back to the jail, they found it empty and quiet. They found a note on the desk that read: "Wayne Newton offered the girls rooms if they needed rest. Will send word or contact you when they are settled in. Doctor Henry Adams."

Captain Adams saw a look on Hurricane's face that bothered him. "What's wrong Sam?" he asked.

"If the girls were at the fort for almost two months, then which girls were being transported in three more days?"

"Are you thinking what I'm thinking, Sam? Are there more girls in those storage bins we just saw?"

"We're both on the same page, my friend. I'm going down to check it out."

"Not without me you're not," Captain Adams said sternly. "You have no clue how many of Quincy's men may be down there. Let's tell the others where we are going so they don't worry where we are."

"Good thinking, John. Let's load up the truck first."

Sam and Captain Adams loaded up some weapons and night-vision glasses, just in case. Then they headed toward Harrah's to find out where the girls were. After the elevator reached their floor and the door opened, Sam and Captain Adams saw two guys trying to peek through the keyhole of their room. They must have seen something good not to have heard Sam and Captain Adams arriving.

"You guys see anything good yet?" Hurricane asked.

"Yeah, man, get away from here. This is our gig. Go play bodyguard some place else."

Hurricane and Captain Adams each grabbed one of the men. Hurricane stood his up and slammed a fist into his stomach. Captain Adams slammed his guy against the wall, and hit him in his kidney. Both men looked startled and tried to fight back. The next thing they knew they were waking up on top of the roof. They were tied back to back against a smoke stack. When they freed themselves, notes were found in their pockets. They read: "Next time, we will not be as understanding. Don't ever spy on anyone else again." They signed it "The Body Guards."

As Sam and Captain Adams were letting the girls know where they were going, Diane and the other girls stood up. "Where do you think you're going?" Sam asked.

"Why, with you, of course, Hurricane," Crystal answered.

"You girls have already helped me enough. You've been a great help, but you need to get back to your families."

"Mr. Hurricane, I'm very happy we found my stepsister," Diane said. "We vowed to help you until this is over. Besides, if they still have more girls in those bins, you're going to need help getting them out of there. So, we're going."

"Janice, please make a note to remind me when we get back home to send each of these ladies' precincts a letter of honor for their bravery above and beyond the call of duty."

"Thank you, Mr. Hurricane, but first, let's get this thing over with so all of us can relax and enjoy this beautiful city," Joann Fisher said.

"Sam. Please just call me 'Sam.' All right, let's get going, shall we?" Hurricane said.

They decided to take the truck in case they had a lot of people to bring back. Since the captain knew the way, he led the convoy, driving the truck up front as Hurricane and the rest followed.

Chapter Ten

Sam seemed like he was in a trance as they traveled down the road. Janice wasn't sure if she should interrupt his thoughts but decided to take a chance.

"Sam, are you all right? Can we talk?"

He smiled at her and said, "Just thinking about how long we've been working on this case so far. If this doesn't end soon we might have to move here."

Janice snickered at his statement and added, "When you decide to take a vacation, does it always end up as an adventure?"

"Lately, it sure seems that way. I figured I'd solve this case in day or two, and then we could enjoy the rest of our visit. It's been almost two weeks now, and I'm still not any closer to knowing if this is the end of the line. I think I have stepped into a hornet's nest that might never end."

"Sam, you told me once that crime is everywhere. It will never end. But if you can put an end to it in one area at a time, maybe, just maybe, one day peace will find its way here."

"I can't believe you still remember that."

"Are you kidding me? That's why I fell in love with you. You have a kind heart and a desire to help people."

"Yeah, I have such a kind heart. That's why I kill others."

"You only kill when they leave you no choice, but they kill for pure pleasure, just to watch others suffer and die," Janice said.

"Why do I have to be so good at it?"

"We're all put on this earth for certain jobs. If your job is to help people by making bad men perish, so be it. Just remember, if not for you doing your job so well, we might not have met each other. My path now is to help you, and I've accepted the challenge."

Just then, Captain Adams pulled the truck over to the side of the road. He pointed toward the cliff side of the road. Sam came over to find out what was going on. When he looked over the side of the road, he saw the storage bins they had spotted from above.

"Good job, John. I'll get the rope and start down this way. You take the rest around to the front." With that said, Sam retrieved his little duffle bag and the big rope he had brought along. After tying it around a broken tree trunk and then attaching it to his safety harness, he was set to go.

"Good luck, Sam," the captain said. "I hope that trunk and the rope are strong enough to hold you. I'd hate to find out you went down faster than you anticipated."

Hurricane smiled and gave a thumbs up before starting down the hill. The captain figured it would be about twenty minutes before he would see Sam again on the other side. The roads around the mountain were long and very narrow. As he drove around the winding road, Captain Adams couldn't help thinking about how fast the Indians traveled it on horseback.

Hurricane was almost out of rope when he realized he still had a ten-foot drop between him and the bottom of the hill. Looking around, he spotted a ledge off to the left. Figuring he could scale down the hill the rest of the way, he started swaying back and forth. On the eighth try, he made it to the ledge.

Sam tugged on the rope, hoping it would release, but it didn't budge. He removed a pair of climbing gloves from his backpack. The gloves had rubber tipped fingers that would make it easier to grip the rock ledge while climbing down. He knew he would have to be very careful because it's more difficult to go down a hill than to climb up. Looking down, he figured he would have to angle his descent. He still had about four feet of rope left as he slowly descended the hill.

Sam knew that when he reached the end of the rope, there would be no turning back, and falling could create a commotion that drew attention. He definitely did not want that. He found a solid grip and released the rope. Slowly, he maneuvered down the mountain. He found that the footing was great for the moment, but knew full well that it could change at any moment. When he was within three feet of the bottom, he released the strap of his backpack and let it fall to the sand below. It felt good to get that extra weight off his back, and he was able to quickly scale down the rest of the mountain.

At the bottom, he retrieved his weapons from the hot sand. When he looked to the west, he could see Captain Adams getting closer. He couldn't believe it took him that long to scale down ten feet. *I must be getting old*, he said to himself.

Sam was close to one of the storage bins and decided to check it out. He placed his stethoscope on the side of the bin and heard voices inside. There was only one way to find out who they were. He struck the side of the bin hoping he would hear female voices. Instead, it became very quiet inside. Deciding to try again, he tapped out a common code, hoping someone would know the end of the code. He was in luck as someone finally tapped back. Suddenly, he heard a female voice. "Please help us. We are being held hostage in here."

Hurricane was cautious. He had been in situations like this enough to know it could be a trap, and he took nothing for granted. He carefully moved around to view the front of the bin. Four guys were on the sandy beach setting up to start a fire. It would most likely be to signal in the boat that was due to arrive in a couple of days. He extracted one of his guns from its holster and crept up on the four dudes. They were talking loudly and goofing around so much that no one noticed Hurricane advancing until he was standing behind them. "Hello, boys. Mind if I join your party?" he asked.

They spun around and looked down the barrel of his .357 magnum. "Listen, buddy," the smallest guy said, "you don't know what you're doing. We don't have any money. We are here strictly on business. Do you know who we work for?"

Before he could say another word, Hurricane spoke up, "Shut up, little man. What are you, maybe five feet tall? I know exactly who you work for. I hope you boys aren't expecting any paychecks soon. Quincy's going to be out of business for a while, a very long while. Now, which one of you choir boys has the keys to these storage bins?"

"We have no keys. We're just paid to watch them so nobody steals what's in them."

"Do you even know what it is you're guarding?" Hurricane asked.

"Yes, they are special packages for President Salvantez."

"They're not packages, my friend, you have women in there. Women who are prisoners soon to be sold as slaves," Hurricane said.

"You're lying. There's fresh produce inside these bins. They are going to be delivered to the poor people in Mexico," the little man said.

"Now why would I risk my life climbing down that big mountain just for a load of food products? We're wasting time here, but just in case I'm wrong, open up one of the bins. If it's produce, I'll walk away, and none of this happened. However, if I'm right and you have women inside, you just turn your backs and let me take them home," Hurricane said.

"Why would we just let you take them away?"

"Because, my friend, if you don't, I will have to kill you, and I don't think risking your life is worth all the fuss. Now, if you have the keys, let's check it out," Hurricane tried to persuade them.

"Wait, you're telling us you're planning on fighting us alone and that we are the ones at a disadvantage?" he asked and started laughing. "Who do you think you are, Jackie Chan or Bruce Lee?"

"No, I'm not like them at all," Hurricane answered. "They would leave you for the police. I'll leave you for the buzzards. When I fight, I leave nothing standing. I will destroy everything in my path, and that's why they call me 'the Hurricane'."

The man to the far right finally spoke up, "That's a bunch of bull, man. That guy's a comic book character. He doesn't even exist. I bet you're not even half as fast as they say he is." He clutched his throat as Hurricane stuck three fingers into his windpipe, dropping him to the ground.

"I'm sick and tired of people trying to tell me who I am. Now, either we do this the easy way and you all go home alive, or I leave you here for buzzard food. The choice, as they say, is yours. Either hand over the keys and leave, or try to fight your way out and die. I'll give you one minute to make up your minds."

"Hey, man, I don't know what's going on here. I was just offered a job, and let me tell you, no job is worth dying over. Honest, mister, I know nothing about any key, but I surely don't feel like dying just yet either."

"All right, you're free to go, but heed my warning: you tell anyone about this, and I'll come after you. No matter where you try to hide, I'll find you, and you'll die a slow and tortuous death." When he saw the look in Hurricane's eyes, he knew he meant what he said.

"I give you my word as a friend, I won't tell a soul," he said, as he looked down toward the man still lying on the ground. Then, when Hurricane motioned for him to leave, he left as fast as his feet would carry him.

Hurricane stuck out his big hand for the keys and saw a shadow on the sand from the sun. Spinning quickly, he kicked his leg out into the chest of a fifth man sneaking up on him. The other three were trying to circle around Hurricane, and then they heard a shot and froze. Within seconds, the truck arrived with the man who ran away draped over the hood.

"Sorry we're a little late, Hurricane, but we caught this guy up in a tree with a gun. Seems like he was pointing it this way to shoot you in the back," Captain Adams said.

"You see, boys, I'm not totally alone. These are my women, and along with Captain Adams, this is my army. How do you feel about the odds now, my little friends?" Hurricane said.

The tallest of the four tossed Hurricane the keys, and then one by one they were handcuffed and loaded into the back of the truck. When they opened the first bin, almost twenty girls came running out.

"All right, ladies, please get into the back of the truck, and we'll take you home," Captain Adams said.

"What about the girls in the other bins?" one of them asked.

Instead of asking questions, Hurricane and Captain Adams went to the other bins and opened them one by one. They found almost fifty more women. Some of them must have been there for a while because they were very skinny and dehydrated and needed help walking out.

Knowing they would need more vehicles to carry the women out, Hurricane used Captain Adams' phone and called his buddy. "Colonel Jones, I need another favor from you."

A few minutes after Hurricane had ended his call, four helicopters were hovering above and lowering one by one to take the ladies for medical treatment. After they were all loaded and on their way to safety, Hurricane started setting up shop.

One by one, they set up booby traps in the storage bins with C-four explosives. Each was devised to blow up in a different way, knowing that as soon as one exploded, they would be even more careful with the others. Besides, why spoil all the fun for the rest.

The front bin was strapped with a hand grenade attached to a C-four pack, which was hooked up to a fishing line that would release the pin when the door was opened. In bin number two, a white sheet was hung up half way back inside the bin, giving the impression that the girls were hiding behind it. Once again, a hand grenade was set up to explode. This time, however, the fishing line was stretched across from side to side. After about ten steps inside, they would trip the line, pulling the curtain down. Because of it being so dark inside, they wouldn't see the wire sewn into the sheet, and boom!

Bin number three was set up with clothes and duffle bags, making it look like the women were sleeping in the back. Hurricane taped a C-four pack with a hand grenade to the top of the bin. He let a string hang down to hit the intruder in the head. He hoped they'd think it was a spider web, and when they pull it, boom!

Number four was a bit over the top. Hurricane not only rigged up the front door but the back as well, thinking that maybe after the first three, they might try the back door first. Either way, it would be louder than the others. He was hoping President Salvantez would be eliminated by one of the bombs, though he knew the chances were slim to none. He was setting up a special surprise for him.

Knowing he had at least twenty-four hours, there was plenty of time to prepare for his surprise party. He had Captain Adams and the girls dig a trench around the perimeter of the camp. Hurricane went around looking for broken bark from the trees. When he came back to camp, he was carrying about a dozen flat pieces.

Captain Adams was curious about what Hurricane was up to, but instead of asking, he figured he would watch and see. Hurricane went to the truck and notched out holes in the middle of the bark pieces. Then he took out one of the duffle bags and pulled out six claymore mines. He taped the bark over the mines with the detonators sticking up through the holes. He was going to use them as landmines. Captain Adams was amazed at what this man had for weapons, and more so at how he was able to acquire them.

Not wanting to waste any more time, he walked over to Hurricane and asked, "Hey, partner, need some help with those booby traps?"

"Yes, as a matter of fact, I'd like the help. I've so much to do in such a short time. Take these mines and spread them out in the trench the girls have dug. Make sure you spread them around evenly, as I only have six. We need to get as many bad guys out of the way as possible."

"Sounds like you're expecting an army to show up," the captain said.

"I think he'll have enough men to escort all those women off of this beach, and I know there were almost eighty women down here. I should have brought more guns and ammo along. I figure they'll have to have at least two boats, and enough men to handle all those women. I just hope they don't figure out this is a set up until it's too late, and I'm hoping a bunch of them get destroyed by these claymore mines. If not, I'll just have to take them out my way. Either way, they'll be just as dead."

"Hurricane, you're such a mean bastard, but that's why you're so good at doing this. I wish I could be half as good as you."

"Don't sell yourself short, Captain. You have a lot of responsibility there on The Strip. Besides, you didn't have to come along on this mission. I think they made a wise choice when they chose you for sheriff. You really care about people. That's hard to do with the type of jobs we have. You just never know when someone is telling you the truth."

"Thanks, Hurricane. I never thought about my job as being that important. You've opened up my eyes to a lot of things I didn't see before."

"If that's the case, how about taking these mines and see where the best spot will be to set them up," Hurricane said in a joking manner.

They both laughed as Captain Adams started walking over to where the boats would be landing. One by one he laid down the mines, spreading them out maybe ten to fifteen feet apart. Hurricane gave a thumb's up as his approval of where Adams was installing them. One by one, the captain buried them in the sand, and then he put little buckets over the top. He didn't want any premature explosions happening, at least not before their guests arrived.

Hurricane and the girls were loading bullets into the extra gun clips, thinking they just might be getting into a bigger fight than expected. After the clips were loaded, Hurricane started separating the hand grenades, guns, and many of the other weapons he had brought along. Diane spotted the long sword in the pile of weapons in the truck. She walked over and started to examine it.

"See something you like, Diane?" Hurricane asked.

"Yes, I haven't seen a sword like this in quite a while. May I hold it?" she asked.

Hurricane shook his head yes. He was amazed at how gracefully she was swinging it around. It was as if she became part of the sword. It was like poetry in motion. "You're very good with that weapon. Would you like to hold on to it for a while?" Hurricane thought her eyes might pop out of their sockets as she said, "Do you really mean what you said? I can use this beautiful weapon?"

"Yes, Diane. It looks like you two were meant for each other."

"Thank you, Hurricane!"

Hurricane had grabbed a few mannequins from the hotel lobby. Captain Adams had wondered why he wanted them before. Now he understood as Hurricane dressed them and then positioned them like they were sitting around the campfire. The enemy wouldn't know they were dummies until it was too late.

Everything was set up, and the truck was camouflaged with tarps and brush. Looking at his watch, Sam saw they had a good six hours before their guests would arrive. He suggested they get some sleep before the action started. He'd wake everyone up in three or four hours and then get them into position to fight these abductors.

Chapter Eleven

It was nearly six-thirty in the morning when Hurricane woke up the others. According to the letter they had found in the house, President Salvantez should be arriving at approximately nine o'clock to pick up his passengers. That would give them a little more than two hours to prepare.

Hurricane had drawn up a plan while the others slept. When everyone was dressed and ready to fight, they joined Hurricane and were shown the game plan. Captain Adams was the first to speak.

"I take it from this drawing you didn't get any sleep? It's a great plan, but I only have one more question. You have a sniper on top of a hill or something. Where exactly is this hill? It's all flat land here, my friend?"

"Roxanne, I figure you're about one hundred and five pounds right?" Hurricane asked.

"No, more like one twenty five, maybe thirty with all this gear on."

"I overheard you tell the other girls you won first place in the sniper shootout."

"Yes, I won this free trip to Las Vegas so I could relax and have fun."

"You think you could lay over the canvas on top of that truck, and give us some fire power? Just remember, this isn't for fun today. Do you think you can shoot to kill?"

"After seeing what they did to those women, it'll be my pleasure to take out a few of those bastards."

"I was hoping you would say that. Take this sniper rifle and case of

171

ammo. I found this big piece of bark we can lay across the top of the canvas for extra support."

After everyone helped Roxanne get set up, they came back for further instructions.

"Crystal, Joann, Diane, Janice, and Captain Adams, I'd like you to spread out twenty feet apart. Position yourselves fifty feet away from the front of the bins. When the mines go off, start shooting. Roxanne, if they don't enter all the bins, I have a red dot on the buildings where the bombs are placed. Shoot toward those spots and blow the hell out of this place," Hurricane said. "I'll be sneaking around toward the boat, hoping we can get the drop on them. I'll be shooting back toward them, and we'll have them in a nice crossfire."

"What are we going to do if they send more than one boat?" Captain Adams asked.

"If that happens, I'll need one of you to help capture the other boat. We'll cross that bridge when we see them coming. For now we'll just stick to our game plan as is. Now we need to make a few sand hills to hide behind. How do you feel about playing in the sand for a while?" Hurricane asked with a smile on his face.

They all grabbed shovels and started piling the sand. After almost a half hour, the sand dunes were in place. They dug shallow valleys between each one so they could lie down and shoot without being seen. Things were going better than planned at this point. It was only eight-fifteen, and they could rest a while before the fun began. Hurricane walked back to the truck, picked up a box, and returned.

"I was going to save these until after we were finished, but I think you deserve them now." He opened the box and handed out bottles of beer. Each of them took one and decided to save the rest for later.

"Here's to good friends, great aim, and lots of luck getting out of this alive," Diane toasted.

"Here's to a better vacation than I had expected," Roxanne said.

"Here's to finding more great friends," Joann added.

"Here's to saving those who were prisoners," Crystal replied.

"Here's to an adventurous two weeks," Janice added.

"Here's to finally stopping the kidnapping," Captain Adams said.

"Here's to six of the best partners I've ever had," Hurricane replied.

They all took a drink for each toast and were just about to say something else when Janice said, "Sam, I think our friends are a little early. Look at the smoke above the trees."

"Okay, troops, let's get into position, and may luck be with you," Hurricane said.

Everyone scattered to their assigned positions. Hurricane retrieved his binoculars from the truck and looked out toward the smoke. What he saw almost turned him a ghostly white. There was one huge boat in the bay, and they were lowering three small boats. Sam knew he had to change a few things. Going over toward his crew he told them what he saw. They decided to stay with the original plan, except for one change. They would all row out toward the bigger boat and, with any luck, take them by surprise. Hopefully, they would not run after hearing the bombs. He knew the President would send in his men and wait for them out past the river.

As the boats advanced closer to the beach, Hurricane slid underneath the boat dock and into the lukewarm water. He could see about ten men per boat. He was stumped as to how they planned to take that many women back to the yacht with so many men per boat.

When they docked the boats, the men started running onto the beach, laughing, but their laughter faded away when they realized the men around the fire were dummies. They were just about to call the President when they found the keys. After passing out the four keys to the storage bins, they began talking about making three trips if necessary.

"Remember, the President wants them all today. Nobody gets left behind this time," one of them stated.

"What's this?" the guy entering the left bin asked. "Those drapes won't do anything for you sluts."

Hurricane was timing his steps. Just as the man was at the tenth step, the bin to the right was opened and two thunderous blasts were heard. *Ten men down, twenty to go*, Hurricane thought.

The rest of the men were reluctant to enter the other two bins and started talking among themselves. Suddenly, two shots rang out. Before Hurricane could blink, the other two bins were exploding, taking about six more men with them.

Hurricane was watching the boat in the river. It was staying still. Holding two machine guns, he started unloading his guns. Just as the remaining guys were about to fire back, the others opened up behind them. Roxanne was fantastic as she hit everything she aimed at. They quit firing after the last man was down.

"We have to take out the head guy now," Hurricane told his team.

"What, he's not here?" Diane asked.

"No. Unfortunately, he's on the boat out there. We will have to go get him," Hurricane said.

"All right, put us in the middle of one of the boats like we are tied up. You and the captain can escort us out to the boat like two of their men. Then we'll get that madman once and for all," Crystal suggested to Hurricane.

"Sounds good. Let's get going before they get suspicious and leave before we can get there."

After getting into the boat, they started up the motor and drove out slowly toward the yacht. Hurricane told them how glad he was to have them along and gave Roxanne a lot of praise for her shooting. Then he told the group that as they were boarding the boat, they shouldn't make any sudden moves until everyone was aboard.

Hurricane and Captain Adams switched clothes with a couple of the dead men, and they had no trouble boarding the ship. Once they were on board, one of the crew said, "Hey, mate, I've never seen you before. Who are you?" He tried to grab Hurricane, but his wrist was suddenly twisted behind his back.

"No matter. Now tell me how many men are on board this boat."

"Twenty," the man replied. "There are twenty men on this boat."

"Excluding the twenty or so we just killed on shore?"

"Yes. The President always likes having more men than needed in case of times like this."

"Is the President on this tug?"

"Yes, he's in the captain's quarters in the lower floor."

"Where are the other men?"

"They are all eating in the mess hall on the second floor in the middle room. Just listen for all the noise."

"Well, thank you, my friend. You've been very helpful. Unfortunately, I can't let you go and tell the others we're on board."

"No, I won't tell a soul mis ..."

Before he could finish, Hurricane slit his throat and sent him overboard.

"All right, team, we can either stay together or split up. You call it," Hurricane told the pack.

"I think if we split up, we'll find him faster, just in case he has an escape route," Captain Adams said.

"Why don't Joann, Roxanne, the captain, and I go one way, and you, Crystal, and Janice circle around the other way? We can meet in the middle," Diane said.

"All right, we'll meet by the mess hall first. If you get there before us, hold on for five minutes before entering. We'll do the same, in case we run into trouble along the way," Hurricane suggested.

They all agreed and synchronized their watches. The captain and his crew went right, and the others traveled left. The yacht had to stretch at least thirty feet long. They decided to stay together as a group, trying not to draw attention. Just as they were circling around the stern, they spotted a man sitting in a recliner, resting. Not knowing who he was, the captain and Joann walked out to the back rail hand in hand.

"Hey, mate, who are you?" he asked in a mean-sounding voice. "I've never seen you two before."

"We're guests of the President," Joann answered.

"I don't think so, mate. Let's go down and see what the President says about this."

"When we left, he was going to lie down and take a nap," the captain told him.

"That's a darn lie. I just left him in the lower galley, and he was wide awake. Now, why don't we get you ready to walk the plank, shall we?"

"Sorry to disappoint you, buddy, but you're not taking our friends anywhere," Diane said. As the startled man turned around, Diane brought her mighty sword straight down and sliced his skull in half.

"Diane," Captain Adams said. "Please remind me to never get you mad at me."

She had a wide smile on her face as she said, "Relax, Captain. I only hurt the ones I love."

They all laughed as they threw the man overboard. "The sharks have to eat, too," Captain Adams stated as they continued on their way.

While Captain Adams and his team of ladies were busy on the stern side, Hurricane and his team encountered their own problems. Circling the bow, they came upon two men eating lunch. Hurricane placed his arms around Janice and Crystal as they walked beside him toward the front rail. They began to laugh and tease as they walked. When the two men saw them, they got up to find out what was going on.

"Hey, man, what gives here?" the taller of the two asked.

Hurricane began laughing when he saw his two front teeth missing. The shorter guy wasn't any better looking and walked with a limp. "What do you mean by that remark?" Sam asked back.

"What's with the two chicks? That's just not fair, man. You have two gorgeous babes in your arms, and we have nobody."

Hurricane figured, with the question just asked, that these guys were as sharp as a pair of marbles. He played around as he said. "Is that all you're wondering about? Heck, I'll give you these two lovely ladies. Just be careful because they bite."

"You're funny," they laughed. "They bite. Well, girls, we like it when you bite, as long as it's not too hard."

"You're a couple of dirty-minded men, and we don't like men who talk like that," Crystal responded.

"I really don't care what you like, and we call the shots around here. You'll do what we say, or we'll throw you overboard for the sharks."

"Well, I'll tell you what," Janice said as both the girls walked toward the men, while running their hands up and down their shapely figures. Both men were getting really excited before Crystal said, "I don't think we want to play with you then."

Just as they were going to protest, Janice and Crystal thrust their arms straight out and stuck a knife into each of their hearts. "I hope you have fun playing with the sharks," Crystal said as they shoved them overboard.

Hurricane heard footsteps running toward them. He motioned for the girls to stay where they were. He crouched down behind a raft that was positioned on the right side of the bow. Two short men came running around the side. They both stood about five-eight. One was more muscular while the other was skinny, but the skinny one had an arrogance about him. He would prove Hurricane right as they stopped in front of the girls.

"Hey, were the hell did you two come from?" the skinny one asked.

"If you can't ask us a little nicer than that, we won't tell you," Roxanne snapped back.

"We'll just see what the President says about that. Let's go," Skinny said, trying to grab Crystal.

"Our boyfriend told us to stay here and not move. If you don't want any trouble, it would be wise if you left before he came back," Crystal said.

"Yes, he gets very jealous of other men pawing us," Janice added.

"And just what is your boyfriend's name? Is he your pimp?"

"I don't like it when someone insults my lady friends like that," Hurricane spoke behind them.

"Hey, where the hell did you come from?" the muscular one asked.

"Well, if you must know, I came from my mother."

"We don't know who you are, scumbag, but you're a dead man," he added in a threatening tone.

"If I had a dime for everyone who has said that to me, I could have retired five years ago."

The skinny guy came after Hurricane, swinging his arms and legs.

"So, you're into martial arts. We'll have to find out just how good you are," Hurricane said as he swiped his legs from one side to the other. "If this is the best you have, I'll have to teach you some new moves." With that Hurricane snapped his right leg straight out, hitting his target in the solar plexus and sending him reeling on his backside. To Hurricane's surprise, he sprang back up with one leap and headed toward him again. Hurricane stepped to his right and tried to give him a straight arm, but the wiry man grabbed his arm, swung his body around, and stuck both his knees into the small of Hurricane's back.

Hurricane was a bit surprised at how quick and tough this little man was. He must have thought Hurricane was an easy target, as he let him catch his wind. He smiled smugly toward Hurricane and said, "Not as fast as I am, old man? I'm going to enjoy killing you."

Hurricane's eyes turned a bright red. "All right, little man, you want to play for blood? Come and get it."

The man laughed as he ran fast toward Hurricane and took a giant leap toward him. As he tried to kick Hurricane behind his head, he was met with a powerful right fist between his legs. The little man fell in a fetal position, gasping for breath. Hurricane walked toward him and said, "I fought the best there was in Vietnam, little man. You're nothing compared to them because they fought with pride and dignity. All you have is a lack of respect for the martial arts." The little man was trying to crawl away as Hurricane came closer, but he couldn't move fast because of the pain. Hurricane noticed the man's right leg was over his left. He came down with a thunderous heel to the kneecap. Not only did the leg break, it was a compound fracture. The blood began to puddle around him rapidly. Sam grabbed the collar of the man's shirt and dragged him to the front of the boat. "The reason I drew blood, little man, is so the sharks will find you faster." Hurricane picked him up over his head and flung him over the side of the boat.

The other man was being taught a lesson about speaking respectfully to ladies. Janice and Crystal used him as a kicking bag. They were both kicking him all over his body and head as he tried to stand up. Janice was pounding one side, and Crystal was equal to the task on the other. He looked like a pinball in an arcade game bouncing back and forth. They stopped after several minutes, and he dropped to the floor. There wasn't a spot they had missed, and he was swollen and bruised all over his body. His nose and mouth were bleeding, and Hurricane noticed that his ears were even red. Knowing he probably had internal bleeding, he was tossed over the side of the boat as well.

"Let's get going, girls. We don't know how many more of them are on this boat," Hurricane said.

They walked together in the shaded areas to avoid being seen. No other resistance was found. When they were near their targeted area, they heard footsteps approaching and froze. The footsteps stopped abruptly, and they could hear some quiet shuffling. Only when they were within five feet of the door did Hurricane see that it was the captain and his girls. They talked to each other using hand signals so as not to be heard. Everyone knew what they had to do, but first they had to be sure who was in the room. Captain Adams peeked into the small porthole on the side of the wall. Looking back at Hurricane, he smiled and shook his head yes. He gestured the count at eighteen men.

Since they were expecting girls to be coming back to the boat, Sam decided to send the girls in first. If the girls could distract them enough, Sam and Captain Adams could sneak up on them. They indeed had the upper hand. They would wait five minutes and then enter after the girls. If the girls needed help sooner, they would scream.

Captain Adams and Hurricane were busy planning the attack while the girls unbuttoned their blouses and folded up their short pant legs, exposing more skin. When they finally looked, both men froze in their tracks. What a magnificent display of beauty. They started to wonder who had the better side of this deal. However, the outcome would hopefully be in their favor.

The ladies entered the room to a round of cheers and yelling. The girls had them almost eating out of their hands, as they paraded around and made sure they were facing away from the door.

"Well, boys, we heard your morale was a bit low lately, so they sent us in here to lift your spirits," Crystal said.

"I've got something here I'd like you to lift, honey," one man said.

"Keep it clean, boys, or we'll leave you high and dry," Janice spoke.

"Sorry, ma'am. It's just been so long since we saw a girl, let alone five knockout angels."

"Now, that's the kind of talk we like to hear," Joann cooed.

The girls started to sing and dance while the men ate, drank, and cheered. The time was getting close for the captain and Hurricane to enter the scene. Since the girls were wearing their swimsuits underneath their clothes, they started peeling off their shirts, revealing their bikini tops.

The men were cheering so loudly that Hurricane and the captain had no trouble sneaking into the room. When they saw the show, they understood why. The girls were beauty in motion.

The two men standing next to the door were so intrigued with the girls that they failed to see Hurricane and Captain Adams sneaking up on them. After having their necks broken, they were tossed over the side of the yacht. If the girls kept this up, it could be easier than they thought.

The length of time these men had been out to sea would determine how much longer the girls could keep them entertained before trouble began. Apparently, they had been at sea long enough because as soon as they went back in for more bodies, the men had started to advance on the women.

When the first five were within range, the girls braced each other and gave a front kick into their stomachs. That sparked a rumble as the guys charged toward the women. Hurricane and the captain started working from back to front. They had the upper hand with the first three men before someone asked, "Who the hell are you guys?"

"Gentlemen, and I do use that term loosely, you are about to be involved in the worst Hurricane you have ever been involved with," Captain Adams explained to them.

"I've been in a couple hurricanes already, and they aren't so bad."

"This Hurricane is the most dangerous one you will ever experience. You'll be lucky to even walk away. If you want to have a family of your own someday, please get on one of the small boats and leave this yacht," Captain Adams said.

"And what happens if we don't?"

"Let's just say the sharks are in for a big feast tonight," Hurricane said.

"Just who are you to come in here threatening us, mister?"

"My friends call me 'Sam.' My enemies call me 'Hurricane.' I know none of you wants to die tonight, but if you stay here, you'll have more to fear than me."

"Looks like you're the ones who don't understand, friend," the guy closer to Hurricane said. "Do you know how many men are on board this ship?"

"Besides the twenty or so we killed on the shore, how many more of you could there be?" he answered.

"You'll soon find out, and it'll be you playing with the sharks. Don't worry though. We'll throw you over a life preserver."

"Well, if that's the case, we might as well go out fighting." Hurricane threw two ninja stars toward the group, hitting one man in both shoulders. The girls were in the corner fighting two men each and holding up well as they were kicking like tornadoes.

Captain Adams had a couple men in the far corner himself, while Hurricane had the majority of them after him. Hurricane figured they'd all charge him at once, but as they circled him, one man said, "Five hundred dollars will go to the man who kills him." Hurricane smiled, knowing they stood a better chance if they charged him all at once. However, if this is what they wanted, he wasn't about to start complaining.

The first victim was a six-foot-four giant, and he must have weighed four hundred pounds. He had massive arms, but he had one thing against him. Hurricane noticed how the veins in his arms and neck protruded from his body. They were so visible that he reached into his jacket pocket and took out a couple of rings.

"Those rings won't help you, little man," the giant said in a low baritone voice.

"Well, my dumb friend, these aren't just rings. They are razors."

"Who are you calling dumb, dwarf. I'll tear off your fingers and shove them down your throat."

Just before he reached out his mighty paw, Hurricane gave him a flying dropkick right in the kneecaps. "Hey, you cheated," the giant yelled as he hit the ground on his knees. Hurricane laughed and said, "I didn't realize we have rules out here. This is, after all, a street fight. Oh, since we are on this boat, it's more like an ocean fight. My, that looks like it really hurt."

Hurricane was a bit surprised when the big man grabbed hold of his vest and started pulling him his way. "You're dead meat now," he said as he pulled Hurricane closer. Just as he was about to swat him, Hurricane turned so fast that he lost his grip. The big man never felt a thing as Sam sliced one of the veins in his arm. "Hey, you're pretty fast there, little man. I'll give you that." Hurricane motioned with his eyes for the man to check his forearm. When he looked down and saw blood pouring out of his arm, he said, "How'd you do that without me noticing? As soon as I get up you're a dead man." When he looked away for a second that's all the time Hurricane needed, as he advanced toward his prey fast and slid his ring against his neck. Blood now was pouring out from his neck. The giant became dizzy and never made it off his knees.

Hurricane noticed fear in the eyes of the rest of the men. He looked toward them and asked, "Okay, which one of you is next?" Nobody made a move until one guy tried to charge Hurricane from behind. Hurricane moved and the man crashed into the table. "So, you like to attack people when they have their backs turned." With that, Hurricane grabbed one of his man's legs and spun fast, striking the inside with his big forearm. Seeing his leg dangle freely from his body, the guy collapsed.

They were just about to attack all at once when five sets of legs kicked their way through the crowd. The ladies were now inside the circle with Hurricane. Some of the men suddenly started falling. Captain Adams had a boat oar and was clubbing them in the head. He took the men out with ease. They were no match for Hurricane's team, and besides, they were sailors, not fighters.

Just as they were about to leave the room, fifteen men came through the door with guns.

"Very impressive, people. Now, unless you join our team, we'll have to kill you all," one of the goons said.

"Where did you guys come from?" the captain asked.

"You really don't think the President wouldn't have extra men and cameras installed on his yacht, do you?"

"So, now that you're here, that means the President is alone, right?" Hurricane asked.

"Not that it really concerns you, but maybe a couple of us stayed back, just in case."

"Can the President see and hear us now?" Hurricane asked.

"Yes, just face the camera inside the cabinet and talk, he'll hear you."

"Mr. President, I'll only say this once, so please listen carefully. Tell your men to drop their weapons and surrender peacefully, and nobody else will get hurt. If not, all of you are going down."

A voice came through the speakers in a laughing tone. "I have to hand it to you, Mr. Hurricane. Even when the odds are against you, you have that never-give-up mentality. What I wouldn't give to have men with your kind of passion. You never seem to realize when you're beaten."

"Well, you see, Mr. President, your yacht is on the ocean, which is federal territory, and you're in violation of federal law."

"Yes, but I have diplomatic immunity in the States."

"Your immunity is automatically revoked when you commit a crime in federal territory."

"That would be true if a crime was actually committed on federal land, but that's not the case here."

"When you intended to transport those kidnapped women on this boat, it became a federal offense. Besides, they were held on the shore lines by Hoover Dam, and that is federal land."

"Enough of this small talk, Mr. Hurricane. You are trying my patience. Now my men will take you to the top deck and watch you jump off the side of the yacht."

"Mr. President, this is your last chance to survive. If you take us out there, you will be put into prison and never let out."

"Have a nice swim, Mr. Hurricane. Our conversation is over."

They were led outside. The sun was overhead and hot on their skin.

Just as they were taken to the side of the boat, three Apache helicopters circled the yacht. A loud speaker from one of the helicopters stated, "This is the United States Marine Corp. Drop your weapons."

The men on the yacht stood their ground until a couple of Coast Guard response boats surrounded the yacht with their big machine guns pointing right at them. When the weapons had been secured, one of the helicopters lowered an officer onto the yacht to take the President into custody.

"Sorry we're a little late, Hurricane," the officer said.

"You were almost a little too late, Colonel Jones. I'm awfully glad to see you again."

"I'm just as glad to see all of you safe, Hurricane. We've been trying to catch this guy for some time now. He always seems to know where we are. This time you distracted him long enough to forget about us. Your plan worked perfectly, like always."

"Except this time we lost our brave leader, Charging Buffalo. Our brothers fought very bravely, Colonel," Hurricane said.

"Yes, they did, and Charging Buffalo's death was a great loss. Two more of their warriors suffered fatal injuries, but the rest of their injured are being very well cared for at the Army hospital. I can promise you that. They are there as we speak."

Colonel Jones knocked on the President's door. After they received no response, they entered the only way possible. Hurricane kicked in the door and entered with the colonel and Captain Adams. It was music to their ears when they heard the officer say, "President Salvantez, we place you under arrest for kidnapping, espionage, extortion, and most of all, murder. You will get a military trial, where, after being found guilty, you will be hung by the neck until dead." Hurricane and Captain Adams proceeded to handcuff the President and his men. They spoke not a word.

The Coast Guard had been cleaning up the rest of the yacht's crew, and they were secured in a chamber with no windows and only one door. Armed guards were posted at the door. The yacht would be taken to the Coast Guard port for storage once the prisoners were on shore. Hurricane, Captain Adams, and the girls were taken back to retrieve their vehicles where they had left them by the storage bins. It was a very quiet ride back to The Strip. Everyone was exhausted, but everyone had survived. Sam was grateful.

Chapter Twelve

Janice punched Sam with her elbow. "At least being on vacation with you isn't boring, Sam," she said. "I realize this wasn't entirely a vacation trip, but I was hoping we could have had at least a couple of days to ourselves."

Sam laughed and said, "I'm sorry, baby. If I had known it was going to be like this, I would never have asked you to come along."

Janice looked intently into Sam's eyes and wrinkled up her nose. "Samuel Rufus, or should I say 'Hurricane,' if you think for one minute that I haven't had fun on this trip, then I think you'd better look around. We've made a big difference in many people's lives, not to mention the friendships we've made with some extraordinary young ladies and an outstanding captain on the Las Vegas Police force."

"I understand what you're saying, but it could have gone in a much worse direction than it did. All of you could have been killed. This went deeper than anyone involved had imagined. I should not have agreed to all of you coming along," Sam said.

"Now, hold on, Mr. Hurricane!" Diane interrupted the conversation. "We were prisoners waiting to be executed when you rescued us. I think I speak for all my sisters here when I say if you thought we did this just to help you, you're dead wrong. We did this to stop this maniac, and we figured we were already dead until you showed up. We may come from different areas of this country, but we are all law enforcement officers.

Better yet, I think we've become closer to being sisters than if we had been born into the same family. I want each and every one of you to know that if you ever need help or need to talk about anything, just pick up the phone and call."

"Better yet," Roxanne spoke up, "let's make a pact that once or twice a year we meet somewhere. We can bring our families and have a reunion."

Everyone agreed with that suggestion just as the ride came to an end. When they exited the truck and stretched their muscles, it was almost night time. The lights from The Strip were magnificent and warmed their hearts. Captain Adams escorted them into Harrah's Casino, and Wayne Newman was there waiting.

He held out his hand toward Hurricane and said, "I'd like to thank you for ending this terrible ordeal and allowing the Las Vegas casinos to operate in a peaceful manner once again. I want all of you to rest here for the night, and if there's anything we can do for you, just let us know."

"That's really generous of you, Mr. Newman. There is one thing you can do for all of us."

"Just name it, Sam, and it's yours," Wayne answered.

"All of these lovely ladies have been talking about getting together once a year with their families to celebrate the outcome of what we've gone through here. Would you be able to accommodate all these lovely ladies and their families for those events?"

"Funny you should bring that up at this time, Sam, because every casino that was involved has granted you just what you've asked. All you have to do is call us with the details, and we'll take care of the rest."

"That's very thoughtful of all of these establishments, but how will you remember who we are?" Crystal curiously asked.

"I'm glad you brought that up. If you would, please follow me to the main lobby," Wayne said.

When they entered the main lobby, there was a gold plague on the wall that read: "For their courage and unselfish efforts to help clean up the streets of Las Vegas and save the lives of many, these brave people shall be honored in every establishment and on every casino wall on this Las Vegas Strip. We will be forever indebted to all of you for making this Strip safe again." The names read "Captain John Adams, Janice Jenkins, Crystal Smith, Joann Fisher, Roxanne Redford, Diane Carter, and the Mighty

Hurricane, Sam Rufus."

"My friends, you will always be remembered by every casino on this Strip, including our neighbors on the downtown Strip. This is our thanks to all of you," Wayne concluded.

"I don't know what to say, Mr. Newman. I've been thanked in all kinds of ways, but never have I ever been so deeply honored. Could you do me another favor, Wayne?"

"Just ask, and it's yours, Sam."

"Since you've already paid for our trip and expenses, I don't feel right taking more money from you. Whatever money you were going to pay me for this job, please split it among the families who have been affected by this tragedy," Sam suggested.

"By all means, Sam. That's what makes you unique. You're always helping those in need. Heaven must have a special place picked out for you. Goodbye, my friend, and don't be a stranger. You come back soon, and I'll be waiting for you," Wayne Newman said as he held out his hand.

Sam shook Wayne's hand, and then they embraced in a strong bear hug. After that, they were escorted to their rooms. All of the women agreed that they were anxious for a long, hot bath and a good night's sleep.

The next morning, the shuttle took all of them to the airport. When everyone had their ticket, they all met in the middle of the main lobby. Everyone hugged and kissed each other and exchanged phone numbers and addresses. One by one, they walked toward their planes to go home. Sam and Janice waited until the last girl was gone. Holding hands, they walked toward where their flight would be. Wayne had made sure their baggage was taken to the airport before they arrived.

It was almost noon when they stepped onto their airplane and sat back for their flight. Janice was watching as Sam leaned his head back and closed his eyes. This was the first time in days that he could let down his guard and rest.

"Why are you watching me?" he asked.

"You rotten snake, I thought you were sleeping," she said with a laugh as she punched him in the ribs.

"Even though this wasn't much of a vacation, we sure saw a lot of Nevada, didn't we?" Sam said.

"Yes, we did, and we were able to make some good friends. I just hope we are all able to keep in touch. I really liked those girls."

"Did you really like those girls?" Sam asked.

"Yes, Sam, I really did, I'm going to miss them."

"Maybe we'll see them next year."

"What in blazes are you talking about, Sam?"

"Well, I was hoping I could do this before everything went south on us. I figured we'd be able to squeeze a day or two to ourselves. It never turned out that way for us, so I guess I'll have to do it here."

"Sam, what are you babbling about?

Sam took a package out of his jacket pocket and handed it to Janice. "I meant to give you this a week ago, but things kind of got out of control."

Janice opened the box to find another smaller box inside. When she opened that one, her eyes lit up. It was a jewelry box. With shaking hands, she opened it to find a gorgeous diamond ring, along with a note that said, "Will you marry me?"

A tear slid slowly from her eye. She felt Sam take her hand in his. He looked deep into her eyes with an intensity she had never seen before and said, "I love you, Janice." Then he pulled her to him and gave her the most loving kiss of her entire life. She was shaken to her core and melted in his strong arms. When he finally let her go, she didn't want to move.

"What do you say about tying the knot and becoming Mrs. Hurricane Rufus?" he asked. "We can fly back to Vegas with your family, invite our new friends, and have a real vacation."

Janice looked at Sam with tears sliding down her cheeks and said, "It's about time you asked me."

"Is that a yes?"

"Yes! Of course, it's a yes. How long have you been planning this?"

"Long before we came to Vegas. I thought maybe we could get married there. But I don't think things could have turned out any better for us."

"What do you mean by that, Sam?"

"Look at all the new friends we've made. And besides, now your mother can see how beautiful Las Vegas is with us."

Janice leaned her head on Sam's shoulder. "I love you, Samuel Hurricane Rufus."

This was going to be a beautiful flight home.

Meet the Author

Joseph J. Cacciotti

Joseph Cacciotti grew up in Racine, Wisconsin, along the shores of Lake Michigan. His desire to write appeared early in life when his high school teachers encouraged him to write poetry and to become a journalist. His drive to write fiction grew stronger as he matured.

Joe made a promise to his friend and mentor, Harold A. Schink, on his deathbed. Harold asked Joe to never stop writing. Joe has been faithful to that promise. In 2006, he published *Poems for the Heart*, an award-winning collection of fifty of his most talked about poems. His second poetry book, *Poems for the Heart, Volume II* was released in April 2012.

Also published in 2006 was *Blue Collar Real Estate Mogul*, a biography based on true life experiences that he and his best friend endured as landlords in Racine and about a friendship that never stopped growing, even after death.

In 2009, Joe completed *Hurricane Cores the Big Apple,* the first in a series about "Hurricane" Samuel James Rufus, an unconventional detective whose methods for getting the bad guys come close to crossing ethical and legal lines in his pursuit of justice. The second book in the Hurricane series, *Hurricane Rocks Wisconsin*, was released in March 2012. *Hurricane Strips Las Vegas* is the third book in the series. Several more adventures are underway and will be released soon.

Joe lives with his wife Diane in Racine, Wisconsin. They have three daughters. Joe continues to write poetry, as well as the "Hurricane Sam Rufus" adventures.

www.ingramcontent.com/pod-product-compliance
Lightning Source LLC
Chambersburg PA
CBHW060645260626
47161CB00008B/3006